THE PUPPET MASTERS

By the same author in Pan Books

RED PLANET

THE DOOR INTO SUMMER

ROBERT A. HEINLEIN

THE PUPPET MASTERS

UNABRIDGED

PAN BOOKS LTD : LONDON

First published in Great Britain as
A Heinlein Triad 1966 by Victor Gollancz Ltd.

This edition published 1969 by Pan Books Ltd.,
33 Tothill Street, London, S.W.1

ISBN 0 330 02235 0

2nd Printing 1973

*The characters, the location, and the incidents in this book
are entirely the product of the author's imagination and
have no relation to any person or event in real life*

*Printed in Great Britain
by Richard Clay (The Chaucer Press), Ltd., Bungay, Suffolk*

I

Were they truly intelligent? By themselves, that is? I don't know and I don't know how we can ever find out.

If they were *not* truly intelligent, I hope I never live to see us tangle with anything at all like them which *is* intelligent. I know who will lose. Me. You. The so-called human race.

For me it started too early on July 12th, '07, with my phone shrilling in a frequency guaranteed to peel off the skull. The sort of phone my Section uses is not standard; the audio relay was buried surgically under the skin back of my left ear – bone conduction. I felt around my person, then recalled that I had left it in my jacket across the room. 'All right,' I growled. 'I hear you. Shut off that damned noise.'

'Emergency,' a voice said in my ear. 'Report in person.'

I told him what to do with his emergency.

'Report to the Old Man,' the voice persisted, 'at once.'

That was different. 'Moving,' I acknowledged and sat up with a jerk that hurt my eyeballs. I went into the bath, injected a grain of 'Gyro' into my arm, then let the vibro shake me apart while the drug put me together. I stepped out a new man, or at least a good mock-up of one, and got my jacket.

I entered our Section offices through a washroom booth in MacArthur Station. You won't find our offices in the phone lists. In fact, it does not exist. All is illusion. Another route is through a little hole-in-the-wall shop with a sign reading RARE STAMPS & COINS. Don't try that route either – they'll try to sell you a Tu'penny Black.

Don't try any route. I told you we didn't exist, didn't I?

There is one thing no head of a country can know, and that is: how good is his intelligence system? He finds out only by having it fail him. Hence our Section. Suspenders *and* belt. United Nations had never heard of us, nor had Central Intelligence – I think. All I really knew about us was the training I had received and the jobs the Old Man sent me on. Interesting jobs if you don't care where you sleep, what you eat, or how long you live. If I had had any sense, I'd have quit and taken a working job.

The only trouble with that would be that I wouldn't have been working for the Old Man any longer. That made the difference.

Not that he was a soft boss. He was quite capable of saying, 'Boys, we need to fertilize this oak tree. Jump in that hole at its base and I'll cover you up.'

We'd have done it. Any of us would.

And the Old Man would bury us alive, too, if he thought that there was as much as a fifty-three per cent probability that it was the Tree of Liberty he was nourishing.

He got up and limped towards me as I came in, with his face split in a wicked smile. His big hairless skull and his strong Roman nose made him look like a cross between Satan and Punch of Punch-and-Judy. 'Welcome, Sam,' he said. 'Sorry to get you out of bed.'

The deuce he was sorry! 'I was on leave,' I answered shortly.

'Ah, but you still are. We're going on a vacation.'

I didn't trust his 'vacations', so I did not rise to the bait. 'So my name is "Sam",' I answered. 'What's my last name?'

'Cavanaugh. And I'm your uncle Charlie – Charles M. Cavanaugh, retired. Meet your sister Mary.'

I had noticed that there was another person in the room, but when the Old Man is present he gets full attention as long as he wants it. Now I looked over my 'sister' and then looked her over again. It was worth it.

I could see why he had set us up as brother and sister if we were to do a job together; it would give him a trouble-free pattern. An indoctrinated agent can't break his assumed character any more than a professional actor can intentionally muff his lines. So this one I must treat as my sister – a dirty trick if I ever met one!

A long, lean body, but pleasingly mammalian. Good legs. Broad shoulders for a woman. Flaming, wavy red hair and the real redheaded saurian bony structure to her skull. Her face was handsome rather than beautiful; she looked me over as if I were a side of beef.

I wanted to drop one wing and run in circles. It must have shown, for the Old Man said gently, 'Tut tut, Sammy. Your sister dotes on you and you are extremely fond of your sister, but in a healthy, clean-cut, sickeningly chivalrous, All-American-Boy sort of way.'

'As bad as that?' I asked, still looking at my 'sister'.

'Worse.'

'Oh, well. Howdy, Sis. Glad to know you.'

She stuck out a hand. It was firm and seemed as strong as mine. 'Hi, Bud.' Her voice was deep contralto, which was all I needed. Damn the Old Man!

'I might add,' the Old Man went on, 'that you are so devoted to your sister that you would gladly die to protect her. I dislike to tell you so, Sammy, but your sister is a leetle more valuable, for the present at least, to the organization than you are.'

'Got it,' I acknowledged. 'Thanks for the polite qualification.'

'Now, Sammy —'

'She's my favourite sister; I protect her from dogs and strange men. Okay, when do we start?'

'Better stop over in Cosmetics; they have a new face for you.'

'Make it a whole new head. See you. 'Bye, Sis.'

They did not quite do that, but they did fit my personal phone under the back of my skull and then cemented hair over it. They dyed my hair to the same shade as that of my newly acquired sister, bleached my skin, and did things to my cheekbones and chin. The mirror showed me to be as good a redhead as Sis. I looked at my hair and tried to recall what its natural shade had been, 'way back when. Then I wondered if Sis were what she seemed to be along

7

those lines. I rather hoped so.

I put on the kit they gave me and somebody handed me a jump bag already packed. The Old Man had evidently been in Cosmetics, too; his skull was now covered by crisp curls of a shade between pink and white. They had done something to his face – I could not tell just what – but we were all three clearly related by blood and were all of that curious sub-race, the redheads.

'Come, Sammy,' he said. 'I'll brief you in the car.' We went up by a route I had not known about and ended up on the Northside launching platform, high above New Brooklyn and overlooking Manhattan Crater.

I drove while the Old Man talked. Once we were out of local control he told me to set it automatic on Des Moines, Iowa. I then joined Mary and 'Uncle Charlie' in the lounge. He gave us our personal histories up to date. 'So here we are,' he concluded, 'a merry family party – tourists. And if we should happen to run into unusual events, that is how we will behave, as nosy and irresponsible tourists.'

'But what is the problem?' I asked. 'Or do we play this one by ear?'

'Mmmm – possibly.'

'Okay. But when you're dead, it's nice to know why. Eh, Mary?'

'Mary' did not answer. She had that quality, rare in babes, of not talking when she had nothing to say. The Old Man looked me over; presently he said, 'Sam, you've heard of "flying saucers".'

'Huh?'

'You've studied history. Come, now!'

'You mean *those*? The flying-saucer craze, 'way back before the Disorders? I thought you meant something recent and real; those were mass hallucinations.'

'Were they?'

'Well, I haven't studied much statistical abnormal psychology, but I seem to remember an equation. That whole period was psychopathic; a man with all his gaskets tight would have been locked up.'

'This present day is sane, eh?'

8

'Oh, I wouldn't go so far as to say that.' I pawed back through my mind and found the answer I wanted. 'I remember that equation now – Digby's evaluating integral for second and higher order data. It gave a 93·7 per cent certainty that the flying-saucer myth, after elimination of explained cases, was hallucination. I remember it because it was the first case of its type in which the instances had been systematically collected and evaluated. A government project, God knows why.'

The Old Man looked benign. 'Brace yourself, Sammy. We are going to inspect a flying saucer today. Maybe we'll even saw off a souvenir, like true tourists.'

II

'Seventeen hours' – the Old Man glanced at his finger watch and added – 'and twenty-three minutes ago an unidentified space ship landed near Grinnell, Iowa. Type, unknown. Approximately disk shaped and about one hundred and fifty feet across. Origin, unknown, but —'

'Didn't they track a trajectory on it?' I interrupted.

'They did not,' he answered. 'Here is a photo of it taken after landing by Space Station Beta.'

I looked it over and passed it to Mary. It was as unsatisfactory as a telephoto taken from five thousand miles out usually is. Trees looking like moss . . . a cloud shadow that loused up the best part of the pic . . . and a grey circle that might have been a disk-shaped ship and could just as well have been an oil tank or a water reservoir.

Mary handed the pic back. I said, 'Looks like a tent for a camp meeting. What else do we know?'

'Nothing.'

'Nothing? After seventeen hours! We ought to have agents pouring out of their ears!'

'We did have. Two within reach and four that were sent in. They failed to report back. I dislike losing agents, Sammy, especially with no results.'

I had a sudden cold realization that the situation must be so serious that the Old Man had chosen to bet his own brain against the loss of the organization – for he *was* the Section. I suddenly felt chilly. Ordinarily an agent has a duty to save his own neck – in order to complete his mission and report back. On this job it was the Old Man who must come back – and after him, Mary. I was as expendable as a paper clip. I didn't like it.

'One agent made a partial report,' the Old Man went on. 'He went in as a casual bystander and reported by phone that it must be a space ship. He then reported that the ship was opening and that he was going to try to get closer, past the police lines. The last thing he said was, "Here they come. They are little creatures, about —" Then he shut off.'

'Little men?'

'He said creatures.'

'Peripheral reports?'

'Plenty. The Des Moines stereocasting station sent mobile units in for spot cast. The pictures they sent out were all long shots, taken from the air. They showed nothing but a disk-shaped object. Then, for about two hours, no pictures and no news, followed later by close-ups and a new news slant.'

The Old Man shut up. I said, 'Well?'

'The thing was a hoax. The "space ship" was a sheet-metal-and-plastic fraud, built by two farm boys, in woods near their home. The fake reports originated with an announcer who had put the boys up to it to make a story. He has been fired and the latest "invasion from outer space" turns out to be a joke.'

I squirmed. 'So it's a hoax – but we lose six men. We're going to look for them?'

'No, for we would not find them. We are going to try to find out why triangulation of this photograph' – he held up the teleshot taken from the space station – 'doesn't quite jibe with the news reports – and why the Des Moines stereo station shut up for a while.'

Mary spoke up for the first time. 'I'd like to talk with those farm boys.'

I roaded the car five miles this side of Grinnell and we started looking for the McLain farm – the news reports had named Vincent and George McLain as the culprits. It wasn't hard to find. At a fork in the road was a big sign: THIS WAY TO THE SPACE SHIP. Shortly the road was parked on both sides with duos and groundcars and triphibs. A couple of stands dispensed cold drinks and souvenirs at the turnoff into the McLain place. A state cop was directing traffic.

'Pull up,' directed the Old Man. 'Might as well see the fun, eh?'

'Right, Uncle Charlie,' I agreed.

The Old Man bounced out, swinging his cane. I handed Mary out and she snuggled up to me, grasping my arm. She looked up at me, managing to look both stupid and demure. 'My, but you're strong, Buddy.'

I wanted to slap her. That poor-little-me routine – from one of the Old Man's agents. A smile from a tiger.

'Uncle Charlie' buzzed around, bothering state police, buttonholing people, stopping to buy cigars at a stand, and giving a picture of a well-to-do, senile old fool, out for a holiday. He turned and waved his cigar at a state sergeant. 'The inspector says it is a fraud, my dears – a prank thought up by boys. Shall we go?'

Mary looked disappointed. 'No space ship?'

'There's a space ship, if you want to call it that,' the cop answered. 'Just follow the suckers. It's "sergeant", not "inspector".'

We set out, across a pasture and into some woods. It cost a dollar to get through the gate and many turned back. The path through the woods was rather deserted. I moved carefully, wishing for eyes in the back of my head instead of a phone. Uncle Charlie and Sis walked ahead, Mary chattering like a fool and somehow managing to be both shorter and younger than she had been on the trip out. We came to a clearing and there was the 'space ship'.

It was more than a hundred feet across, but it was whipped together out of light-gauge metal and sheet plastic, sprayed with aluminium. It was the shape of two pie plates, face to face. Aside from that, it looked like nothing in particular. Nevertheless, Mary squealed, 'Oh, how exiting!'

A youngster, eighteen or nineteen, with a permanent sunburn and a pimply face, stuck his head out of a hatch in the top of the monstrosity. 'Care to see inside?' he called out. He added that it would be fifty cents apiece more, and Uncle Charlie shelled out.

Mary hesitated at the hatch. Pimple face was joined by what appeared to be his twin and they started to hand her down in. She drew back and I moved in fast, intending to do any handling myself. My reasons were ninety-nine per cent professional; I could feel danger all through the place.

'It's dark,' she quavered.

'It's safe,' the second young man said. 'We've been taking sightseers through all day. I'm Vinc McLain. Come on, lady.'

Uncle Charlie peered down the hatch, like a cautious mother hen. 'Might be snakes in there,' he decided. 'Mary, I don't think you had better go in.'

'Nothing to fear,' the first McLain said insistently. 'It's safe.'

'Keep the money, gentlemen.' Uncle Charlie glanced at his finger. 'We're late. Let's go, my dears.'

I followed them back up the path, my hackles up the whole way.

We got back to the car. Once we were rolling, the Old Man said sharply, 'Well? What did you see?'

I countered with, 'Any doubt about the first report? The one that broke off?'

'None.'

'That thing wouldn't have fooled an agent, even in the dark. This wasn't the ship he saw.'

'Of course not. What else?'

'How much would you say that fake cost – new sheet

metal, fresh paint, and, from what I saw through the hatch, probably a thousand feet of lumber to brace it.'

'Go on.'

'Well, the McLain place had "mortgage" spelled out all over it. If the boys were in on the gag, they didn't foot the bill.'

'Obviously. You, Mary?'

'Uncle Charlie, did you notice how they treated me?'

'Who?' I said sharply.

'The state sergeant and the two boys. When I use the sweet-little-bundle-of-sex routine, something should happen. Nothing did.'

'They were all attentive,' I objected.

'You don't understand – but I *know*. I always know. Something was wrong with them. They were dead inside. Harem guards, if you know what I mean.'

'Hypnosis?' asked the Old Man.

'Possibly. Or drugs perhaps.' She frowned and looked puzzled.

'Hmm —' he answered. 'Sammy, take the next turn to the left. We're investigating a point two miles south of here.'

'The triangulated location by the pic?'

'What else?'

But we didn't get there. First it was a bridge out and I didn't have room enough to make the car hop it, quite aside from traffic regulations for a duo on the ground. We circled south and came in again, the only remaining route. We were stopped by a highway cop. A brush fire, he told us; go any farther and we would probably be impressed into fire fighting. He didn't know but what he ought to send me up to the fire lines anyhow.

Mary waved her lashes at him and he relented. She pointed out that neither she nor Uncle Charlie could drive, a double lie.

After we pulled away, I asked her, 'How about that one?'

'What about him?'

'Harem guard?'

'Oh my, no! A most attractive man.'

Her answer annoyed me.

13

The Old Man vetoed taking to the air and making a pass over the spot. He said it was useless. We headed for Des Moines. Instead of parking at the tollgates we paid to take the car into the city and ended up at the studios of Des Moines stereo. 'Uncle Charlie' blustered our way into the office of the general manager. He told several lies – or perhaps 'Charles M. Cavanaugh' was actually a big wheel with the Federal Communications Authority.

Once inside, he continued the Big Brass act. 'Now, sir, what is this nonsense about a space-ship hoax? Speak plainly, sir: your licence may depend on it.'

The manager was a little round-shouldered man, but he did not seem cowed, merely annoyed. 'We've made full explanation over the channels,' he said. 'We were victimized. The man has been discharged.'

'Hardly adequate, sir.'

The little man – Barnes, his name was – shrugged. 'What do you expect? Shall we string him up by his thumbs?'

Uncle Charlie pointed his cigar at him. 'I warn you, sir. I am not to be trifled with. I am not convinced that two farm louts and a junior announcer could have pulled off this preposterous business. There was money in it, sir. Yes, sir – money. Now tell me, sir, just what did you —'

Mary had seated herself close by Barnes's desk. She had done something to her costume and her pose put me in mind of Goya's *Disrobed Lady*. She made a thumbs-down signal to the Old Man.

Barnes should not have caught it; his attention appeared to be turned to the Old Man. But he did. He turned towards Mary and his face went dead. He reached for his desk.

'Sam! Kill him!' the Old Man rapped.

I burned his legs off and his trunk fell to the floor. It was a poor shot; I had intended to burn his belly.

I stepped in and kicked his gun away from still-groping fingers. I was about to give him *coup de grâce* – a man burned that way is dead, but it takes a while to die – when the Old Man snapped, 'Don't touch him! Mary, stand back!'

He sidled towards the body, like a cat investigating the unknown. Barnes gave a long sigh and was quiet. The Old Man poked him gently with his cane.

'Boss,' I said, 'time to git, isn't it?'

Without looking around he answered, 'We're as safe here as anywhere. This building may be swarming with them.'

'Swarming with what?'

'How would I know? Swarming with whatever *he* was.' He pointed at Barnes's body. 'That's what I've got to find out.'

Mary gave a choked sob and gasped, 'He's still breathing. Look!'

The body lay face down; the back of the jacket heaved as if the chest were rising. The Old Man looked and poked at it with his cane. 'Sam. Come here.'

I came. 'Strip it,' he went on. 'Use gloves. And be careful.'

'Booby trap?'

'Shut up. Use care.'

He must have had a hunch that was close to truth. I think the Old Man's brain has a built-in integrator which arrives at logical necessity from minimum facts the way a museum johnny reconstructs an animal from a single bone. First pulling on gloves – agent's gloves; I could have stirred boiling acid, yet I could feel a coin in the dark and call heads or tails – once gloved, I started to turn him over to undress him.

The back was still heaving; I did not like the look of it – unnatural. I placed a palm between the shoulder blades.

A man's back is bone and muscle. This was soft and undulating. I snatched my hand away.

Without a word Mary handed me a pair of scissors from Barnes's desk. I took them and cut the jacket away. Underneath, the body was dressed in a light singlet. Between this and the skin, from the neck halfway down the back, was something which was not flesh. A couple of inches thick, it gave the corpse a round-shouldered, or slightly humped, appearance.

It pulsed.

15

As we watched, it slid slowly off the back, away from us. I reached out to peel up the singlet; my hand was knocked away by the Old Man's cane. 'Make up your mind,' I said and rubbed my knuckles.

He did not answer but tucked his cane under the shirt and worried it up the trunk. The thing was uncovered.

Greyish, faintly translucent, and shot through with darker structure, shapeless – but it was clearly alive. As we watched, it flowed down into the space between Barnes's arm and chest, filled it and stayed there, unable to go farther.

'The poor devil,' the Old Man said softly.

'Huh? *That?*'

'No – Barnes. Remind me to see that he gets the Purple Heart, when this is over. If it ever is over.' The Old Man straightened up and stumped around the room, as if he had forgotten completely the thing nestling in the crook of Barnes's arm.

I drew back and continued to stare at it, my gun ready. It could not move fast; it obviously could not fly; but I did not know what it could do. Mary moved and pressed her shoulder against mine, as if for human comfort. I put my free arm around her.

On a side table there was a stack of cans, the sort used for stereo tapes. The Old Man took one, spilled out the reels and came back with it. 'This will do, I think.' He placed the can on the floor, near the thing, and began chivvying it with his cane, trying to irritate it into crawling into the can.

Instead it oozed back until it was almost entirely under the body. I grabbed the free arm and heaved Barnes away; the thing clung, then flopped to the floor. Under dear old Uncle Charlie's directions, Mary and I used our guns at lowest power to force it, by burning the floor close to it, into the can. We got it in, a close fit, and I slapped the cover on.

The Old Man tucked the can under his arm. 'On our way, my dears.'

On the way out he paused in the door to call out a parting, then, after closing the door, stopped at the desk of Barnes's secretary. 'I'll be seeing Mr Barnes tomorrow,' he told her. 'No, no appointment. I'll phone.'

Out we went, slow march, the Old Man with the can full of thing under his arm and me with my ears cocked for alarms. Mary played the silly little moron, with a running monologue. The Old Man even paused in the lobby, bought a cigar, and inquired directions, with bumbling, self-important good nature.

Once in the car, he gave the directions, then cautioned me against driving fast. The directions led us into a garage. The Old Man sent for the manager and said, 'Mr Malone wants this car – immediately.' It was a signal I had had occasion to use myself; the duo would cease to exist in about twenty minutes, save as anonymous spare parts in the service bins.

The manager looked us over, then answered quietly, 'Through that door over there.' He sent the two mechanics in the room away and we ducked through the door.

We ended up in the apartment of an elderly couple; there we became brunettes and the Old Man got his bald head back. I acquired a moustache; Mary looked as well dark as she had as a redhead. The 'Cavanaugh' combination was dropped; Mary got a nurse's costume and I was togged out as a chauffeur, while the Old Man became our elderly, invalid employer, complete with shawl and tantrums.

A car was waiting for us. The trip back was no trouble; we could have remained the carrot-topped Cavanaughs. I kept the screen tuned to Des Moines, but if the cops had turned up the late Mr Barnes, the newsboys hadn't heard about it.

We went straight to the Old Man's office and there we opened the can. The Old Man sent for Dr Graves, head of the Section's bio lab, and the job was done with handling equipment.

What we needed were gas masks, not handling equipment. A stink of decaying organic matter filled the room and forced us to slap the cover on and speed up the blowers.

Graves wrinkled his nose. 'What in the world was that?' he demanded.

The Old Man was swearing softly. 'You are to find out,' he said. 'Work it in suits, in a germ-free compartment, and *don't* assume that it is dead.'

'If that is alive, I'm Queen Anne.'

'Maybe you are, but don't take chances. It's a parasite, capable of attaching itself to a host, such as a man, and controlling the host. It is almost certainly extraterrestrial in origin and metabolism.'

The lab boss sniffed. 'Extraterrestrial parasite on a terrestrial host? Ridiculous! The body chemistries would be incompatible.'

The Old Man grunted. 'Damn your theories. When we captured it, it was living on a man. If that means it has to be a terrestrial organism, show me where it fits into the scheme of things and where to look for its mates. And quit jumping to conclusions; I want facts.'

The biologist stiffened. 'You'll get them!'

'Get going. And don't persist in the silly assumption that the thing is dead; that perfume may be a protective weapon. That thing, if alive, is fantastically dangerous. If it gets on one of your laboratory men, I'll almost certainly have to kill him.'

The lab director left without some of his cockiness.

The Old Man settled back in his chair, sighed, and closed his eyes. After five minutes or so he opened his eyes and said, 'How many mustard plasters the size of that thing can arrive in a space ship as big as that fraud we looked at?'

'Was there a space ship?' I asked. 'The evidence seems slim.'

'Slim but utterly incontrovertible. There was a ship. There still is.'

'We should have examined the site.'

'That site would have been our last sight. The other six boys weren't fools. Answer my question.'

'How big the ship was doesn't tell me anything about its pay load, when I don't know its propulsion method, the jump it made, or what the passengers require. How long is a piece of rope? If you want a guess, I'd say several hundred, maybe several thousand.'

'Mmm ... yes. So there are maybe several thousand zombies in Iowa tonight. Or harem guards, as Mary puts it.' He thought for a moment. 'But how am I to get past them to the harem? We can't go around shooting every round-shouldered man in Iowa; it would cause talk.' He smiled feebly.

'I'll put you another question,' I said. 'If one space ship lands in Iowa yesterday, how many will land in North Dakota tomorrow? Or Brazil?'

'Yes.' He looked still more troubled. 'I'll tell you how long is your piece of rope.'

'Huh?'

'Long enough to choke you. You kids go enjoy yourselves; you may not have another chance. Don't leave the offices.'

I went back to Cosmetics, got my own skin colour back and resumed my normal appearance, had a soak and a massage, and then went to the staff lounge in search of a drink and company. I looked around, not knowing whether I was looking for a blonde, brunette, or redhead, but fairly sure that I could spot the chassis.

It was a redhead. Mary was in a booth, sucking on a drink and looking much as she had looked at first.

'Hi, Sis,' I said, sliding in beside her.

She smiled and answered, 'Hello, Bud. Drag up a rock,' while moving to make room for me.

I dialled for bourbon and water and then said, 'Is this your *real* appearance?'

She shook her head. 'Not at all. Zebra stripes and two heads. What's yours?'

'My mother smothered me with a pillow, so I never got a chance to find out.'

She again looked me over with that side-of-beef scrutiny, then said, 'I can understand her actions, but I am more hardened than she was. You'll do, Bud.'

'Thanks.' I went on, 'Let's drop this Bud-and-Sis routine; it gives me inhibitions.'

'Hmm . . . I think you need inhibitions.'

'Me? Never any violence with me; I'm the "Barkis-is-willing" type.' I might have added that, if I laid a hand on her and she happened not to like it, I'd bet that I would draw back a bloody stump. The Old Man's kids are never sissies.

She smiled. 'So? Well, Miss Barkis is *not* willing, not this evening.' She put down her glass. 'Drink up and re-order.'

We did so and continued to sit there, feeling warm and good. There aren't many hours like that in our profession; it makes one savour them.

While we sat there, I got to thinking how well she would look on the other side of a fireplace. My job being what it was, I had never thought seriously about getting married. And after all, a babe is just a babe; why get excited? But Mary was an agent herself; talking to her would not be like shouting off Echo Mountain. I realized that I had been lonely for one hell of a long time.

'Mary —'

'Yes?'

'Are you married?'

'Eh? Why do you ask? As a matter of fact, I'm not. But what business – I mean, why does it matter?'

'Well, it might,' I persisted.

She shook her head.

'I'm serious,' I went on. 'Look me over. I've got both hands and feet, I'm fairly young, and I don't track mud in the house. You could do worse.'

She laughed, but her laugh was kindly. 'And you could work up better lines. I am sure they must have been extemporaneous.'

'They were.'

'And I won't hold them against you. Listen, wolf, your technique is down; just because a woman turns you down is no reason to lose your head and offer her a contract. Some women would be mean enough to hold you to it.'

'I meant it,' I said peevishly.

'So? What salary do you offer?'

'Damn your pretty eyes! If you want that type of contract, I'll go along; you can keep your pay and I'll allot half of mine to you – unless you want to retire.'

She shook her head. 'I'd never insist on a settlement contract, not with a man I was willing to marry in the first place —'

'I didn't think you would.'

'I was just trying to make you see that you yourself were not serious.' She looked me over. 'But perhaps you are,' she added in a warm, soft voice.

'I am.'

She shook her head again. 'Agents should not marry.'

'Agents shouldn't marry anyone but agents.'

She started to answer, but stopped suddenly. My own phone was talking in my ear, the Old Man's voice, and I knew she was hearing the same thing. 'Come into my office,' he said.

We both got up without saying anything. Mary stopped me at the door and looked up into my eyes. '*That* is why it is silly to talk about marriage. We've got this job to finish. All the time we've been talking, you've been thinking about the job and so have I.'

'I have not.'

'Don't play with me! Sam – suppose you were married and you woke up to find one of those things on your wife's shoulders, possessing her.' There was horror in her eyes as she went on. 'Suppose I found one of them on *your* shoulders.'

'I'll chance it. And I won't let one get to you.'

She touched my cheek. 'I don't believe you would.'

We went on into the Old Man's office.

He looked up to say, 'Come along. We're leaving.'

'Where?' I answered. 'Or shouldn't I ask?'

'White House. See the President. Shut up.'

I shut.

III

At the beginning of a forest fire or an epidemic there is a short time when a minimum of correct action will contain and destroy. What the President needed to do the Old Man had already figured out – declare a national emergency, fence off the Des Moines area, and shoot anybody who tried to slip out. Then let them out one at a time, searching them for parasites. Meantime, use the radar screen, the rocket boys, and the space stations to spot and smash any new landings.

Warn all the other nations, ask for their help – but don't be fussy about international law, for this was a fight for racial survival against an outside invader. It did not matter where they came from – Mars, Venus, the Jovian satellites, or outside the system entirely. Repel the invasion.

The Old Man's unique gift was the ability to reason logically with unfamiliar, hard-to-believe facts as easily as with the commonplace. Not much, eh? Most minds stall dead when faced with facts which conflict with basic beliefs; 'I-just-can't-believe-it' is all one word to highbrows and dimwits alike.

But not to the Old Man – and he had the ear of the President.

The Secret Service guards gave us the works. An X-ray went *beep!* and I surrendered my heater. Mary turned out to be a walking arsenal; the machine gave four beeps and a hiccough, although you would have sworn she couldn't hide a tax receipt. The Old Man surrendered his cane without waiting to be asked.

Our audio capsules showed up both by X-ray and by metal detector, but the guards weren't equipped for surgical operations. There was a hurried conference and the head guard ruled that anything embedded in the flesh need not be classed as a weapon. They printed us, photographed our retinas, and ushered us into a waiting room. The Old Man was whisked out and in to see the President alone.

After quite a while we were ushered in. The Old Man introduced us and I stammered. Mary just bowed. The President said he was glad to see us and turned on that smile, the way you see it in the stereocasts – and he made us feel that he *was* glad to see us. I felt warm inside and no longer embarrassed.

The Old Man directed me to report all that I had done and seen and heard on this assignment. I tried to catch his eye when it came to the part about killing Barnes, but he wasn't having any – so I left out the Old Man's order to shoot and made it clear that I had shot to protect another agent – Mary – when I saw Barnes reach for his gun. The Old Man interrupted me. 'Make your report complete.'

So I filled in the Old Man's order to shoot. The President threw the Old Man a glance, the only expression he showed. I went on about the parasite thing, on up to that present moment, as nobody told me to stop.

Then it was Mary's turn. She fumbled in trying to explain to the President why she expected to get a response out of normal men – and had not gotten it out of the McLain boys, the state sergeant, and Barnes. The President helped her – by smiling warmly and saying, 'My dear young lady, I quite believe it.'

Mary blushed. The President listened gravely while she finished, then sat still for several minutes. Presently he spoke to the Old Man. 'Andrew, your Section has been invaluable. Your reports have sometimes tipped the balance in crucial occasions in history.'

The Old Man snorted. 'So it's "no", is it?'

'I did not say so.'

'You were about to.'

The President shrugged. 'I was going to suggest that your young people withdraw. Andrew, you are a genius, but even geniuses make mistakes.'

'See here, Tom, I anticipated this; that's why I brought witnesses. They are neither drugged nor instructed. Call in

23

your psych crew; try to shake their stories.'

The President shook his head. 'I'm sure you are cleverer about such things than anyone whom I could bring in to test them. Take this young man – he was willing to risk a murder charge to protect you. You inspire loyalty, Andrew. As for the young lady – really, Andrew, I can't start what amounts to war on a woman's intuition.'

Mary took a step forward. 'Mr President,' she said very earnestly, 'I do know. I know every time. I can't tell you how I know – *but those were not normal male men.*'

He answered, 'You have not considered an obvious explanation - that they actually were, ah, "harem guards". Pardon me, miss. There are always such unfortunates. By laws of chance you ran across four in one day.'

Mary shut up. The Old Man did not. 'God damn it, Tom' – I shuddered; you don't talk to the President that way – 'I knew you when you were an investigating senator and I was a key man in your investigations. You know I wouldn't bring you this fairy tale if there were any way to explain it away. How about that space ship? What was in it? Why couldn't I even reach the spot where it landed?' He hauled out the photograph taken by Space Station Beta and shoved it under the President's nose.

The President seemed unperturbed. 'Ah yes, facts. Andrew, you and I have a passion for facts. But I have sources of information other than your Section. Take this photo. You made a point of it when you phoned. The metes and bounds of the McLain farm as recorded in the local county courthouse check with the triangulated latitude and longitude of this object on this photograph.' The President looked up. 'Once I got lost in my own neighbourhood. You weren't even in your own neighbourhood, Andrew.'

'Tom —'

'Yes, Andrew?'

'You did not trot out there and check those courthouse maps yourself?'

'Of course not.'

'Thank God – or you would be carrying three pounds of pulsing tapioca between your shoulders – and God save the

United States! Be sure of this: the courthouse clerk and whatever agent was sent, both are hagridden this very moment. Yes, and the Des Moines chief of police, editors around there, dispatchers, cops – all sorts of key people. Tom, I don't know what we are up against, but *they* know what *we* are, and they are pinching off the nerve cells of our social organism before true messages can get back – or they cover up true reports with false, just as they did with Barnes. Mr President, you must order an immediate, drastic quarantine of the area. There is no other hope!'

'"Barnes",' the President repeated softly. 'Andrew, I had hoped to spare you this, but —' He flipped a key at his desk. 'Get me stereo station WDES, Des Moines, the manager's office.'

Shortly a screen lighted on his desk; he touched another switch and a solid display in the wall lighted up. We were looking into the room we had been in a few hours before.

Looking into it past a man who filled most of the screen – Barnes.

Or his twin. When I kill a man, I expect him to stay dead. I was shaken, but I still believed in myself – and my heater.

The man said, 'You asked for me, Mr President?' He sounded as if he were dazzled by the honour.

'Yes, thank you. Mr Barnes, do you recognize these people?'

He looked surprised. 'I'm afraid not. Should I?'

The Old Man interrupted. 'Tell him to call in his office force.'

The President looked quizzical but did so. They trooped in, girls mostly, and I recognized the secretary who sat outside the door. One of them squealed, 'Oooh – it's the *President.*'

None of them identified us – not surprising with the Old Man and me, but Mary's appearance was just as it had been, and I will bet that Mary's looks would be burned into the mind of any woman who had ever seen her.

But I noticed one thing about them – every one of them was round-shouldered.

25

The President eased us out. He put a hand on the Old Man's shoulder. 'Seriously, Andrew, the Republic won't fall – we'll worry it through.'

Ten minutes later we were standing in the wind on the Rock Creek platform. The Old Man seemed shrunken and old.

'What now, Boss?'

'Eh? For you two, nothing. You are both on leave until recalled.'

'I'd like to take another look at Barnes's office.'

'Stay out of Iowa. That's an order.'

'Mmm—what are you going to do, if I may ask?'

'I am going down to Florida and lie in the sun and wait for the world to go to hell. If you have any sense, you'll do the same. There's damned little time.'

He squared his shoulders and stumped away. I turned to speak to Mary, but she was gone. I looked around but could not spot her. I trotted off and overtook the Old Man. 'Excuse me, Boss. Where did Mary go?'

'Huh? On leave, no doubt. Don't bother me.'

I considered trying to relay to her through the Section circuit, when I remembered that I did not know her right name, or her code, or her ID number. I thought of trying to bull it through by describing her, but that was foolishness. Only Cosmetics Records knows the original appearance of an agent – and they won't talk. All I knew was that she had twice appeared as a redhead – and that, for my taste, she was 'why men fight'. Try punching that into a phone!

Instead I found a room for the night.

IV

I woke up at dusk and looked out as the capital came to life for the night. The river swept away in a wide band past the memorial; they were adding fluorescin to the water above the District so the river stood out in curving sweeps of glowing rose and amber and emerald and shining fire. Pleasure boats cut through the colours, each filled, I had no doubt, with couples up to no good and enjoying it.

On the land, here and there among older buildings, bubble domes were lighting up, giving the city a glowing fairyland look. To the east, where the bomb had landed, there were no old buildings at all, and the area was an Easter basket of colour – giant eggs, lighted from within.

I've seen the capital at night oftener than most and had never thought much about it. But tonight I had that 'last ride together' feeling. It was not its beauty that choked me up; it was knowing that down under those warm lights were people, alive and individual, going about their lawful occasions, making love or having spats, whichever suited them – doing whatever they damn well pleased, each under his own vine and fig tree, as it says, with nobody to make him afraid.

I thought about all those gentle, kindly people – each with a grey slug clinging to his neck, twitching his legs and arms, making his voice say what the slug wished, going where the slug wanted to go.

I made myself a solemn promise: if the parasites won, I'd be dead before I would let one of those things ride me. For an agent it would be simple; just bite my nails – or, if your hands happen to be off, there are other ways. The Old Man planned for all professional necessities.

But the Old Man had not planned such arrangements for such a purpose and I knew it. It was his business – and mine – to keep those people down there safe, not to run out when the going got tough.

I turned away. There was not a confounded thing I could do about it now; I decided that what I needed was company. The room contained the usual catalogue of 'escort bureaus' and 'model agencies' that you'll find in almost any big hotel. I thumbed through it, then slammed it shut. I didn't want a whoopee girl; I wanted one particular girl – one who would as soon shoot as shake hands. And I did not know where she had gone.

I always carry a tube of 'tempus fugit' pills, as one never knows when giving your reflexes a jolt will get you through a tight spot. Despite the scare propaganda, tempus pills are not habit-forming, not the way hashish is.

Nevertheless, a purist would say I was addicted, for I took them occasionally to make a twenty-four-hour leave seem like a week. I enjoyed the mild euphoria which the pills induced. Primarily, though, they just stretch your subjective time by a factor of ten or more – chop time into finer bits so that you live longer for the same amount of clock-and-calendar. Sure, I know the horrible example of the man who died of old age in a month through taking the pills steadily, but I took them only once in a while.

Maybe he had the right idea. He lived a long and happy life – you can be sure it was happy – and died happy at the end. What matter that the sun rose only thirty times? Who is keeping score and what are the rules?

I sat there, staring at my tube of pills and thinking that I had enough to keep me hopped up for what would be, to me, at least two 'years'. I could crawl in my hole and pull it in after me.

I took out two pills and got a glass of water. Then I put them back in the tube, put on my gun and phone, left the hotel, and headed for the Library of Congress.

On the way I stopped in a bar and looked at a newscast. There was no news from Iowa, but when is there any news from Iowa?

At the library I went to the catalogue, put on blinkers, and started scanning for references. 'Flying Saucers' led to 'Flying Disks', then to 'Project Saucer', then 'Lights in the Sky', 'Fireballs', 'Cosmic Diffusion Theory of Life Origins',

and two dozen blind alleys and screwball branches of litera-
ture. I needed a Geiger counter to tell me what was pay dirt,
especially as what I wanted was certain to carry a semantic-
content key classing it between Aesop's fables and the Lost
Continent myths.

Nevertheless, in an hour I had a handful of selector
cards. I handed them to the vestal virgin at the desk and
waited while she fed them into the hopper. Presently she
said, 'Most of the films you want are in use. The rest will be
delivered to study room 9-A. Take the escalator, puhlease.'

Room 9-A had one occupant, who looked up and said,
'Well! The wolf in person. How did you pick me up? I
could swear I gave you a clean miss.'

I said, 'Hello, Mary.'

'Hello,' she answered, 'and now, goodbye. Miss Barkis still
ain't willin' and I've got work to do.'

I got annoyed. 'Listen, you conceited twerp, odd as it may
seem, I did not come here looking for your no-doubt
beautiful body. I occasionally do some work myself. When
my spools arrive, I'll get the hell out and find another study
room – a stag one!'

Instead of flaring back, she immediately softened. 'I beg
your pardon, Sam. A woman hears the same thing so many
thousand times. Sit down.'

'No,' I answered, 'thanks, but I'll leave. I really want to
work.'

'Stay,' she insisted. 'Read that notice. If you remove
spools from the room to which they are delivered, you will
not only cause the sorter to blow a dozen tubes, but you'll
give the chief reference librarian a nervous breakdown.'

'I'll bring them back when I'm through.'

She took my arm and warm tingles went up it. 'Please,
Sam. I'm sorry.'

I sat down and grinned. 'Nothing could persuade me to
leave. I don't intend to let you out of sight until I know
your phone code, your home address, and the true colour of
your hair.'

'Wolf,' she said softly. 'You'll never know any of them.'
She made a great business of fitting her head back into her

study machine while ignoring me.

The delivery tube went *thunk!* and my spools spilled into the basket. I stacked them on the table by the other machine. One rolled over against the ones Mary had stacked up and knocked them down. I picked up what I thought was my spool and glanced at the end—the wrong end, as all it held was the serial number and that pattern of dots the selector reads. I turned it over, read the label, and placed it in my pile.

'Hey!' said Mary. 'That's mine.'

'In a pig's eye,' I said politely.

'But it is. It's the one I want next.'

Sooner or later, I can see the obvious. Mary wouldn't be there to study the history of footgear. I picked up others of hers and read the labels. 'So that's why nothing I wanted was in,' I said. 'But you didn't do a thorough job.' I handed her my selection.

Mary looked them over, then pushed all into a single pile. 'Shall we split them, or both of us see them all?'

'Fifty-fifty to weed out the junk, then we'll both go over the remainder,' I decided. 'Let's get busy.'

Even after having seen the parasite on poor Barnes's back, even after being assured by the Old Man that a 'flying saucer' had in fact landed, I was not prepared for the pile of evidence to be found buried in a public library. A pest on Digby and his evaluating formula! The evidence was unmistakable; Earth had been visited by ships from outer space not once but many times.

The reports long antedated our own achievement of space travel; some ran back into the seventeenth century – earlier than that, but it was impossible to judge reports dating back to a time when 'science' meant an appeal to Aristotle. The first systematic data came from the 1940s and 1950s; the next flurry was in the 1980s. I noticed something and started taking down dates. Strange objects in the sky appeared to hit a cycle at about thirty-year intervals. A statistical analyst might make something of it.

'Flying saucers' were tied in with 'mysterious disappearances', not only through being in the same category as sea serpents, bloody rain, and suchlike wild data, but also because, in well-documented instances, pilots had chased 'saucers' and never come back, or down, anywhere, i.e. officially classed as crashed in wild country and not recovered—an 'easy out' explanation.

I got another wild hunch and tried to see whether or not there was a thirty-year cycle in mysterious disappearances and, if so, did it match the objects-in-the-sky cycle? I could not be sure – too much data and not enough fluctuation; there are too many people disappearing every year for other reasons. But vital records had been kept for a long time and not all were lost in the bombings. I noted it down to farm out for professional analysis.

Mary and I did not exchange three words all night. Eventually we got up and stretched, then I lent Mary change to pay the machine for the spools of notes she had taken (*why* don't women carry change?) and got my wires out of hock too. 'Well, what's the verdict?' I asked.

'I feel like a sparrow who has built a nice nest in a rain spout.'

I recited the old jingle. 'And we'll do the same – refuse to learn and build again in the spout.'

'Oh no! Sam, we've got to do something! It makes a full pattern; this time they are moving in to stay.'

'Could be. I think they are.'

'Well, what do we *do*?'

'Honey chile, you are about to learn that in the Country of the Blind the one-eyed man is in for a hell of a rough ride.'

'Don't be cynical. There isn't time.'

'No, there isn't. Let's get out of here.'

Dawn was on us and the library was almost deserted. I said, 'Tell you what – let's find a barrel of beer, take it to my hotel room, bust in the head, and talk this over.'

She shook her head. 'Not to your room.'

'Damn it, this is business.'

'Let's go to my apartment. It's only a couple of hundred miles away; I'll fix breakfast there.'

I recalled my purpose in life in time to leer. 'That's the

best offer I've had all night. Seriously – why not the hotel? We'd save a half hour's travel.'

'You don't want to come to my apartment? I won't bite you.'

'I was hoping you would. No, I was wondering why the sudden switch?'

'Well – perhaps I wanted to show you the bear traps around my bed. Or perhaps I wanted to prove to you I could cook.' She dimpled.

I flagged a taxi and we went to her apartment.

When we got inside she made a careful search of the place, then came back and said, 'Turn around. I want to feel your back.'

'Why do —'

'Turn around!'

I shut up. She gave it a good knuckling, then said, 'Now you feel mine.'

'With pleasure!' Nevertheless I did a proper job, for I saw what she was driving at. There was nothing under her clothes but girl and assorted items of lethal hardware.

She turned around and let out a sigh. 'That's why I didn't want to go to your hotel. Now I *know* we are safe for the first time since I saw that *thing* on the station manager's back. This apartment is tight; I turn off the air and leave it sealed like a vault every time I leave it.'

'Say, how about the air-conditioning ducts?'

'I didn't turn on the conditioner system; I cracked one of the air-raid reserve bottles instead. Never mind; what would you like to eat?'

'Any chance of a steak, just warmed through?'

There was. While we chomped, we watched the newscast. Still no news from Iowa.

V

I did not get to see the bear traps; she locked her bedroom door. Three hours later she woke me and we had a second breakfast. Presently we struck cigarettes and I switched off the newscast. It was principally a display of the entries for 'Miss America'. Ordinarily I would have watched with interest, but since none of the babes was round-shouldered and their contest costumes could not possibly have concealed humps, it seemed to lack importance.

I said, 'Well?'

Mary said, 'We've got to arrange the facts and rub the President's nose in them.'

'How?'

'We've got to see him again.'

I repeated, 'How?'

She had no answer.

I said, 'We've got only one route – through the Old Man.'

I put in the call, using both our codes so that Mary could hear. Presently I heard, 'Chief Deputy Oldfield, for the Old Man. Shoot.'

'It's got to be the Old Man.'

There was a pause, then, 'Is this official or unofficial?'

'Uh, I guess you'd call it unofficial.'

'Well, I won't put you through for anything unofficial. And anything official I am handling.'

I switched off before I used any bad language. Then I coded again. The Old Man has a special code which is guaranteed to raise him up out of his coffin – but God help the agent who uses it unnecessarily.

He answered with a burst of profanity.

'Boss,' I said, 'on the Iowa matter —'

He broke off short. 'Yes?'

'Mary and I spent all night digging data out of the files. We want to talk it over.'

The profanity resumed. Presently he told me to turn it in for analysis and added that he intended to have my ears fried for a sandwich.

'Boss!' I said sharply.

'Eh?'

'If you can run out, so can we. Mary and I are resigning right now. That's official!'

Mary's eyebrows went up but she said nothing. There was a long silence, then he said, in a tired voice, 'Palmglade Hotel, North Miami Beach.'

'Right away.' I sent for a taxi and we went up on the roof. I had the hackie swing out over the ocean to avoid the Carolina speed trap; we made good time.

The Old Man lay there, looking sullen and letting sand dribble through his fingers while we reported. I had brought along a buzz box so that he could get it directly off the wire.

He looked up when we came to the point about thirty-year cycles, but he let it ride until my later query about possible similar cycles in disappearances, whereupon he called the Section. 'Get me Analysis. Hello – Peter? This is the boss. I want a curve on unexplained disappearances, starting with 1800. Huh? Smooth out known factors and discount steady load. What I want is humps and valleys. When? Two hours ago; what are you waiting for?'

He struggled to his feet, let me hand him his cane, and said, 'Well, back to the jute mill.'

'To the White House?' Mary asked eagerly.

'Eh? Be your age. You two have picked up nothing that would change the President's mind.'

'Oh. Then what?'

'I don't know. Keep quiet unless you have a bright idea.'

The Old Man had a car and I drove us back. After I turned it over to block control I said, 'Boss, I've got a caper that might convince the President.'

He grunted. 'Like this,' I went on. 'Send two agents in, me and one other. The other agent carries a portable scanning rig and keeps it trained on me. You get the President to watch.'

34

'Suppose nothing happens?'

'I'll make it happen. I am going where the space ship landed, bull my way through. We'll get close-up pix of the real ship, piped into the White House. Then I'll go to Barnes's office and investigate those round shoulders. I'll tear shirts off right in front of the camera. There won't be any finesse; I'll just bust things wide open.'

'You realize you have the same chance as a mouse at a cat convention.'

'I'm not so sure. As I see it, these things haven't super-human powers. I'll bet they are limited to whatever the human being they are riding can do. I don't plan on being a martyr. In any case, I'll get you pix.'

'Hmm —'

'It might work,' Mary put in. 'I'll be the other agent. I can —'

The Old Man and I said 'No' together – and then I flushed; it was not my prerogative. Mary went on, 'I was going to say that I am the logical one, because of the, uh, talent I have for spotting a man with a parasite.'

'No,' the Old Man repeated. 'Where he's going they'll all have riders – assumed so until proved otherwise. Besides, I am saving you for something.'

She should have shut up, but did not. 'For what? This is important.'

The Old Man said quietly, 'So is the other job. I'm planning to make you a Presidential bodyguard.'

'Oh.' She thought and answered, 'Uh, Boss – I'm not certain I could spot a woman who was possessed. I'm not, uh, equipped for it.'

'So we take his women secretaries away from him. And, Mary – you'll be watching him too.'

She thought that over. 'And suppose I find that one has gotten to him, in spite of everything?'

'You take necessary action, the Vice-President succeeds to the chair, and you get shot for treason. Now about this mission. We'll send Jarvis with the scanner and include Davidson as hatchet man. While Jarvis keeps the pickup on

35

you, Davidson can keep his eyes on Jarvis – and you can try to keep one eye on him.'

'You think it will work, then?'

'No – but any plan is better than no plan. Maybe it will stir up something.'

While we headed for Iowa – Jarvis, Davidson, and I – the Old Man went to Washington. Mary cornered me as we were about to leave, grabbed me by the ears, kissed me firmly, and said, 'Sam – come back.'

I got all tingly and felt like a fifteen-year-old.

Davidson roaded the car beyond the place where I had found a bridge out. I was navigating, using a map on which the landing site of the real space ship had been pin-pointed. The bridge gave a precise reference point. We turned off the road two-tenths of a mile due east of the site and jeeped through the scrub to the spot.

Almost to the spot, I should say. We ran into burned-over ground and decided to walk. The site shown by the space-station photograph was in the brush-fire area – and there was no 'flying saucer'. It would have taken a better detective than I to show that one had ever landed. The fire had destroyed any traces.

Jarvis scanned everything, anyhow, but I knew that the slugs had won another round. As we came out we ran into an elderly farmer; following doctrine, we kept a wary distance.

'Quite a fire,' I remarked, sidling away.

'Sure was,' he said dolefully. 'Killed two of my best milch cows, the poor dumb brutes. You fellows reporters?'

'Yes,' I agreed, 'but we've been sent on a wild goose chase.' I wished Mary were along. Probably this character was naturally round-shouldered. But assuming that the Old Man was right about the space ship – and he *had* to be right – then this too-innocent bumpkin must know about it and was covering up. Ergo, he was hagridden.

I had to do it. The chances of capturing a parasite and getting its picture on channels to the White House were better here than they were in a crowd. I threw a glance at my team mates; they were alert and Jarvis was scanning.

As the farmer turned I tripped him. He went down with me on his back, clawing at his shirt. Jarvis moved in and got a close-up. I had his back bare before he got his wind.

And it was *bare* – no parasite, no sign of one. Nor any place on his body, which I made sure of.

I helped him up and brushed him off; his clothes were filthy with ashes. 'I'm terribly sorry,' I said.

He was trembling with anger. 'You young —' He couldn't find a word bad enough for me. He looked at us and his mouth quivered. 'I'll have the law on you. If I were twenty years younger I'd lick all three of you.'

'Believe me, old-timer, it was a mistake.'

'Mistake!' His face broke and I thought he was going to cry. 'I come back from Omaha and find my place burned, half my stock gone, and my son-in-law no place around. I come out to find out why strangers are snooping around my land and I like to get torn to pieces. "Mistake!" What's the world coming to?'

I thought I could answer that last one, but I did not try. I did try to pay him for the indignity but he slapped my money to the ground. We tucked in our tails and got out.

When we were rolling again, Davidson said, 'Are you sure you know what you are up to?'

'I can make a mistake,' I said savagely, 'but have you ever known the Old Man to?'

'Mmm – no. Where next?'

'WDES main station. This one won't be a mistake.'

At the tollgates into Des Moines the gatekeeper hesitated. He glanced at a notebook and then at our plates. 'Sheriff has a call out for this car,' he said. 'Pull over to the right.' He left the barrier down.

'Right it is,' I agreed, backed up thirty feet and gunned her. The Section's cars are beefed up and hopped up – a good thing, for the barrier was stout. I did not slow down on the far side.

'This,' said Davidson dreamily, 'is interesting. Do you still know what you are doing?'

'Cut the chatter,' I snapped. 'Get this, both of you: we aren't likely to get out. *But we are going to get those pix.*'

'As you say, Chief.'

I was running ahead of any pursuit. I slammed to a stop in front of the station and we poured out. None of 'Uncle Charlie's' indirect methods – we swarmed into the first elevator and punched for Barnes's floor. When we got there I left the door of the car open. As we came into the outer office the receptionist tried to stop us, but we pushed on by. The girls looked up, startled. I went straight to Barnes's inner door and tried it; it was locked. I turned to his secretary. 'Where's Barnes?'

'Who is calling, please?' she said, polite as a fish.

I looked down at her shoulders. Humped. By God, I said to myself, this one *has* to be. She was here when I killed Barnes.

I bent over and pulled up her sweater.

I was right. I had to be right. For the second time I stared at one of the parasites.

She struggled and clawed and tried to bite. I judo-cut her neck, almost getting my hand in the mess, and she went limp. I gave her three fingers in the pit of her stomach, then swung her around. 'Jarvis,' I yelled, 'get a close-up.'

The idiot was fiddling with his gear, his big hind end between me and the pickup. He straightened up. 'School's out,' he said. 'Blew a tube.'

'Replace it – *hurry!*'

A stenographer stood up on the other side of the room and fired, at the scanner. Hit it, too – and Davidson burned her down. As if it had been a signal, about six of them jumped Davidson. They did not seem to have guns; they just swarmed over him.

I hung on to the secretary and shot from where I was. I caught a movement out of the corner of my eye and turned to find Barnes – 'Barnes number two' – standing in his doorway. I shot him through the chest to get the slug I knew was on his back. I turned back to the slaughter.

Davidson was up again. A girl crawled towards him; she seemed wounded. He shot her in the face and she stopped.

His next bolt was just past my ear. I said, 'Thanks! Let's get out of here. Jarvis – come on!'

The elevator was open; we rushed in, me still burdened with Barnes's secretary. I slammed the door and started it. Davidson was trembling and Jarvis was white. 'Buck up,' I said, 'you weren't shooting people, but *things*. Like this.' I held the girl up and looked down at her back.

Then I almost collapsed. My specimen, the one I had grabbed to take back alive, was gone. Slipped to the floor, probably, and oozed away during the ruckus. 'Jarvis,' I said, 'did you get *anything*?' He shook his head.

The girl's back was covered with a rash like a million pin-pricks, where the thing had ridden her. I settled her on the floor against the wall of the car. She was still unconscious, so we left her in the car. There was no hue and cry as we went through the lobby to the street.

A policeman had his foot on our car while making out a ticket. He handed it to me and said, 'You can't park in this area, Mac.'

I said, 'Sorry,' and signed his copy. Then I gunned the car away, got as clear as I could of traffic – and blasted off, right from a city street. I wondered whether he added that to the ticket. When I had her at altitude I switched licence plates and identification code. The Old Man thinks of everything.

But he did not think much of me. I tried to report on the way in but he cut me short and ordered us into the Section offices. Mary was there with him. He let me report, inter-rupting with only an occasional grunt. 'How much did you see?' I asked when I had finished.

'Transmission cut off when you hit the toll barrier,' he informed me. 'The President was not impressed by what he saw.'

'I suppose not.'

'He told me to fire you.'

I stiffened. 'I am perfectly will —' I started out.

'Pipe down!' the Old Man snapped. 'I told him that he could fire me, but not my subordinates. You are a thumb-fingered dolt,' he went on quietly, 'but you can't be spared now.'

'Thanks.'

Mary had been wandering around the room. I tried to catch her eye, but she was not having any. Now she stopped back of Jarvis's chair – and gave the Old Man the sign she had given about Barnes.

I hit Jarvis in the head with my heater and he sagged out of his chair.

'Stand back, Davidson!' the Old Man rapped. His gun was out and pointed at Davidson's chest. 'Mary, how about him?'

'He's all right.'

'And him.'

'Sam's clean.'

The Old Man's eyes moved over us and I have never felt closer to death. 'Peel off your shirts,' he said sourly.

We did – and Mary was right. I had begun to wonder whether I would know it if I *did* have a parasite on me. 'Now him,' the Old Man ordered. 'Gloves.'

We stretched Jarvis out and carefully cut his clothing away. We had our live specimen.

VI

I felt myself ready to retch. The thought of that *thing* right behind me all the way from Iowa was more than my stomach could stand. I'm not squeamish – but you don't know what the sight of one can do unless you yourself have seen one while knowing what it was.

I swallowed and said, 'Let's work it off. Maybe we can still save Jarvis.' I did not really think so; I had a deep-down hunch that anyone who had been ridden by one of those things was spoiled, permanently.

The Old Man waved us back. 'Forget Jarvis!'

'But —'

'Stow it! If he can be saved, a bit longer won't matter. In any case —' He shut up and so did I. I knew what he meant; we were expendable; the people of the United States were not.

The Old Man, gun drawn and wary, continued to watch the thing on Jarvis's back. He said to Mary, 'Get the President. Special code zero zero zero seven.'

Mary went to his desk. I heard her talking into the muffler, but my own attention was on the parasite. It made no move to leave its host.

Presently Mary reported, 'I can't get him, sir. One of his assistants is on the screen. Mr McDonough.'

The Old Man winced. McDonough was an intelligent, likable man who hadn't changed his mind on anything since he was housebroken. The President used him as a buffer.

The Old Man bellowed, not bothering with the muffler.

No, the President was not available. No, he could not be reached with a message. No, Mr McDonough was not exceeding his authority; the Old Man was not on the list of exceptions – if there was such a list. Yes, Mr McDonough would be happy to make an appointment; that was a promise. How would next Friday do? Today? Out of the question. Tomorrow? Impossible.

The Old Man switched off and seemed about to have a stroke. Then he took two deep breaths, his features relaxed, and he said, 'Dave, ask Doc Graves to step in. The rest of you keep your distance.'

The head of the biological lab came in shortly. 'Doc,' said the Old Man, 'there is one that isn't dead.'

Graves looked closely at Jarvis's back. 'Interesting,' he said. He dropped to one knee.

'Stand back!'

Graves looked up. 'But I must have an opportunity —'

'You and my half-wit aunt! I want you to study it, yes, but first you've got to keep it alive. Second, you've got to keep it from escaping. Third, you've got to protect yourself.'

Graves smiled. 'I'm not afraid of it. I —'

'Be afraid of it! That's an order.'

41

'I was about to say that I must rig up an incubator to care for it after we remove it from the host. It is evident that these things need oxygen – not free oxygen, but oxygen from its host. Perhaps a large dog would suffice.'

'No,' snapped the Old Man. 'Leave it where it is.'

'Eh? Is this man a volunteer?'

The Old Man did not answer. Graves went on, 'Human laboratory subjects must be volunteers. Professional ethics, you know.'

These scientific laddies never do get broken to harness; the Old Man said quietly, 'Dr Graves, every agent in this Section is a volunteer for whatever I find necessary. Please carry out my orders. Get a stretcher in here. Use care.'

After they had carted Jarvis away, Davidson and Mary and I went to the lounge for a drink or four. We needed them. Davidson had the shakes. When the first drink failed to fix him I said, 'Look, Dave, I feel as bad about those girls as you do – but it could not be helped. Get that through your head.'

'How bad was it?' asked Mary.

'Pretty bad. I don't know how many we killed. There was no time to be careful. We weren't shooting people; we were shooting parasites.' I turned to Davidson. 'Don't you see that?'

'That's just it. They weren't human.' He went on, 'I think I could shoot my own brother if the job required it. But these things aren't human. You shoot and they keep coming towards you. They don't —' He broke off.

All I felt was pity. After a bit he left and Mary and I talked a while, trying for answers and getting nowhere. Then she announced that she was sleepy and headed for the women's dormitory. The Old Man had ordered all hands to sleep in that night, so I went to the boys' wing and crawled in a sack.

The air-raid alarm woke me. I stumbled into clothes as blowers sighed off, then the inter-com bawled in the Old Man's voice, 'Anti-gas and anti-radiation procedures! Seal everything! All hands gather in the conference hall. Move!'

Being a field agent, I had no local duties. I shuffled down the tunnel to the offices. The Old Man was in the big hall, looking grim. I wanted to ask what was up, but there were a dozen clerks, agents, stenos, and such there before me. After a bit the Old Man sent me out to get the door tally from the guard on watch. The Old Man called the roll and presently it was clear that every person listed on the door tally was now inside the hall, from old Miss Haines, the Old Man's secretary, down to the steward of the lounge – except the door guard and Jarvis. The tally had to be right; we keep track of who goes in and out a bit more carefully than a bank keeps track of money.

I was sent out again for the door guard. It took a call back to the Old Man before he would leave his post; he then threw the bolt switch and followed me. When we got back Jarvis was there, attended by Graves and a lab man. He was wrapped in a hospital robe, apparently conscious, but dopey.

I began to have some notion of what it was all about. The Old Man was facing the assembled staff and keeping his distance; now he drew his gun. 'One of the invading parasites is loose among us,' he said. 'To some of you that means too much. To the rest of you I will have to explain, as the safety of all of us – of our whole race – depends on complete co-operation and utter obedience.' He went on to explain briefly but with ugly exactness what a parasite was, what the situation was. 'In short,' he concluded, 'the parasite is almost certainly in this room. One of us looks human but is an automaton, moving at the will of our deadliest enemy.'

There was a murmur. People stole glances at each other. Some tried to draw away. A moment before we had been a team; now we were a mob, each suspicious of the other. I found myself edging away from the man closest to me – Ronald the lounge steward; I had known him for years.

Graves cleared his throat. 'Chief,' he started in, 'I took every reasonable —'

'Stow it. Bring Jarvis out in front. Take his robe off.' Graves shut up and he and his assistant complied. Jarvis

43

seemed only partly aware of his surroundings. Graves must have drugged him.

'Turn him around,' the Old Man ordered. Jarvis let himself be turned; there was the mark of the slug, a red rash on shoulders and neck. 'You can see,' the Old Man went on, 'where the thing rode him.' There had been whispers and one embarrassed giggle when Jarvis had been stripped; now there was a dead hush.

'Now,' said the Old Man, 'we are going to *get that slug*! Furthermore, we are going to capture it alive. You have all seen where a parasite rides a man. I'm warning you; if the parasite gets burned, I'll burn the man who did it. If you have to shoot to catch it, shoot low. Come here!' He pointed his gun at me.

He halted me halfway between the crowd and himself. 'Graves! Sit Jarvis down behind me. No, leave his robe off.' The Old Man turned back to me. 'Drop your gun on the floor.'

The Old Man's gun was pointed at my belly; I was very careful how I drew mine. I slid it six feet away from me. 'Take off all your clothes.'

That is an awkward order to carry out. The Old Man's gun overcame my inhibitions. It did not help to have some of the girls giggling as I got down to the buff. One of them whispered, 'Not bad!' and another replied, 'Knobby, I'd say.' I blushed.

After he looked me over the Old Man told me to pick up my gun. 'Back me up,' he ordered, 'and keep an eye on the door. You! Dotty Something-or-other – you're next.'

Dotty was a girl from the clerical pool. She had no gun, of course, and was dressed in a floor-length négligé. She stepped forward, stopped, but did nothing more.

The Old Man waved his gun. 'Come on – get 'em off!'

'You really mean it?' she said incredulously.

'*Move!*'

She almost jumped. 'Well!' she said, 'no need to take a person's head off.' She bit her lip and then unfastened the clasp at her waist. 'I ought to get a bonus for this,' she said defiantly, then threw the robe from her.

'Over against the wall,' the Old Man said savagely. 'Renfrew!'

After my ordeal the men were businesslike though some were embarrassed. As to the women, some giggled and some blushed, but none of them objected too much. In twenty minutes there were more square yards of goose flesh exposed than I had ever seen before, and the pile of guns looked like an arsenal.

When Mary's turn came, she took her clothes off quickly and without a fuss. She made nothing of it, and wore her skin with quiet dignity. She added considerably to the pile of hardware. I decided she just plain liked guns.

Finally we were all skinned and quite evidently free of parasites, except the Old Man and his old-maid secretary. I think he was a bit in awe of Miss Haines. He looked distressed and poked about in the pile of clothing with his cane. Finally he looked up at her. 'Miss Haines – if you please.'

I thought to myself, Brother, this time you are going to have to use force.

She stood there, facing him down, a statue of offended modesty. I moved closer and said, out of the corner of my mouth, 'Boss – how about yourself? Take 'em off.'

He looked startled. 'I mean it,' I said. 'It's you or she. Might be either. Out of those duds.'

The Old Man can relax to the inevitable. He said, 'Have her stripped.' He began fumbling at his zippers, looking grim. I told Mary to take a couple of women and peel Miss Haines. When I turned back the Old Man had his trousers at half mast – and Miss Haines made a break for it.

The Old Man was between us; I couldn't get in a clean shot – and every other agent in the place was disarmed! I don't think it was accident; the Old Man did not trust them not to shoot. He wanted that slug – alive.

She was out the door and running down the passage by the time I could get organized. I could have winged her in the passageway, but I was inhibited. First, I could not shift gears emotionally that fast. I mean to say, she was still Old Lady Haines, secretary to the boss, the one who bawled me out for poor grammar in my reports. In the second place, if she was carrying a parasite, I did not want to risk burning it.

She ducked into a room; again I hesitated – sheer habit: it was the ladies' room.

But only a moment. I slammed the door open and looked around, gun ready.

Something hit me back of my right ear.

I can give no clear account of the next few moments. I was out cold, for a time at least. I remember a struggle and some shouts: 'Look out!' 'Damn her – she's bitten me!' 'Watch your hands!' Then somebody said quietly, 'By her hands and feet – careful.' Somebody said, 'How about him?' and someone answered, 'Later, he's not hurt.'

I was still practically out as they left, but I began to feel a flood of life stirring back into me. I sat up, feeling extreme urgency about something. I got up, staggering, and went to the door. I looked out cautiously; nobody was in sight. I trotted down the corridor, away from the conference hall.

At the outer door, I realized with a shock that I was naked, and tore on down the hallway to the men's wing. There I grabbed the first clothes I could find and pulled them on. The shoes were much too small for me; it did not seem to matter.

I ran back to the exit, found the switch; the door opened. I thought I had made a clean escape, but somebody shouted, 'Sam!' just as I was going out. I plunged on out. At once I had my choice of six doors and then three more beyond the one I picked. The warren we called the offices was served by a spaghetti-like mess of tunnels. I came up finally inside a subway fruit-and-bookstall, nodded to the proprietor, and swung the counter gate up and mingled with the crowd.

I caught the up-river jet express and got off at the first station. I crossed over to the down-river, waited around the change window until a man came up who displayed quite a bit of money as he bought his counter. I got on the same train and got off when he did. At the first dark spot I rabbit-

46

punched him. Now I had money and was ready to operate. I did not know why I had to have money, but I knew that I needed it for what I was about to do.

VII

I saw things around me with a curious double vision, as if I stared through rippling water – yet I felt no surprise and no curiosity. I moved like a sleepwalker, unaware of what I was about to do – but I was wide awake, aware of who I was, where I was, what my job at the Section had been. And, although I did not know what I was about to do, I was always aware of what I was doing and sure that each act was the necessary act at that moment.

I felt no emotion most of the time, except the contentment that comes from work which needs to be done. That was on the conscious level; someplace, more levels down than I understand about, I was excruciatingly unhappy, terrified, and filled with guilt, but that was down, 'way down, locked, suppressed; I was hardly aware of it and not affected by it.

I knew that I had been seen to leave. That shout of 'Sam!' was for me; two persons only knew me by that name and the Old Man would have used my right name. So Mary had seen me leave. It was a good thing, I thought, that she had let me find out where her apartment was. It would be necessary to booby-trap it against her next use of it. In the meantime I must get on with work and keep from being picked up.

I was moving through a warehouse district, all my training at work to avoid notice. Shortly I found a satisfactory building; there was a sign: LOFT FOR LEASE – SEE RENTAL AGENT ON GROUND FLOOR. I scouted it, noted the address, then doubled back to a Western Union booth two squares back. There I took a vacant machine and sent this message: EXPEDITE TWO CASES TINY TOTS TALKY TALES SAME DISCOUNT CONSIGNED JOEL FREEMAN, and added the address of the loft. I sent it to Roscoe & Dillard, Jobbers and Manufacturers Agents, Des Moines, Iowa.

As I left the booth the sight of one of the Kwikfede restaurants reminded me that I was hungry, but the reflex cut off and I thought no more about it. I returned to the warehouse, found a dark corner in the 'rear, and settled back to wait for dawn and business hours.

I have a dim recollection of ever-repeating, claustrophobic nightmares.

At nine o'clock I met the rental agent as he unlocked his office, and leased the loft, paying him a fat squeeze for immediate possession. I went up to the loft, unlocked it, and waited.

About ten-thirty my crates were delivered. After the expressmen were gone, I opened a crate, took out one cell, warmed it, and got it ready. Then I found the rental agent again and said, 'Mr Greenberg, could you come up for a moment? I want to see about making changes in the lighting.'

He fussed, but did so. When we entered the loft I closed the door and led him to the open crate. 'Here,' I said, 'if you will lean over there, you will see what I mean. If I could just —'

I got him with a grip that cut off his wind, ripped his jacket and shirt up, and, with my free hand, transferred a master from the cell to his bare back, then held him tight until he relaxed. I let him up, tucked his shirt in, and dusted him off. When he caught his breath, I said, 'What news from Des Moines?'

'What do you want to know?' he asked. 'How long have you been out?'

I started to explain, but he interrupted with, 'Let's have direct conference and not waste time.' I skinned up my shirt; he did the same; and we sat down on the unopened crate, back to back, so that our masters could be in contact. My own mind was blank; I have no idea how long it went

48

on. I watched a fly droning around a dusty cobweb.

The building superintendent was our next recruit. He was a large Swede and it took both of us. After that Mr Greenberg called up the owner and insisted that he had to come down and see some mishap that had occurred to the structure – just what, I don't know; I was busy with the super, opening and warming more cells.

The owner of the building was a prize and we all felt pleased, including, of course, himself. He belonged to the Constitution Club, the membership of which read like Who's Who in Finance, Government, and Industry.

It was pushing noon; we had no time to lose. The super went out to buy clothes and a satchel for me and sent the owner's chauffeur up to be recruited as he did so. At twelve-thirty we left, the owner and I, in his town car; the satchel contained twelve masters, in their cells but ready.

The owner signed: *J. Hardwick Potter & Guest*. A flunky tried to take my bag, but I insisted that I needed it to change my shirt before lunch. We fiddled in the washroom until we had it to ourselves, save for the attendant – where-upon we recruited him and sent him with a message to the manager that a guest had taken ill in the washroom.

After we took care of the manager he obtained a white coat and I became another washroom attendant. I had only ten masters left, but the cases would be picked up from the loft and delivered to the club shortly. The regular atten-dant and I used up the rest of those I had before the lunch-hour rush was over. One guest surprised us while we were busy and I had to kill him. We stuffed him into the mop closet. There was a lull after that, as the cases had not yet arrived. Hunger reflex nearly doubled me over, then it dropped off but persisted; I told the manager, who had me served lunch in his office. The cases arrived as I was finish-ing.

During the drowsy period in the mid-afternoon we secured the place. By four o'clock everyone in the building – members, staff, and guests – were with us; from then on we processed them in the lobby as the doorman passed them in. Later in the day the manager phoned Des Moines for more cases. Our big prize came that evening – the Assistant Secretary of the Treasury. We saw a real victory; the Treasury Department is charged with the safety of the President.

VIII

The capture of a high key official was felt by me as absent-minded satisfaction, then I thought no more about it. We – the human recruits, I mean – hardly thought at all; we knew what we were to do, but we knew it only at the moment of action, as a 'high school' horse gets his orders, responds to them, and is ready for the next signal from his rider.

High school horse and rider is a good comparison, but it does not go nearly far enough. The masters had at their disposal not only our full intelligences, they were also able to tap directly our memory and experiences. We communicated for them between masters too; sometimes we knew what we were talking about; sometimes not. Spoken words went through the servant, but we the servants had no part in more important, direct, master-to-master conferences. During these we sat quietly and waited until our riders were through, then straightened out clothing and did what was necessary.

I had no more to do with words spoken by me for my master than has a telephone. I was a communication instrument, nothing more. Some days after I was recruited I gave the club manager instructions about shipments of masters' carrying cells. I was fleetingly aware, as I did so, that three more ships had landed, but my overt knowledge was limited to a single address in New Orleans.

I thought nothing about it; I went on with my work. I was a new 'special assistant to Mr Potter' and spent the days in his office – and the nights too. Actually, the relationship may have reversed; I frequently gave oral instructions to Potter. Or perhaps I understand the social organization of the parasites as little now as I did then.

I knew – and my master knew – that it was well for me to stay out of sight. Through me, my master knew as much as I did; it knew that I was one human known to the Old Man to have been recruited – and my master knew, I am sure, that the Old Man would not cease to search for me, to recapture me or kill me.

It seems odd that it did not change bodies and kill mine; we had many more recruits available than we had masters. It could not have felt anything parallel to human squeamishness; masters newly delivered from their transit cells frequently damaged their hosts; we always destroyed the host and found a new one. On the other hand, would a skilled cowhand have destroyed a well-trained work horse in favour of an untried, strange mount? That may have been why I was hidden and saved.

After a time the city was 'secured' and my master started taking me out on the streets. I do not mean that every inhabitant wore a hump – no; the humans were very numerous and the masters still very few – but the key positions in the city were held by our own recruits, from the cop on the corner to the mayor and the chief of police, not forgetting ward bosses, church ministers, board members, and any and all in public communication and news. The majority continued their usual affairs, not only undisturbed by the masquerade but unaware of it.

Unless, of course, one of them happened to be in the way of some purpose of a master – in which case he was disposed of.

One of the disadvantages our masters worked under was the difficulty of long-distance communication. It was limited to what human hosts could say in human speech over ordinary channels, and was further limited, unless the channel was secured throughout, to code messages such as the one I had sent ordering the first shipment of masters. Such communications through servants was almost certainly not adequate to the purposes of the masters; they seemed to need frequent body-to-body conference to co-ordinate their actions.

I was sent to New Orleans for such a conference.

I went out on the street as usual one morning, then went to the uptown launching platform and ordered a cab. After a wait my cab was lifted to the loading ramp and I started to get in – as an old gentleman bustled up and climbed into it ahead of me.

I received an order to dispose of him, which order was immediately countermanded by one telling me to go slow and be careful. I said, 'Excuse me, sir, but this cab is taken.'

'Quite,' the elderly man replied. 'I've taken it.'

'You will have to find another,' I said reasonably. 'Let's see your queue ticket.'

I had him; the cab carried the launching number shown on my ticket, but he did not stir. 'Where you going?' he demanded.

'New Orleans,' I answered and learned for the first time my destination.

'Then you can drop me off in Memphis.'

I shook my head. 'It's out of my way.'

'All of fifteen minutes!' He seemed to have difficulty controlling his temper. 'You cannot pre-empt a public vehicle unreasonably.' He turned from me. 'Driver! Explain the rules to this person.'

The driver stopped picking his teeth. 'It's nothing to me. I pick 'em up, I take 'em, I drop 'em. Settle it yourselves or I'll ask the dispatcher for another fare.'

I hesitated, not yet having been instructed. Then I found myself climbing inside. 'New Orleans,' I said, 'with stop at Memphis.' The driver shrugged and signalled the control tower. The other passenger snorted and paid me no attention.

Once in the air, he opened his brief case and spread papers across his knees. I watched him with disinterest. I found myself shifting position to let me get at my gun easily. The man shot out a hand, grabbed my wrist. 'Not so fast, son,' he said, and his features broke into the satanic grin of the Old Man himself.

My reflexes are fast, but I was at the disadvantage of having everything routed from me to my master, passed on by it, and action routed back to me. How much delay is that? I don't know. As I was drawing, I felt the bell of a gun against my ribs. 'Take it easy.'

With his other hand he thrust something against my side; I felt a prick, and then through me spread the warm tingle of a jolt of 'Morpheus' taking hold. I made one more attempt to pull my gun free and sank forward.

I was vaguely aware of voices. Someone was handling me roughly and someone was saying, 'Watch out for that ape!' Another voice replied, 'It's all right; his tendons are cut,' to which the first retorted, 'He's still got *teeth*, hasn't he?'

Yes, I thought fretfully, and if you get close I'll bite you with them. The remark about cut tendons seemed to be true; none of my limbs would move, but that did not worry me as much as being called an ape. It was a shame, I thought, to call a man names when he couldn't protect himself.

I wept a little and then fell into a stupor.

'Feeling better, son?'

The Old Man was leaning over the end of my bed, staring thoughtfully. His chest was bare and covered with grizzled hair.

'Unh,' I said, 'pretty good, I guess.' I started to sit up and found I could not.

The Old Man came around to the side. 'We can take those restraints off,' he said, fiddling with clasps. 'Didn't want you hurting yourself. There!'

I sat up, rubbing myself. 'Now,' said the Old Man, 'how much do you remember? Report.'

'Remember?'

'They caught you. Do you remember anything after the parasite got to you?'

I felt a sudden wild fear and clutched at the bed. 'Boss!

53

They know where this place is! *I told them.*'

'No, they don't,' he answered quietly, 'because these aren't the offices you remember. I had the old offices evacuated. They don't know about this hangout – I think. So you remember?'

'Of course I remember. I got out of here – I mean out of the old offices and went up —' My thoughts raced ahead; I had a sudden image of holding a live master in my bare hand, ready to place it on the rental agent.

I threw up. The Old Man wiped my mouth and said gently, 'Go ahead.'

I swallowed and said, 'Boss – they're all around. They've got the city.'

'I know. Same as Des Moines. And Minneapolis, St Paul, New Orleans, and Kansas City. Maybe more. I don't know – I can't be everyplace.' He scowled and added, 'It's like fighting with your feet in a sack. We're losing, fast. We can't even clamp down on the cities we know about.'

'Good grief! Why not?'

'You should know. Because "older and wiser heads" are still unconvinced. Because when they take over a city, everything goes on as before.'

I stared. 'Never mind,' he said gently. 'You are the first break we've had. You're the first victim to be recaptured alive – and now we find you remember what happened. That's important. And your parasite is the first one we've managed to capture and keep alive. We'll have a chance to —'

My face must have been a mask of terror; the notion that my master was still alive – and might get to me again – was more than I could stand.

The Old Man shook me. 'Take it easy,' he said mildly. 'You are still pretty weak.'

'*Where is it?*'

'Eh? The parasite? Don't worry about it. It's living off your opposite number, a red orang-utan, name of Napoleon. It's safe.'

'*Kill it!*'

'Hardly. We need it alive, for study.'

I must have gone to pieces, for he slapped me. 'Take a brace,' he said. 'I hate to bother you when you are sick, but I've got to. We've got to get everything you remember down on wire. So level off and fly right.'

I pulled myself together and started making a careful report of all that I could remember. I described renting the loft and recruiting my first victim, then how we moved on to the Constitution Club. The Old Man nodded. 'Logical. You were a good agent, even for *them*.'

'You don't understand,' I objected. '*I* didn't do any thinking. I knew what was going on, but that was all. It was as if, uh, as if —' I paused, stuck for words.

'Never mind. Get on.'

'After we recruited the club manager the rest was easy. We took them as they came in and —'

'Names?'

'Oh, certainly. M. C. Greenberg, Thor Hansen, J. Hardwick Potter, his chauffeur Jim Wakeley, a little guy called "Jake" who was washroom attendant, but he had to be disposed of later – his master would not let him take time out for necessities. Then there was the manager; I never did get his name.' I paused, letting my mind run back, trying to make sure of each recruit. 'Oh my God!'

'What is it?'

'The Assistant Secretary of the *Treasury*.'

'You got *him*?'

'Yes. The first day. How long has it been? God, Chief, the Treasury Department *protects the President*!'

But there was just a hole in the air where the Old Man had been.

I lay back exhausted. I started sobbing into my pillow. After a while I went to sleep.

IX

I woke up with my mouth foul, head buzzing, and a sense of impending disaster. Nevertheless I felt fine, by comparison. A cheerful voice said, 'Feeling better?'

A small brunette creature was bending over me. She was a cute little bug and I was well enough to appreciate the fact, faintly. She was dressed in an odd costume: white shorts, a wisp of stuff that restrained her breasts, and a sort of metal carapace that covered the neck, shoulders, and spine.

'Better,' I admitted, making a face.

'Mouth taste unpleasant?'

'Like a Balkan cabinet meeting.'

'Here.' She gave me some stuff in a glass; it burned a little and washed away the bad taste. 'No,' she went on, 'don't swallow it. 'Pit it out and I'll get you water.' I obeyed.

'I'm Doris Marsden,' she went on, 'your day nurse.'

'Glad to know you, Doris,' I answered and stared at her. 'Say – why the getup? Not that I don't like it, but you look like a refugee from a comic book.'

She giggled. 'I feel like a chorus girl. But you'll get used to it – I did.'

'I like it. But why?'

'Old Man's orders.'

Then I knew why, and I started feeling worse again. Doris went on, 'Now for supper.' She got a tray.

'I don't want anything to eat.'

'Open up,' she said firmly, 'or I'll rub it in your hair.'

Between gulps, taken in self-defence, I managed to get out, 'I feel pretty good. One jolt of Gyro and I'll be on my feet.'

'No stimulants,' she said flatly, still shovelling it in. 'Special diet and lots of rest, with a sleepy pill later. That's what the man says.'

'What's wrong with me?'

'Exhaustion, starvation, and incipient scurvy. As well as scabies and lice – but we got those whipped. Now you know – and if you tell the doctor, I'll call you a liar to your face. Turn over.'

I did so and she started changing dressings; I appeared to be spotted with sores; I thought about what she had told me and tried to remember how I had lived under my master.

'Stop trembling,' she said. 'Having a bad one?'

'I'm all right,' I told her. As near as I could remember I had not eaten oftener than every second or third day. Bathing? Let me see. Why, I hadn't bathed at all! I had shaved every day and put on a clean shirt; that was necessary to the masquerade and the master knew it.

On the other hand, I had never taken off my shoes from the time I had stolen them until the Old Man had recaptured me – and they had been too tight to start with. 'What shape are my feet in?' I asked.

'Don't be nosy,' Doris advised me.

I like nurses; they are calm and earthy and tolerant. Miss Briggs, my night nurse, was not the cute job that Doris was; she had a face like a horse. She wore the same musical-comedy rig that Doris sported, but she wore it with a no-nonsense air and walked like a grenadier. Doris, bless her heart, jiggled pleasantly as she walked.

Miss Briggs refused me a second sleeping pill when I woke up in the night and had the horrors, but she did play poker with me and skinned me out of half a month's pay. I tried to find out from her about the President matter, but she wasn't talking. She would not admit that she knew anything about parasites, flying saucers, or whatnot – and she herself dressed in a costume that could have only one purpose!

I asked her what the public news was, then. She maintained that she had been too busy to look at a 'cast. So I asked to have a stereo box moved into my room. She said I would have to ask the doctor; I was on the 'quiet' list. I asked when I was going to see this so-called doctor. About then her call bell sounded and she left.

I fixed her. While she was gone, I cold-decked the deal, so that she got a pat hand – then I wouldn't bet against her.

I got to sleep later on and was awakened by Miss Briggs slapping me in the face with a washcloth. She got me ready for breakfast, then Doris relieved her and brought it to me. While I was chomping I tackled her for news – with the same score I had made with Miss Briggs. Nurses run a hospital as if it were a nursery for backward children.

Davidson came to see me after breakfast. 'Heard you were here,' he said. He was wearing shorts and nothing else, except that his left arm was covered by a dressing.

'More than I've heard,' I complained. 'What happened to you?'

'Bee stung me.'

If he didn't want to tell me how he had got burned, that was his business. I went on, 'The Old Man was in here yesterday and left very suddenly. Seen him since?'

'Yep.'

'Well?' I answered.

'Well, how about *you*? Have the psych boys cleared you for classified matters, or not?'

'Is there any doubt about it?'

'You're darn tootin' there is. Poor old Jarvis never did pull out of it.'

'Huh?' I hadn't thought about Jarvis. 'How is he now?'

'He isn't. Dropped into a coma and died – the day after you left. I mean the day after you were captured.' Davidson looked me over. 'You must be tough.'

I did not feel tough. Tears of weakness welled up again and I blinked them back. Davidson pretended not to see and went on, 'You should have seen the ruckus after you gave us the slip. The Old Man took out after you wearing nothing but a gun and a look of grim determination. He would have caught you, but the police picked him up and we had to get him out of hock.' Davidson grinned.

I grinned feebly. There was something both gallant and silly about the Old Man charging out to save the world in his birthday suit. 'Sorry I missed it. What else has happened – lately?'

Davidson looked me over, then said, 'Wait a minute.' He stepped out and was gone a short time. When he came back, he said, 'The Old Man says okay. What do you want to know?'

'Everything! What happened yesterday?'

'That's how I got this.' He waved his damaged wing at me. 'I was lucky,' he added. 'Three agents were killed. Quite a fracas.'

'But how about the President? Was he —'

Doris bustled in. 'Oh, there you are!' she said to Davidson. 'I told you to stay in bed. You're due at Mercy Hospital right now. The ambulance has been waiting ten minutes.'

He stood up, grinned, and pinched her with his good hand. 'The party can't start until I get there.'

'Well, hurry!'

'Coming.'

I called out, 'Hey! How about the *President*?'

Davidson looked back over his shoulder. 'Oh, him? He's all right – not a scratch.' He went on.

Doris came back a few minutes later, fuming. 'Patients!' she said, like a swear word. 'I should have had twenty minutes for his injection to take hold; as it was I gave it to him when he got into the ambulance.'

'Injection for what?'

'Didn't he tell you?'

'No.'

'Well – no reason not to tell you. Amputation and graft, lower left arm.'

'Oh.' Well, I thought, I won't hear the end of the story from Davidson; grafting on a new limb is a shock. They keep the patient hopped up for at least ten days. I tackled Doris again. 'How about the Old Man? Was he wounded? Or would it be against your sacred rules to tell me?'

'You talk too much,' she answered. 'It's time for morning nourishment and your nap.' She produced a glass of milky slop.

'Speak up, wench, or I'll spit it in your face.'

'The Old Man? You mean the Chief of Section?'

'Who else?'

'*He's* not on the sick list.' She made a face. 'I wouldn't want *him* as a patient.'

X

For two or three more days I was kept in bed and treated like a child. I didn't care; it was the first real rest I had had in years. The sores got better and presently I was encouraged – 'required' I should say – to take light exercise around the room.

The Old Man called on me. 'Well,' he said, 'still malingering.'

I flushed. 'Damn your black, flabby heart,' I told him. 'Get me some pants and I'll show you who is malingering.'

'Slow down.' He took my chart and looked it over. 'Nurse,' he said, 'get this man a pair of shorts. I'm restoring him to duty.'

Doris faced up to him like a banty hen. 'You may be the big boss, but you can't give orders here. The doctor will —'

'Stow it!' he said, 'and get those drawers.'

'But —'

He picked her up, swung her around, paddled her behind, and said, 'Git!'

She went out, squawking and sputtering, and came back with the doctor. The Old Man said mildly, 'Doc, I sent for pants, not for you.'

The medico said stiffly, 'I'll thank you not to interfere with my patients.'

'He's not your patient. I'm restoring him to duty.'

'Yes? Sir, if you do not like the way I run my department, you may have my resignation.'

The Old Man answered, 'I beg your pardon, sir. Sometimes I become too preoccupied to remember to follow correct procedure. Will you do me the favour of examining this patient? If he can be restored to duty, it would help me to have his services at once.'

The doctor's jaw muscles were jumping, but he said, 'Certainly, sir!' He went through a show of studying my chart, then tested my reflexes. 'He needs more recuperation time – but you may have him. Nurse – fetch clothing for this man.'

Clothing consisted of shorts and shoes. But everybody else was dressed the same way, and it was comforting to see all those bare shoulders with no masters clinging to them. I told the Old Man so. 'Best defence we've got,' he growled, 'even if it does make the joint look like a summer colony. If we don't win this set-to before winter weather, we're licked.'

He stopped at a door with a sign: BIOLOGICAL LABORATORY – STAY OUT!

I hung back. 'Where are we going?'

'To take a look at your twin, the ape with your parasite.'

'That's what I thought. Not for me – no, thanks!' I could feel myself tremble.

'Now look, son,' he said patiently, 'get over your panic. The best way is to face up to it. I know it's hard – I've spent hours staring at the thing, getting used to it.'

'You don't know – you *can't* know!' I had the shakes so badly that I had to steady myself by the door frame.

'I suppose it's different,' he said slowly, 'when you've actually had it. Jarvis —' He broke off.

'You're darn right it's different! You're not going to get *me* in *there*!'

'No, I guess not. Well, the doctor was right. Go on back, son, and turn yourself in at the infirmary.' He stared into the laboratory.

He had gotten three or four steps away before I called out, 'Boss!'

He stopped and turned, his face expressionless. 'Wait,' I added, 'I'm coming.'

'You don't have to.'

'I'll do it. It – it just takes – a while – to get your nerve back.'

As I came alongside him he grasped my upper arm, warmly and affectionately, and continued to hold it as we walked. We went on in, through another locked door and into a room conditioned warm and moist. The ape was there, caged.

His torso was supported and restrained by a strap-metal framework. His arms and legs hung limply, as if he had no control over them. He looked up and at us with eyes malevolent and intelligent; then the fire died out and they were merely the eyes of a dumb brute, a brute in pain.

'Around to the side,' the Old Man said softly. I would have hung back, but he still had me by the arm. The ape followed us with his eyes, but his body was held by the frame. From the new position I could see – it.

My master. The thing that had ridden my back for an endless time, spoken with my mouth – thought with my brain. My master.

'Steady,' the Old Man said softly. 'You'll get used to it. Look away for a bit. It helps.'

I did so and it did help. I took a couple of deep breaths and managed to slow my heart down. I made myself stare at it.

It is not the appearance of a parasite which arouses horror. Nor is the horror entirely from knowing what they can do, for I felt the horror the first time I saw one, before I knew what it was. I tried to tell the Old Man so. He nodded, his eyes on the parasite. 'It's the same with everybody,' he said. 'Unreasoned fear, like a bird with a snake. Probably its prime weapon.' He let his eyes drift away, as if too long a sight was too much even for his rawhide nerves.

I stuck with him, trying to get used to it and gulping at my breakfast. I kept telling myself that it couldn't harm *me*. I looked away again and found the Old Man's eyes on me. 'How about it?' he said. 'Getting hardened?'

I looked back at it. 'A little.' I went on savagely, 'All I want is to kill it! I want to kill all of them – I could spend my life killing them and killing them.' I began to shake again.

The Old Man studied me. 'Here,' he said, and handed me his gun.

It startled me. I was unarmed, having come straight from bed. I took it but looked at him questioningly. 'Huh? What for?'

'You want to kill it. If you have to – go ahead. Kill it. Right now.'

'Huh? But – Boss, you told me you needed this one for study.'

'I do. But if you feel that you have to kill it, do so. This particular one is your baby. If you need to kill it, to make you a whole man again, go ahead.'

' "To make me a whole man again —" ' The thought rang through my head. The Old Man knew what medicine it would take to cure me. I was no longer trembling; the gun was cradled in my hand, ready to spit and kill. My master. . . .

If I killed *this* one I would be a free man, but I would never be free as long as *it* lived. I wanted to kill every one of them, search them out, burn them – but *this* one above all.

My master . . . still my master unless I killed it. I had a dark and certain thought that if I were alone with it, I would be able to do nothing, that I would freeze while it crawled up me and settled again between my shoulder blades, searched out my spinal column, took possession of my brain and my very self.

But now I could kill it!

No longer frightened but fiercely exultant, I raised the gun.

The Old Man watched me.

I lowered the gun and said uncertainly, 'Boss, suppose I do. You've got others?'

'No.'

'But you need it.'

'Yes.'

'Well, but — For the love o' God, why did you give me the gun?'

'You know why. If you have to, go ahead. If you can pass

it up, then the Section will use it.'

I *had* to. Even if we killed all the others, while this one was alive I would still crouch and tremble in the dark. As for others – why, we could capture a dozen at the Constitution Club. With this one dead I'd lead the raid myself. Breathing rapidly, I raised the gun again.

Then I turned and chucked the gun to the Old Man; he plucked it out of the air. 'What happened?' he asked.

'Uh? I don't know. When I got to it, it was enough to know that I could.'

'I figured it would be.'

I felt warm and relaxed, as if I had just killed a man or had a woman – as if I had just killed *it*. I was able to turn my back on it. I was not even angry with the Old Man for what he had done. 'I know you did, damn you. How does it feel to be a puppet master?'

He did not take the jibe as a joke. He answered soberly, 'Not me. The most I ever do is to lead a man on the path he wants to follow. *There* is the puppet master.'

I looked around at it. 'Yes,' I agreed softly, ' "the puppet master". You think you know what you mean – but you don't. And, Boss . . . I hope you never do.'

'I hope so too,' he answered seriously.

I could look now without trembling. Still staring at it, I went on, 'Boss, when you are through with it, then I'll kill it.'

'That's a promise.'

We were interrupted by a man bustling in. He was dressed in shorts and a lab coat; it made him look silly. It was not Graves; I never saw Graves again; I imagine the Old Man ate him for lunch.

'Chief,' he said, 'I didn't know you were in here. I —'

'Well, I am,' the Old Man cut in. 'Why are you wearing a coat?' The Old Man's gun was out and pointed at him.

The man stared at the gun as if it were a bad joke. 'Why, I was working. There is always a chance of splattering one's self. Some of our solutions are rather —'

'Take it off!'

'Eh?'

The Old Man waggled his gun. To me he said, 'Get ready to take him.'

The man took his coat off. His shoulders were bare, nor was there the telltale rash. 'Take that damned coat and burn it,' the Old Man told him. 'Then get back to work.'

The man hurried away, his face red, then stopped and said, 'Chief, are you ready for that, uh, procedure?'

'Shortly. I'll let you know.'

He left. The Old Man wearily put his gun away. 'Post an order,' he muttered. 'Read it aloud. Make them initial it. Tattoo it on their narrow little chests – and some smart aleck thinks it doesn't mean him. Scientists!'

I turned back to my former master. It still revolted me, but there was a gusty feeling of danger, too, that was not totally unpleasant. 'Boss,' I asked, 'what are you going to do with this thing?'

'I plan to interview it.'

'To what? But how? What I want to say is – the ape, I mean —'

'No, the ape can't talk. We'll have to have a volunteer – a human volunteer.'

When I began to visualize what he meant the horror struck me again almost full force. 'You can't mean that. You wouldn't do that – not to anybody.'

'I could and I will. What needs to be done will be done.'

'You won't get any volunteers!'

'I've got one.'

'You have? Who?'

'But I don't want to use the one I've got. I'm still looking for the right man.'

I was disgusted and showed it. 'You ought not to be looking for anyone, volunteer or not. If you've got one, you won't find another; there can't be two people that crazy.'

'Possibly,' he agreed. 'But I still don't want the one I've got. The interview is a "must", son; we are fighting with a total lack of military intelligence. We don't know our enemy. We can't negotiate with him, we don't know where he comes from, nor what makes him tick. We've got to find out; our existence depends on it. The *only* way to talk to these critters is through a human. So it will be done. But I'm still looking for a volunteer.'

'Don't look at me!'

'I *am* looking at you.'

My answer had been half wisecrack; his answer startled me speechless. I managed to splutter, 'You're crazy! I should have killed it when I had your gun. I would have if I had known why you wanted it. But as for volunteering to let you put that thing — No! I've had it.'

He ploughed on as if he had not heard me. 'It can't be just anyone; it has to be a man who can take it. Jarvis wasn't stable enough, nor tough enough. We know you are.'

'Me? All you know is that I lived through it once. I – I couldn't *stand* it again.'

'Well,' he answered calmly, 'it is less likely to kill you than someone else. You are proved and salted; with anyone else I run more risk of losing an agent.'

'Since when did you worry about risking an agent?' I said bitterly.

'Always, believe me. I am giving you one more chance, son: are you going to do this, knowing that it has to be done and that you stand the best chance of anybody – and can be of most use to us, because you *are* used to it – or are you going to let some other agent risk his reason and his life in your place?'

I started to try to explain how I felt. I could not stand the thought of dying while possessed by a parasite. Somehow I felt that to die so would be to die already consigned to an endless unbearable hell. Even worse was the prospect of *not* dying once the slug touched me. But I could not find words for it.

I shrugged. 'You can have my appointment back. There is a limit to what one man can go through. I won't do it.'

He turned to the inter-com on the wall. 'Laboratory,' he called out, 'we'll start now. Hurry up!'

I recognized the voice of the man who had walked in on us. 'Which subject?' he asked.

'The original volunteer.'

'The smaller rig?' the voice asked doubtfully.

'Right. Get it in here.'

I started for the door. The Old Man snapped, 'Where are you going?'

'Out,' I snapped back. 'I want no part of this.'

He grabbed me and spun me around. 'No, you don't. You know about these creatures; your advice could help.'

'Let go of me.'

'You'll stay!' he said savagely, 'strapped down or free to move. I've made allowance for your illness, but I've had enough of your nonsense.'

I was too weary to buck him. 'You're the boss.'

The lab people wheeled in a sort of chair, more like a Sing Sing special than anything else. There were clamps for ankles and knees and for wrists and elbows. There was a corselet to restrain the waist and chest, but the back was cut away so that the shoulders of the victim would be free.

They placed it beside the ape's cage, then removed the side of the cage nearest the 'chair'. The ape watched with intent, aware eyes, but his limbs still dangled helplessly. Nevertheless, I became still more disturbed at the cage being opened. Only the Old Man's threat of restraint kept me there. The technicians stood back, apparently ready. The outer door opened and several people came in, among them Mary.

I was caught off balance; I had been wanting to see her and had tried several times to get word to her through the nurses, but they either could not identify her or had received instructions. Now I saw her under *these* circumstances. I cursed the Old Man to myself – it was no sort of a show to bring a woman to, even a woman agent. There ought to be decent limits somewhere.

Mary looked surprised and nodded. I let it go at that; it was no time for small talk. She was looking good, though very sober. She was dressed in the costume the nurses had worn, but she did not have the ludicrous helmet and back plate. The others were men, loaded with recording and stereo equipment as well as other apparatus.

'Ready?' inquired the lab chief.

'Get going,' answered the Old Man.

Mary walked straight to the 'chair' and sat down. Two technicians knelt and started fastening the clamps. I watched in a frozen daze. Then I grabbed the Old Man and literally threw him aside and I was by the chair, kicking the technicians out of the way. 'Mary!' I screamed, 'get up from there!'

Now the Old Man had his gun on me. 'Away from her,' he ordered. 'You three – grab him and tie him.'

I looked at the gun, then down at Mary. She did not move; her feet were already bound. She simply looked at me with compassionate eyes. 'Get up, Mary,' I said dully, 'I want to sit down.'

They removed the chair and brought in a larger one. I could not have used hers; both were tailored to size. When they finished clamping me I might as well have been cast into concrete. My back began to itch unbearably, although nothing, as yet, had touched it.

Mary was no longer in the room; I had not seen her leave and it did not seem to matter. After I had been prepared the Old Man laid a hand on my arm and said quietly, 'Thanks, son.' I did not answer.

I did not see them handle the parasite as it took its place behind my back. I was not interested enough to look, even if I had been able to turn my head, which I couldn't. Once the ape barked and screamed and someone shouted, 'Watch it!'

There was silence, as if everyone was holding his breath – then something moist touched my neck and I fainted.

I came out of it with the same tingling energy I had experienced before. I knew I was in a tight spot, but I was warily determined to think my way out. I was not afraid; I was contemptuous and sure that I could outwit them.

The Old Man said sharply, 'Can you hear me?'

I answered, 'Quit shouting.'

'Do you remember what we are here for?'

I said, 'You want to ask questions. What are you waiting for?'

'*What are you?*'

'That's a silly question. I'm six feet one, more muscle than brain, and I weigh —'

'Not you. You know to whom I am talking – *you*.'

'Guessing games?'

The Old Man waited before replying, 'It's no good to pretend that I don't know what you are —'

'Ah, but you don't.'

'You know that I have been studying you all the time you have been living on the body of that ape. I know things which give me an advantage. One —' He started ticking them off.

'You can be killed.

'Two, you can be hurt. You don't like electric shock and you can't stand the heat even a man can stand.

'Three, you are helpless without your host. I could have you removed and you would die.

'Four, you have no powers except those you borrow – and your host is helpless. Try your bonds. You must co-operate – or die.'

I had already been trying my bonds, finding them, as I expected, impossible to escape. This did not worry me; I was oddly contented to be back with my master, to be free of troubles and tensions. My business was to serve; the future would take care of itself. One ankle strap seemed less tight than the other; possibly I might drag my foot through it. I checked on the arm clamps; perhaps if I relaxed completely . . .

An instruction came at once – or I made a decision; the words mean the same. There was no conflict between my master and me; we were one. Instruction or decision, I knew it was not time to risk an escape. I ran my eyes around the room, trying to figure who was armed. It was my guess that only the Old Man was; that bettered the chances.

Somewhere, deep down, was that ache of guilt and despair never experienced by any but the servants of the masters, but I was much too busy to be troubled by it.

'Well?' the Old Man went on. 'Do you answer questions, or do I punish you?'

'What questions?' I asked. 'Up to now you've been talking nonsense.'

The Old Man turned to a technician. 'Give me the tickler.' I felt no apprehension, being still busy checking my bonds. If I could tempt him into placing his gun within reach – assuming that I could get one arm free – then I might . . .

He reached past my shoulders with a rod. I felt a shocking pain; the room blacked out as if a switch had been thrown. I was split apart; for the moment I was masterless.

The pain left, leaving only searing memory behind. Before I could think coherently the splitting away had ended and I was again safe in the arms of my master. But for the first and only time in my service to him I was not myself free of worry; some of his own wild fear and pain was passed on to me.

'Well,' asked the Old Man, 'how did you like the taste?'

The panic washed away; I was again filled with unworried well-being, albeit wary and watchful. My wrists and ankles, which had begun to pain me, stopped hurting. 'Why did you do that?' I asked. 'Certainly, you can hurt me – but why?'

'Answer my questions.'

'Ask them.'

'*What are you?*'

The answer did not come at once. The Old Man reached for the rod; I heard myself saying, 'We are the people.'

'What people?'

'The only people. We have studied you and we know your ways. We —' I stopped suddenly.

'Keep talking,' the Old Man said grimly, and gestured with the rod.

'We come,' I went on, 'to bring you —'

'To bring us what?'

I wanted to talk; the rod was terrifyingly close. But there

was some difficulty with words. 'To bring you peace,' I blurted out.

The Old Man snorted.

'Peace,' I went on, 'and contentment – and the joy of – of surrender.' I hesitated again; 'surrender' was not the word. I struggled the way one struggles with a foreign language. 'The joy,' I repeated, 'the joy of ... *nirvana*.' The word fitted. I felt like a dog being patted for fetching a stick; I wriggled with pleasure.

'Let me get this,' the Old Man said. 'You are promising the human race that, if we will just surrender, you will take care of us and make us happy. Right?'

'Exactly!'

The Old Man studied this while looking past my shoulders. He spat on the floor. 'You know,' he said slowly, 'me and my kind, we have often been offered that bargain. It never worked out worth a damn.'

'Try it yourself,' I suggested. 'It can be done quickly – then you will *know*.'

He stared this time in my face. 'Maybe I should. Maybe I owe it to – somebody, to try it. Maybe I will, someday. But right now,' he went on briskly, 'you have questions to answer. Answer quick and proper and stay healthy. Be slow and I'll step up the current.' He brandished the rod.

I shrank back, feeling dismay and defeat. For a moment I had thought he was going to accept and had been planning the possibilities of escape. 'Now,' he went on, 'where do you come from?'

No answer. I felt no urge to answer.

The rod came closer. 'Far away!' I burst out.

'That's no news. Where's your home base, your own planet?'

The Old Man waited, then said, 'I'll have to touch up your memory.' I watched dully, thinking nothing. He was interrupted by an assistant. 'Eh?' said the Old Man.

'There may be a semantic difficulty,' the other repeated. 'Different astronomical concepts.'

'Why?' asked the Old Man. 'That slug knows what his host knows; we've proved that.' But he turned back and started a different tack. 'See here. You savvy the solar system. Is your planet inside it or outside?'

I hesitated, then answered, 'All planets are ours.'

The Old Man pulled at his lip. 'I wonder,' he mused, 'what you mean.' He went on: 'Never mind; you can claim the whole damned universe. Where is your nest? Where do your ships come from?'

I could not have told him; I sat silent.

Suddenly he reached behind me; I felt one smashing blow. 'Talk, damn you! What planet? Mars? Venus? Jupiter? Saturn? Uranus? Neptune? Pluto?' As he ticked them off, I saw them – and I have never been as far off Earth as the space stations. When he came to the right one, I knew – and the thought was instantly snatched from me.

'Speak up,' he went on, 'or feel the whip.'

I heard myself saying, 'None of them. Our home is much farther away.'

He looked past my shoulders and then into my eyes. 'You are lying. You need some juice to keep you honest.'

'No, no!'

'No harm to try.' Slowly he thrust the rod behind me. I knew the answer again and was about to give it when something grabbed my throat. Then the pain started.

It did not stop. I was being torn apart; I tried to talk – anything to stop the pain, but the hand still clutched my throat.

Through a blur of pain I saw the Old Man's face, shimmering and floating. 'Had enough?' he asked. I started to answer, but choked and gagged. I saw him reach out again with the rod.

I burst into pieces and died.

They were leaning over me. Someone said, 'He's coming around.'

The Old Man's face was over mine. 'You all right, son?' he asked anxiously. I turned my face away.

'One side, please,' another voice said. 'Let me give him the injection.' The speaker knelt by me and gave me a shot.

He stood up, looked at his hands, then wiped them on his shorts.

Gyro, I thought absently, or something like it. Whatever it was, it was pulling me back together. Shortly I sat up, unassisted. I was still in the cage room, directly in front of that damnable chair. I started to get to my feet; the Old Man gave me a hand. I shook him off. 'Don't touch me!'

'Sorry,' he answered, then snapped, 'Jones! You and Ito – get the litter. Take him to the infirmary. Doc, you go along.'

'Certainly.' The man who had given me the shot started to take my arm. I drew back. 'Keep your hands off me!'

The doctor looked at the Old Man, who shrugged, then motioned them all back. Alone, I went to the door and on out through the outer door into the passageway. I paused there, looked at my wrists and ankles and decided that I might as well go to the infirmary. Doris would take care of me and then maybe I could sleep. I felt as if I had gone fifteen rounds and lost them all.

'Sam, Sam!'

I knew that voice. Mary hurried up and was standing before me, looking at me with great sorrowful eyes. 'Oh, Sam! What have they done to you?' Her voice was so choked that I could hardly understand her.

'You should know,' I answered and had strength enough left to slap her.

'Bitch,' I added.

My room was still empty, but I did not find Doris. I closed the door, then lay face down on the bed and tried to stop thinking or feeling. Presently I heard a gasp, and opened one eye; there was Doris. 'What in the world?' she exclaimed. I felt her gentle hands on me. 'Why, you poor, poor baby!' Then she added, 'Stay there, don't move. I'll get the doctor.'

'No!'

'But you've got to have the doctor.'

'I won't see him. You help me.'

She did not answer. Presently I heard her go out. She

73

came back shortly – I think it was shortly – and started to bathe my wounds. I wanted to scream when she touched my back. But she dressed it quickly and said, 'Over easy, now.'

'I'll stay face down.'

'No,' she denied, 'I want you to drink something, that's a good boy.'

I turned over, with her doing most of the work, and drank what she gave me. After a bit I went to sleep.

I seem to remember being awakened, seeing the Old Man and cursing him. The doctor was there too – or it could have been a dream.

Miss Briggs woke me, and Doris brought me breakfast; it was as if I had never been off the sick list. I wasn't in too bad shape. I felt as if I had gone over Niagara Falls in a barrel; there were dressings on both arms and both legs where I had cut myself on the clamps, but no bones were broken. Where I was sick was in my soul.

Don't misunderstand me. The Old Man could send me into a dangerous spot. That I had signed up for. But I had not signed up for what he had done to me. He knew what made me tick and he had used it to force me into something I would never have done willingly. Then after he had gotten me where he wanted me, he had used me unmercifully. Oh, I've slapped men around to make them talk. Sometimes you have to. This was different. Believe me.

It was the Old Man that really hurt. Mary? After all, what was she? Just another babe. True, I was disgusted with her for letting herself be used as bait. It was all right for her to use her femaleness as an agent; the Section had to have female operatives. There have always been female spies, and the young and pretty ones have always used the same tools.

But she should not have agreed to use them against a fellow agent – at least, she should not have used them against *me*.

Not very logical, is it? It was logical to me. I'd had it; they could go ahead with 'Operation Parasite' without me; I owned a cabin in the Adirondacks; I had stuff there in deep freeze to carry me a year, anyhow. I had plenty of tempus pills; I would go up there and use them – and the world could save itself, or go to hell, without me.

If anyone came within a hundred yards, he would either show a bare back or be burned down.

XI

I had to tell somebody about it and Doris was the goat. She was indignant. Shucks, she was sore as a boiled owl. She had dressed what they had done to me. Being a nurse, she had dressed a lot worse, but this had been done *by our own people.* I blurted out how I felt about Mary's part in it.

'Do I understand that you had wanted to *marry* this girl?'

'Correct. Stupid, ain't I?'

'Then she knew what she could do to you. It wasn't fair.' She stopped massaging me, her eyes snapping. 'I've never met your redhead – but if I do, I'll scratch her face!'

I smiled at her. 'You're a good kid, Doris. I believe you would play fair with a man.'

'Oh, I've pulled some fast ones. But if I did anything halfway like that, I'd have to break every mirror I own. Turn and I'll get the other leg.'

Mary showed up. The first I knew was hearing Doris say angrily, 'You can't come in.'

Mary's voice answered, 'I'm going in.'

Doris squealed, 'Get back – or I'll pull that hennaed hair out by the roots!'

There were sounds of a scuffle – and the *smack!* of some-one getting slapped. I yelled, 'Hey! What goes on?'

They appeared in the doorway together. Doris was breathing hard and her hair was mussed. Mary managed to look dignified, but there was a bright red patch on her cheek the size of Doris's hand.

Doris caught her breath and said, 'You get out. He doesn't want to see you.'

Mary said, 'I'll hear that from him.'

I looked at them both, then said, 'Oh, what the hell. She's here and I've got some things to tell her. Thanks for trying, Doris.'

Doris said, 'You're a fool!' and flounced out.

Mary came over to the bed. 'Sam,' she said. 'Sam.'

'My name isn't "Sam".'

'I've never known your right name.'

It was no time to explain that my parents had burdened me with 'Elihu'. I answered, 'What of it? "Sam" will do.'

'Sam,' she repeated. 'Oh, Sam, my dear.'

'I am not your "dear".'

She inclined her head. 'Yes, I know. I don't know why. Sam, I came to find out why you hate me. Perhaps I can't change it, but I must know.'

I made a sound of disgust. 'After what you did, you don't know why? Mary, you may be a cold fish, but you aren't stupid.'

She shook her head. 'Just backwards, Sam. I'm not cold, but I'm frequently stupid. Look at me, please. I know what they did to you. I know that you let it be done to save me from it. I know and I'm deeply grateful. But I don't know why you hate me. I did not ask you to do it and I did not want you to do it.'

I didn't answer; presently she said, 'You don't believe me?'

I reared up on one elbow. 'I believe you have yourself convinced that that is how it was. Now I'll tell *you* how it was.'

'Do, please.'

'You sat down in that trick chair knowing that I would never let you go through with it. You *knew* that, whether your devious female mind admitted it or not. The Old Man could not have forced me, not with a gun, not even with drugs. *You* could. You did. You forced me to do something

76

which I would rather have been dead than touch – a thing that leaves me dirty and spoiled. You did it.'

She grew steadily whiter, until her face was almost green against her hair. She caught her breath and said, 'You believe that, Sam?'

'What else?'

'Sam, that is not the way it was. I did not know you were going to be there. I was terribly startled. But I had to go through with it; I had promised.'

' "Promised",' I repeated. 'That covers everything, a schoolgirl promise.'

'Hardly a schoolgirl promise.'

'No matter. And it doesn't matter whether you are telling the truth about knowing that I would be in there. The point is: *you* were there and *I* was there – and you could figure what would happen if you did what you did.'

'Oh.' She waited, then went on, 'That's the way it looks to you, and I can't dispute the facts.'

'Hardly.'

She stood very still for a long time. I let her. Finally she said, 'Sam – once you said something about wanting to marry me.'

'That was another day.'

'I didn't expect you to renew the offer. But there was a sort of corollary. Sam, no matter what you think of me, I want to tell you that I am deeply grateful for what you did for me. Uh – Miss Barkis is willing, Sam. You understand me?'

I grinned at her. 'Honest, so help me, the workings of the female mind delight and astound me. You always think you can cancel the score and start over with that one trump play.' I continued to grin while she turned red. 'It won't work. I shan't inconvenience you by taking up your generous offer.'

She came back at me in a steady voice, 'I let myself in for that. Nevertheless, I meant it. That – or anything else I can ever do for you.'

I sank back and lay down. 'Sure, you can do something for me.'

Her face lit up. 'What?'

'Quit bothering me. I'm tired.'

I turned my face away.

The Old Man put his head in late that afternoon. My immediate response was pleasure; the Old Man's personality is hard to shake off. Then I remembered and went cold.

'I want to talk to you,' he started in.

'I don't want to talk to you. Get out.'

He ignored it, and came in. 'Mind if I sit?'

'You seem to be doing so.'

He ignored that too. 'You know, son, you are one of my best boys, but sometimes you are hasty.'

'Don't let that worry you,' I answered. 'As soon as the doctor lets me up, I'm through.'

He was not hearing anything that he did not choose to hear. 'You jump to conclusions. Now take this girl Mary —'

'Mary who?'

'You know who I mean; you know her as "Mary Cavanaugh".'

'*You* take her.'

'You jumped all over her without knowing the score. You've got her all upset. You may have ruined a good agent for me.'

'Humph! I'm in tears.'

'Listen, you young snot, you didn't have any call to be rough on her. You don't know the facts.'

I did not answer; explanations are a poor defence.

'Oh, I know what you think,' he went on. 'You think she let herself be used as bait. Well, you've got it slightly wrong. She was being used, but *I* was using *her*. I planned it that way.'

'I know you did.'

'Then why blame her?'

'Because you couldn't have carried it out without her co-operation. It's big of you, you no-good, heartless bastard, to take all the blame – but you can't.'

He did not hear my profanity either. He went on, 'You understand everything but the key point, which is – *the girl didn't know.*'

'Hell's bells, she was *there*.'

'So she was. Son, did I ever lie to you?'

'No,' I admitted, 'but I don't think you would hesitate.'

He answered, 'Maybe I deserve that. I'd lie to one of my own people if the country's safety depended on it. I haven't found it necessary, because I've been choosy about who works for me. But this time the country's welfare doesn't depend on it and I'm not lying and you'll just have to test it for yourself and make up your mind whether or not I'm lying. That girl didn't know. She didn't know you were going to be in that room. She didn't know why you were there. She didn't know that there was any question about who was going to sit in that chair. She didn't have the faintest suspicion that I didn't mean for her to go through with it, or that I had already decided that you were the only party who would suit me, even if I had to have you tied down and forced – which I would have done, if I hadn't had a double whammy up my sleeve to trick you into volunteering. Hell's bells yourself, son; she didn't even know you were off the sick list.'

I wanted to believe it, so I did my damnedest not to. As to whether he would bother to lie – well, getting two prime agents back into the groove might be something he would class, just now, as involving the country's safety. The Old Man had a complex mind.

'Look at me!' he added. 'There is something I want to rub your nose in. First off, everybody – including me – appreciates what you did, regardless of motives. I'm putting in a letter, and no doubt you'll get a medal. That stands, whether you stay with the Section or not.'

He went on. 'But don't give yourself airs like a little tin hero —'

'I won't!'

'– because that medal is going to the wrong person. Mary ought to get it.

'Now hush up; I'm not through. You had to be forced into it. No criticism; you had been through plenty. But Mary was a real, simon-pure volunteer. When she sat down in that chair, she didn't expect any last-minute reprieve, and she had every reason to believe that, if she got up alive, her mind would be gone, which is worse. But she did it – because she is a hero, which you miss by a couple of points.'

He went on without waiting for me to reply; 'Listen, son – most women are damn fools and children. But they've got more range than we've got. The brave ones are braver, the good ones are better – and the vile ones are viler. What I'm trying to tell you is: this one is more of a man than you are, and you've done her a serious wrong.'

I was so churned up that I could not judge whether he was telling the truth, or manipulating me again. I said, 'Maybe I lashed out at the wrong person. But if what you say is true —'

'It is.'

'– it doesn't make what you did any sweeter; it makes it worse.'

He took it without flinching. 'Son, I'm sorry if I've lost your respect. But I can't be choosy any more than can a commander in battle. Less, because I fight with different weapons. I've always been able to shoot my own dog. Maybe that's bad – but that is what my job takes. If you are ever in my shoes, you'll have to do it too.'

'I'm not likely to be.'

'Why don't you rest up, and think about it?'

'I'll take leave – terminal leave.'

'Very well.'

He started to leave. I said, 'Wait —'

'Yes?'

'You made me one promise and I'm holding you to it. About that parasite – you said I could kill it, personally. Are you through with it?'

'Yes, but —'

I started to get up. 'No "buts". Give me your gun; I'll do it now.'

'You can't. It's already dead.'

'What! You *promised* me.'

'I know. But it died while we were trying to force you – force *it* – to talk.'

I started to shake with laughter. I got started and could not stop.

The Old Man shook me. 'Snap out of it! You'll get yourself sick. I'm sorry about it, but there's nothing to laugh at.'

'Ah, but there is,' I answered, sobbing and chuckling. 'It's the funniest thing that ever happened. All that – and for nothing. You dirtied yourself and you loused up me and Mary – and all for no use.'

'Huh? What gave you that idea?'

'Eh? I *know*. You didn't even get small change out of it – out of us. You didn't learn anything you didn't know before.'

'The hell we didn't!'

'The hell you did.'

'It was a bigger success than you'd ever guess, son. True, we didn't squeeze anything out of it directly, before it died – but we got something out of you.'

'Me?'

'Last night. We put you through it last night. You were doped, psyched, brain-waved, analysed, wrung out and hung out to dry. The parasite spilled things to you and they were still there for the hypno-analysts to pick up after you were free of it.'

'What?'

'Where they live. We know where they come from and can fight back – Titan, sixth satellite of Saturn.'

When he said it, I felt a gagging constriction of my throat – and I knew that he was right.

'You certainly fought before we could get it,' he went on reminiscently. 'We had to hold you down to keep you from hurting yourself – more.'

He threw his game leg over the edge of the bed and struck a cigarette. He seemed anxious to be friendly. As for me, I did not want to fight with him; my head was spinning and I had things to get straight. Titan – that was a long way out. Mars was the farthest men had ever been, unless the Seagraves Expedition, the one that never came back, got out to the Jovian moons.

Still, we could get there if there were a reason to go. We would burn out their nest!

Finally he got up to go. He had limped to the door when I stopped him. 'Dad —'

I had not called him that in years. He turned, his expression surprised and defenceless. 'Yes, son?'

'Why did you and Mother name me "Elihu"?'

'Eh? Why, it was your maternal grandfather's name.'

'Oh. Not enough reason, I'd say.'

'Perhaps not.' He turned and again I stopped him.

'Dad – what sort of a person was my mother?'

'Your mother? I don't know exactly how to tell you. Well – she was much like Mary. Yes, sir, a great deal like her.' He stumped out without giving me further chance to talk.

I turned my face to the wall. After a while I steadied down.

XII

When the doctor released me I went looking for Mary. I still had nothing but the Old Man's word, but I had more than a suspicion that I had made a big hairy thing of myself. I did not expect her to be glad to see me, but I had to speak my piece.

You would think that a tall, handsome redhead would be as easy to find as flat ground in Kansas. But field agents come and go, and the resident staff are encouraged to mind their own business. The personnel office gave me the bland brush off. They referred me to Operations, meaning the Old Man. That did not suit me.

I met with even more suspicion when I tried the door tally; I began to feel like a spy in my own Section.

I went to the bio lab, could not find its chief, and talked to an assistant. He did not know anything about a girl in connection with 'Project Interview'; he went back to scratching himself and shuffling reports. I left and went to the Old Man's office. There seemed to be no choice.

There was a new face at Miss Haines's desk. I never saw Miss Haines again, nor did I ask what had become of her; I did not want to know. The new secretary passed in my ID code, and, for a wonder, the Old Man was in and would see me.

'What do you want?' he said grumpily.

I said, 'Thought you might have some work for me,' which was not at all what I intended to say.

'Matter of fact, I was just fixing to send for you. You're loafed long enough.' He barked something at his desk phone, stood up and said, 'Come!'

I felt suddenly at peace. 'Cosmetics?' I asked.

'Your own ugly face will do. We're headed for Washington.' Nevertheless we did stop in Cosmetics, but only for street clothes. I drew a gun and had my phone checked.

The door guard made us bare our backs before he would let us approach and check out. We went on up, coming out in the lower levels of New Philadelphia. 'I take it this burg is clean?' I said to the Old Man.

'If you do, you are rusty in the head,' he answered. 'Keep your eyes peeled.'

There was no opportunity for more questions. The presence of so many fully clothed humans bothered me; I found myself drawing away and watching for round shoulders. Getting into a crowded elevator to go up to the launching platform seemed downright reckless. When we were in our car and the controls set, I said so. 'What in the devil do the authorities think they are doing? I could swear that one cop we passed was wearing a hump.'

'Possibly. Even probably.'

'Well, for crying in church! I thought you had this job taped and were fighting back on all fronts.'

'What would you suggest?'

'Why, it's obvious. Even if it were freezing cold, we ought not to see a back covered up anywhere, not until we know they are all dead.'

83

'That's right.'

'Well, then — Look, the President knows the score, doesn't he?'

'He knows it.'

'What's he waiting for? He should declare martial law and get action.'

The Old Man stared down at the countryside. 'Son, are you under the impression that the President runs the country?'

'Of course not. But he is the only man who can act.'

'Mmmm – they sometimes call Premier Tsvetkov "the Prisoner of the Kremlin". True or not, the President is the prisoner of Congress.'

'You mean Congress *hasn't acted*?'

'I have spent the past several days – ever since we stopped the attempt on the President – trying to help the President convince them. Ever been worked over by a Congressional committee, son?'

I tried to figure it out. Here we sat, as stupid as dodoes – yes, and *homo sapiens* would be as extinct as the dodo if we did not move. Presently the Old Man said, 'It's time you learned the political facts of life. Congresses have refused to act in the face of dangers more obvious than this. This one isn't obvious. The evidence is slim and hard to believe.'

'But how about the Assistant Secretary of the Treasury? They can't ignore that.'

'Can't they? The Assistant Secretary had one snatched off his back, right in the East Wing, and we killed two of his Secret Service guards. And now the honourable gent is in Walter Reed with a nervous breakdown and can't recall what happened. The Treasury Department gave out that an attempt to assassinate the President had been foiled. True, but not the way they meant it.'

'And the President held still for that?'

'His advisers told him to wait. His majority is uncertain – and there are men in both houses who want his head on a platter. Party politics is a rough game.'

'Good lord, partisanship doesn't figure in a case like this!'

The Old Man cocked an eyebrow. 'You think not, eh?'

I finally managed to ask him the question I had come into his office to ask: where was Mary?

'Odd question from you,' he grunted. I let it ride; he went on, 'Where she should be. Guarding the President.'

We went first to a closed session of a joint special committee. When we got there they were running stereos of my anthropoid friend, Napoleon – shots of him with the titan on his back, then close-ups of the titan. One parasite looks like another; but I knew which one this was and I was deeply glad it was dead.

The ape gave way to me myself. I saw myself being clamped into the chair. I hate to admit how I looked; real funk is not pretty. I saw them lift the titan off the ape and on to my own bare back. Then I fainted in the picture – and almost fainted again. I won't describe it; it upsets me to tell about it.

But I saw the thing *die*. That was worth sitting through the rest.

The film ended and the chairman said, 'Well, gentlemen?'

'Mr Chairman!'

'The gentleman from Indiana is recognized.'

'Speaking without prejudice to the issue, I have seen better trick photography from Hollywood.' They tittered and someone called out, 'Hear! Hear!'

The head of our bio lab testified, then I found myself called to the stand. I gave my name, address, and occupation, then perfunctorily was asked about my experiences under the titans. The questions were read from a sheet. The thing that got me was that they did not *want* to hear my answers. Two of them were reading newspapers.

There were only two questions from the floor. One senator said to me, 'Mr Nivens – your name *is* Nivens?'

I agreed. 'Mr Nivens,' he went on, 'you say that you are an investigator?'

'Yes.'

'FBI, no doubt?'

'No, my chief reports directly to the President.'

The senator smiled. '*Just* as I thought. Now, Mr Nivens,

as a matter of fact you are an actor, are you not?' He seemed to be consulting notes.

I tried to tell too much truth. I wanted to say that I had once acted one season of summer stock but that I was, nevertheless, a real, live, sure-enough investigator. I got no chance. 'That will *do*, Mr Nivens. Thank you.'

The other question was put by an elderly senator who wanted to know my views on using tax money to arm other countries – and he used the question to express his own views. My views on that subject are mixed, but I did not get to express them. The next thing I knew the clerk was saying, 'Stand down, Mr Nivens.'

I sat tight. 'Look here,' I said. 'It's evident that you think this is a put-up job. Well, for the love of heaven, bring in a lie detector! Or use the sleep test. This hearing is a joke.'

The chairman banged his gavel. 'Stand down, Mr Nivens.'

I stood.

The Old Man had told me that the purpose of the meeting was to report out a joint resolution declaring total emergency and vesting war powers in the President. We were ejected before the vote. I said to the Old Man, 'It looks bad.'

'Forget it,' he said. 'The President knew this gambit had failed when he heard the names of the committee.'

'Where does that leave us? Do we wait for the slugs to take over Congress too?'

'The President goes right ahead with a message to Congress requesting full powers.'

'Will he get them?'

The Old Man simply scowled.

The joint session was secret, but we were present – direct orders of the President. The Old Man and I were on that little balcony business back of the Speaker's rostrum. They opened with full rigmarole and then went through the ceremony of notifying the President. He came in at once, escorted by the delegation. His guards were with him, but they were all our men.

Mary was with him too. Somebody set up a folding chair

for her, right by the President. She fiddled with a notebook and handed papers to him, pretending to be a secretary. But the disguise ended there; she looked like Cleopatra on a warm night – and as out of place as a bed in church. She got as much attention as the President.

I caught her eye – and she gave me a long, sweet smile. I grinned like a collie pup until the Old Man dug me in the ribs. Then I settled back and tried to behave.

The President made a reasoned explanation of the situation. It was as straightforward and rational as an engineering report, and about as moving. He simply stated facts. He put aside his notes at the end. 'This is such a strange and terrible emergency, so totally beyond any previous experience, that I must ask broad powers to cope with it. In some areas, martial law must be declared. Grave invasions of civil guarantees will be necessary, for a time. The right of free movement must be abridged. The right to be secure from arbitrary search and seizure must give way to the right of safety for everyone. Because any citizen, no matter how respected or loyal, may be the unwilling servant of these secret enemies, all citizens must face some loss of rights and personal dignities until this plague is killed.

'With utmost reluctance, I ask that you authorize these necessary steps.' With that he sat down.

You can feel a crowd. They were uneasy, but he did not carry them. The President of the Senate looked at the Senate majority leader; it had been programmed for him to propose the resolution.

I don't know whether the floor leader shook his head or signalled, but he did not take the floor. Meanwhile the delay was awkward and there were cries of, 'Mr President!' and 'Order!'

The Senate President passed over several others and gave the floor to a member of his party – Senator Gottlieb, a wheel horse who would vote for his own lynching if it were on his party's programme. He started out by yielding to none in his respect for the Constitution, the Bill of Rights, and, probably, the Grand Canyon. He pointed modestly to his own long service and spoke well of America's place in history. I thought he was stalling while the boys worked out a new shift – when I suddenly realized that his words were adding up to meaning: he was proposing to suspend the order of business and get on with the impeachment and trial of the President of the United States!

I tumbled to it as quickly as anyone; the senator had his proposal so decked out in ritualistic verbiage that it was hard to tell what he was saying. I looked at the Old Man.

The Old Man was looking at Mary.

She was looking back at him with an expression of extreme urgency.

The Old Man snatched a pad from his pocket, scrawled something, wadded it up, and threw it down to Mary. She caught it and read it – and passed it to the President.

He was sitting, relaxed and easy – as if one of his oldest friends were not tearing his name to shreds and, with it, the safety of the Republic. He read the note, then glanced unhurriedly at the Old Man. The Old Man nodded.

The President nudged the Senate President, who, at the President's gesture, bent over him. They exchanged whispers.

Gottlieb was still rumbling along. The Senate President banged his gavel. 'If the senator please!'

Gottlieb looked startled and said, 'I do not yield.'

'The senator is not asked to yield. Because of the importance of what you are saying, the senator is asked to come to the rostrum to speak.'

Gottlieb looked puzzled but walked slowly towards the front of the house. Mary's chair blocked the steps up to the rostrum. Instead of getting out of the way, she bumbled around, turning and picking up the chair, so that she got even more in the way. Gottlieb stopped and she brushed against him. He caught her arm, as much to steady himself as her. She spoke to him and he to her, but no one else could hear the words. Finally he went on to the front of the rostrum.

The Old Man was quivering like a dog in point. Mary looked up and nodded. The Old Man said, 'Take him!'

I was over that rail in a flying leap and landed on Gottlieb's shoulders. I heard the Old Man shout, 'Gloves, son! Gloves!' I did not stop for them. I split the senator's jacket with my bare hands and I could see the slug pulsing under his shirt. I tore the shirt away and anybody could see it.

Six stereo cameras could not have recorded what happened in the next few seconds. I slugged Gottlieb to stop his thrashing. Mary was sitting on his legs. The President was standing over me and shouting, 'There! There! Now you can *all* see.' The Senate President was standing stupefied, waggling his gavel. Congress was a mob, yelling and women screaming. Above me the Old Man was shouting orders to the Presidential guards.

Between the guns of the guards and pounding of the gavel some order was restored. The President started to talk. He told them that fortune had given them a chance to see the nature of the enemy and he suggested that they file past and see for themselves one of the titans from Saturn's largest moon. Without waiting for consent, he pointed to the front row and told them to come up.

They came.

Mary stayed on the platform. About twenty had filed by and a female congressman had gotten hysterics when I saw Mary signal the Old Man. This time I was a hair ahead of his order. I might have had quite a fight if two of the boys had not been close by; this one was young and tough, an ex-marine. We laid him beside Gottlieb.

Then it was 'inspection and search' whether they liked it or not. I patted the women on the back as they came by and caught one. I thought I had caught another, but it was an embarrassing mistake; she was so blubber fat that I guessed wrong. Mary spotted two more, then there was a long stretch, three hundred or more, with no jackpots. It was evident that some were hanging back.

Eight men with guns were not enough – eleven, counting the Old Man, Mary, and me. Most of the slugs would have gotten away if the Whip of the House had not organized help. With their assistance, we caught thirteen, ten alive. Only one of the hosts was badly wounded.

XIII

So the President got the authority and the Old Man was his
de facto chief of staff; at last we could move. The Old Man
had a simple campaign in mind. It could not be the quarantine he had proposed when the infection was limited to the
Des Moines area; before we could fight, we had to locate
them. But government agents couldn't search two hundred
million people; the people had to do it themselves.

'Schedule Bare Back' was to be the first phase of 'Opera
tion Parasite'. The idea was that everybody – *everybody* –
was to peel to the waist and stay peeled, until all titans were
spotted and killed. Oh, women could have halter strings
across their backs; a parasite could not hide under a bra
string.

We whipped up a display to go with the stereocast speech
the President would make to the nation. Fast work had
saved seven of the parasites we had flushed in the sacred
halls of Congress; they were alive on animal hosts. We
could show them and the less grisly parts of the film taken
of me. The President himself would appear in shorts, and
models would demonstrate what the Well-Undressed Citizen Would Wear This Season, including the metal head-
and-spine armour which was intended to protect a person
even when asleep.

We got it ready in one black-coffee night. The smash
finish was to show Congress in session, discussing the emergency, and every man, woman, and page boy showing a
bare back.

With twenty-eight minutes left until stereocast time the
President got a call from up the street. I was present; the
Old Man had been with the President all night and had
kept me around for chores. We were all in shorts; Schedule
Bare Back had already started in the White House. The
President did not bother to cut us out of his end of the

conversation. 'Speaking,' he said. Presently he added, 'You feel certain? Very well, John, what do you advise? . . . I see. No, I don't think that would work. . . . I had better come up the street. Tell them to be ready.' He pushed back the phone and turned to an assistant. 'Tell them to hold up the stereocast.' He turned to the Old Man. 'Come, Andrew, we must go to the Capitol.'

He sent for his valet and retired into a dressing room adjoining his office; when he came out, he was formally dressed for a state occasion. He offered no explanation. The rest of us stayed in our gooseflesh specials and so we went to the Capitol.

It was a joint session – and I got that no-pants-in-church nightmare feeling, for the congressmen and senators were dressed as usual. Then I saw that the page boys were in shorts without shirts and felt better.

Apparently some people would rather be dead than lose dignity, with senators high on the list. Congressmen too. They had given the President the authority he asked for; Schedule Bare Back itself had been discussed and approved – but they did not see that it applied to them. After all, they had been searched and cleaned out. Maybe some saw holes in the argument, but not one wanted to be first in a public strip tease. They sat tight, fully dressed.

When the President took the rostrum, he waited until he got dead silence. Then slowly, calmly, he started taking off clothes. He stopped when he was bare to the waist. He then turned around, lifting his arms. At last he spoke.

'I did that,' he said, 'so that you might see that your Chief Executive is not a prisoner of the enemy.' He paused.

'But how about *you*?' That last word was flung at them.

The President punched a finger at the junior Whip. 'Mark Cummings – are you a loyal citizen – or are you a zombie spy? Get your shirt off!'

'Mr President —' It was Charity Evans, from the state of Maine, looking like a pretty schoolteacher. She stood and I saw that, while she was fully dressed, she was in evening dress. Her gown reached to the floor, but was cut as deep as could be above. She turned like a mannequin; in back the dress ended at the base of her spine. 'Is this satisfactory, Mr President?'

'Quite satisfactory, madam.'

Cummings was fumbling at his jacket; his face was scarlet. Someone stood up in the middle of the hall – Senator Gottlieb. He looked as if he should have been in bed; his cheeks were grey and sunken; his lips showed cyanosis. But he held himself erect and, with incredible dignity, followed the President's example. Then he, too, turned all the way around; on his back was the scarlet mark of the parasite.

He spoke. 'Last night I stood here and said things I would rather have been flayed alive than utter. Last night I was not my own master. Today I am. Can you not see that Rome is burning?' Suddenly he had a gun in his hand. 'Up on your feet, you ward heelers, you courthouse loafers! Two minutes to show a bare back – then I shoot!'

Men close to him tried to grab his arm, but he swung the gun around like a fly swatter, smashing one of them in the face. I had my own out, ready to back his play, but it was not necessary. They could see that he was as dangerous as an old bull; they backed away.

It hung in balance, then they started shucking clothes like Doukhobors. One man bolted for a door; he was tripped. No, he was not wearing a parasite. But we did catch three. After that the show went on the channels ten minutes late and Congress started the first of its 'bare back' sessions.

XIV

'LOCK YOUR DOORS!'
'CLOSE THE DAMPERS ON YOUR FIREPLACES!'
'NEVER ENTER A DARK PLACE!'
'BE WARY OF CROWDS!'
'A MAN WEARING A COAT IS AN ENEMY – SHOOT!'

In addition to a steady barrage of propaganda the country was being quartered and sectioned from the air, searched for flying saucers on the ground. Our radar screen was on full alert for unidentified blips. Military units, from airborne troops to guided-rocket stations, were ready to smear any that landed.

In the uncontaminated areas people took off their shirts, willingly or reluctantly, looked around them and found no parasites. They watched their newscasts and wondered and waited for the government to tell them that the danger was over. But nothing happened, and both laymen and local officials began to doubt the necessity of running around the streets in sunbathing costumes.

The contaminated areas? The reports from the contaminated areas were *not materially different from the reports from other areas.*

Back in the days of radio it could not have happened; the Washington station where the 'cast originated could have blanketed the country. But stereo-video rides wavelengths so short that horizon-to-horizon relay is necessary, and local channels must be squirted out of local stations; it's the price we pay for plenty of channels and high-resolution pictures.

In the infected areas *the slugs* controlled the local stations; the people never heard the warning.

But in Washington, we had every reason to believe that they *had* heard the warning. Reports came back from – well, Iowa, for example, just like those from California. The governor of Iowa was one of the first to send a message to the President, promising full co-operation. There was even a relayed stereo of the governor addressing his constituents, bare to the waist. He faced the camera and I wanted to tell him to turn around. Then they cut to another camera and we had a close up of a bare back, while the governor's voice continued. We listened to it in a conference room off the President's office. The President had kept the Old Man with him. I tagged along, and Mary was still on watch. Secretary of Security Martinez was there, as well as the Supreme Chief of Staff, Air Marshal Rexton.

The President watched the 'cast and turned to the Old Man. 'Well, Andrew? I thought Iowa was a place we would have to fence off.'

The Old Man grunted.

Marshal Rexton said, 'As I figure it – mind you, I have not had much time – they have gone underground. We may have to comb every inch of every suspicious area.'

The Old Man grunted again. 'Combing Iowa, corn shock by corn shock, does not appeal to me.'

'How else would you tackle it, sir?'

'Figure your enemy! He can't go underground. He can't live without a host.'

'Very well – assuming that is true, how many parasites would you say there are in Iowa?'

'Damn it, how should I know? They didn't take me into their confidence.'

'Suppose we make a top estimate. If —'

The Old Man interrupted him. 'You've got no basis for an estimate. Can't you folks see that the titans have won another round?'

'Eh?'

'You just heard the governor; they let us look at his back – or somebody's back. Did you notice that he didn't turn around in front of the camera?'

'But he did,' someone said. 'I saw him.'

'I certainly had the impression that I saw him turn,' said the President slowly. 'You are suggesting that Governor Packer is himself possessed?'

'Correct. You saw what you were meant to see. There was a camera cut just before he was fully turned; people hardly ever notice them. Depend on it, Mr President; every message out of Iowa is faked.'

The President looked thoughtful. Secretary Martinez said, 'Impossible! Granted that the governor's message could have been faked – a clever character actor could have faked it. But we've had our choice of dozens of 'casts from Iowa. How about that street scene in Des Moines? Don't tell me that you can fake hundreds of people dashing around stripped to their waists – or do your parasites practise mass hypnotic control?'

'They can't that I know of,' conceded the Old Man. 'If they can, we might as well throw in the towel. But what made you think that that 'cast came from Iowa?'

'Eh? Why, damn it, sir, it came over the Iowa channel.'

'Proving what? Did you read any street signs? It looked like any typical street in a downtown retail district. Never mind what city the announcer *told* you it was; what city was it?'

The Secretary let his mouth hang open. I've got fairly close to the 'camera eye' that detectives are supposed to have; I let that picture run through my mind – and I not only could not tell what city, I could not even place the part of the country. It could have been Memphis, Seattle, or Boston – or none of them. Most downtown districts in American cities are as standardized as barber shops.

'Never mind,' the Old Man went on. 'I couldn't tell and I was looking for landmarks. The explanation is simple; the Des Moines station picked up a Schedule Bare Back street scene from some city not contaminated and rechannelled it under their own commentary. They chopped out anything that would localize it – and we swallowed it. Gentlemen, this enemy knows us. This campaign has been planned in detail and they are ready to outwit us in almost any move we can make.'

'Aren't you being an alarmist, Andrew?' said the President. 'There is another possibility, that the titans have moved somewhere else.'

'They are still in Iowa,' the Old Man said flatly, 'but you won't prove it with that thing.' He gestured at the stereo tank.

Secretary Martinez squirmed. 'This is ridiculous! You are saying that we can't get a correct report out of Iowa, as if it were occupied territory.'

'That is what it is.'

'But I stopped off in Des Moines two days ago. Everything was normal. Mind you, I grant the existence of your parasites, though I haven't seen one. But let's find them where they are and root them out, instead of dreaming up fantasies.'

The Old Man looked tired. Finally he replied, 'Control the communications of a country and you control the country. You had better move fast, Mr Secretary, or you won't have any communications left.'

'But I was merely —'

'*You* root 'em out!' the Old Man said rudely. 'I've told you they are in Iowa – and in New Orleans, and a dozen other spots. My job is finished.' He stood up and said, 'Mr President, I've had a long pull for a man my age; when I lose sleep I lose my temper. Could I be excused?'

'Certainly, Andrew.' He had not lost his temper and I think the President knew it. He doesn't lose his temper; he makes other people lose theirs.

Secretary Martinez interrupted. 'Wait a moment! You've made some flat-footed statements. Let's check up.' He turned to the Chief of Staff. 'Rexton!'

'Uh – yes, sir.'

'That new post near Des Moines, Fort something-or-other, named after what's-his-name.'

'Fort Patton.'

'That's it, that's it. Well, let's not dally; get them on the command circuit —'

'With visual,' put in the Old Man.

'With visual, of course, and we'll show this – I mean we'll get the true situation in Iowa.'

The air marshal handed a by-your-leave-sir to the President, went to the stereo tank and patched in with Security

General Headquarters. He asked for the officer of the watch at Fort Patton, Iowa.

Shortly thereafter the tank showed the inside of a communications centre. Filling the foreground was a young officer. His rank and corps showed on his cap, but his chest was bare. Martinez turned triumphantly to the Old Man, 'You see?'

'I see.'

'Now to make certain. Lieutenant!'

'Yes, sir!' The young fellow looked awestruck and kept glancing from one famous face to another. Reception and biangle were in synch; the eyes of the image looked where they seemed to look.

'Stand up and turn around,' Martinez continued.

'Uh? Why, certainly, sir.' He seemed puzzled, but did so – and it took him almost out of scan. We could see his bare back up to the short ribs – no higher.

'Confound it!' shouted Martinez. '*Sit down* and turn around.'

'Yessir!' The youth seemed flustered. He added, 'Just a moment while I widen the view angle, sir.'

The picture melted and rippling rainbows chased across the tank. The young officer's voice was still coming over the audio channel. 'There – is that better, sir?'

'Damn it, we can't see a thing!'

'You can't? Just a moment, sir.'

Suddenly the tank came to life and I thought for a moment that we were back at Fort Patton. But it was a major in the screen this time and the place looked larger. 'Supreme Headquarters,' the image announced. 'Communications officer of the watch, Major Donovan.'

'Major,' Martinez said in controlled tones, 'I was hooked in with Fort Patton. What happened?'

'Yes, sir; I was monitoring it. We've had a slight technical difficulty. We'll put your call through again in a moment.'

'Well, hurry!'

'Yes, sir.' The tank rippled and went empty.

The Old Man stood up. 'Call me when you've cleared up that "slight technical difficulty". I'm going to bed.'

XV

If I have given the impression that Secretary Martinez was stupid, I am sorry. Everyone had trouble at first believing what the slugs could do. You have to see one – then you believe in the pit of your stomach.

There were no flies on Marshal Rexton, either. The two worked all night, after convincing themselves by more calls to known danger spots that 'technical interruptions' do not occur so conveniently. They called the Old Man about 4 A.M. and he called me.

They were in the same room, Martinez, Rexton, a couple of his brass, and the Old Man. The President came in, wearing a bathrobe and followed by Mary, as I arrived. Martinez started to speak, but the Old Man cut in. 'Let's see your back, Tom!'

Mary signalled that everything was okay, but the Old Man chose not to see her. 'I mean it,' he persisted.

The President said quietly, 'Perfectly correct, Andrew,' and slipped the robe off his shoulders. His back was clean. 'If I don't set an example, how can I expect others to co-operate?'

Martinez and Rexton had been shoving pins into a map, red for bad, green for good, and a few amber ones. Iowa looked like measles; New Orleans and the Teche country were as bad. So was Kansas City. The upper end of the Missouri–Mississippi system, from Minneapolis and St Paul down to St Louis, was clearly enemy territory. There were fewer red pins from there down to New Orleans – but no green ones. There was a hot spot around El Paso and two on the east coast.

The President looked it over. 'We shall need the help of Canada and Mexico,' he said. 'Any reports?'

'None that mean anything, sir.'

'Canada and Mexico,' the Old Man said seriously, 'will be

just a start. You're going to need the whole world.'

Rexton said, 'We will, eh? How about Russia?'

Nobody had an answer to that one. Too big to occupy and too big to ignore, World War III had not settled the Russian problem, and no war ever would. The parasites might feel right at home there.

The President said, 'We'll deal with that when we come to it.' He drew a finger across the map. 'Any trouble getting messages to the coast?'

'Apparently not, sir,' Rexton told him. 'They don't seem to interfere with straight-through relay. But all military communications I have shifted to relay through the space stations.' He glanced at his watch finger. 'Station Gamma, at the moment.'

'Hmmm —' said the President. 'Andrew, could these things storm a space station?'

'How would I know?' the Old Man answered testily. 'I don't know whether their ships are built for it or not. More probably they would do it by infiltration, through the supply rockets.'

There was discussion as to whether the space stations could already have been taken over; Schedule Bare Back did not apply to the stations. Although we had built them and paid for them, they were technically United Nations territory.

'Don't worry about it,' Rexton said suddenly.

'Why not?' the President asked.

'I am probably the only one here who has done duty in a space station. Gentlemen, the costume we are wearing is customary in a station. A man fully dressed would stand out like an overcoat on the beach. But we'll see.' He gave orders to an assistant.

The President resumed studying the map. 'So far as we know,' he said, pointing to Grinnell, Iowa, 'all this derives from a single landing, here.'

The Old Man answered, 'So far as we know.'

I said, 'Oh no!'

They all looked at me. 'Go ahead,' said the President.

'There were at least three more landings – I *know* there were – before I was rescued.'

The Old Man looked dumbfounded. 'Are you sure, son? We thought we had wrung you dry.'

'Of course I'm sure.'

'Why didn't you mention it?'

'I never thought of it before.' I tried to explain how it feels to be possessed, how you know what is going on, but everything seems dreamy, equally important and equally unimportant. I grew quite upset. I am not the jittery type, but being ridden by a master does something to you.

The Old Man said, 'Steady down, son,' and the President gave me a reassuring smile.

Rexton said, 'The point is: where did they land? We might still capture one.'

'I doubt it,' the Old Man answered. 'They did a cover-up on the first one in a matter of hours. If it was the first,' he added thoughtfully.

I went to the map and tried to think. Sweating, I pointed to New Orleans. 'I'm pretty sure one was about here.' I stared at the map. 'I don't know where the others landed.'

'How about here?' Rexton asked, pointing to the east coast.

'I don't know. I don't know.'

'Can't you remember anything else?' Martinez said testily. 'Think, man!'

'I just don't know. We never knew what they were up to, not really.' I thought until my skull ached, then pointed to Kansas City. 'I sent several messages here, but I don't know whether they were shipment orders, or not.'

Rexton looked at the map. 'We'll assume a landing near Kansas City. The technical boys can do a problem on it. It may be subject to logistic analysis; we might derive the other landing.'

'Or landings,' added the Old Man.

'Eh? "Or landings." Certainly.' He turned back to the map and stared at it.

XVI

Hindsight is confoundedly futile. At the moment the first saucer landed the menace could have been stamped out by one bomb. At the time Mary, the Old Man, and I reconnoitered around Grinnell we three alone might have killed every slug had we known where they all were.

Had Schedule Bare Back been ordered during the first week it alone might have turned the trick. But it was quickly clear that Schedule Bare Back had failed as an offensive measure. As a defence it was useful; the uncontaminated areas could be kept so. It had even had mild success in offence; areas contaminated but not 'secured' were cleaned up – Washington itself, and New Philadelphia. New Brooklyn, too. There I had been able to give specific advice. The entire east coast turned from red to green.

But as the middle of the country filled in on the map, it filled in red. The infected areas stood out in ruby light now, for the wall map studded with pins had been replaced by a huge electronic military map, ten miles to the inch, covering one wall of the conference room. It was a repeater map, the master being down in the sublevels of the New Pentagon.

The country was split in two, as if a giant had washed red pigment down the central valley. Two amber paths bordered the band held by the slugs; these were the only areas of real activity, places where line-of-sight reception was possible both from stations held by the enemy and from stations still in the hands of free men. One started near Minneapolis, swung west of Chicago and east of St Louis, then meandered through Tennessee and Alabama to the Gulf. The other cut a path through the Great Plains and came out near Corpus Christi. El Paso was the centre of a ruby area unconnected with the main body.

I wondered what was going on in those border strips. I was alone; the Cabinet was meeting and the President had taken the Old Man with him. Rexton and his brass had left earlier. I stayed because I hesitated to wander around in the White House. So I fretted and watched amber lights blink red and, much less frequently, red lights blink amber or green.

I wondered how a visitor with no status managed to get breakfast. I had been up since four and so far I had had one cup of coffee, served by the President's valet. Even more urgently I wanted to find a washroom. At last I got desperate enough to try doors. The first two were locked; the third was what I wanted. It was not marked 'Sacred to the Chief', so I used it.

When I came back, Mary was there.

I looked at her stupidly. 'I thought you were with the President.'

She smiled. 'I got chased out. The Old Man took over.'

I said, 'Say, Mary, I've been wanting to talk with you and this is the first chance I've had. I guess I — Well, anyway, I shouldn't have – I mean, according to the Old Man —' I stopped, my carefully rehearsed speech in ruins. 'Anyhow, I shouldn't have said what I did,' I concluded miserably.

She put a hand on my arm. 'Sam. Sam, my very dear, do not be troubled. What you said and what you did was fair enough from what you knew. The important thing, *to me*, is what you did *for me*. The rest does not matter – except that I am happy again to know that you don't despise me.'

'Well, but — Damn it, don't be so noble! I can't stand it!'

She gave me a merry smile, not at all like the gentle one with which she had greeted me. 'Sam, I think you *like* your women to be a bit bitchy. I warn you, I can be so.' She went on, 'You are still worried about that slap too. All right, I'll pay it back.' She reached up and patted me gently on the cheek. 'There, it's paid and you can forget it.'

Her expression suddenly changed. She swung on me – and I thought my head was coming off. 'And that,' she said

102

in a tense whisper, 'pays you back the one I got from your girl friend!'

My ears were ringing and my eyes did not want to focus. I could have sworn that she had used at least a two-by-four. She looked at me, wary and defiant – angry, if dilated nostrils meant anything. I raised a hand and she tensed, but I just wanted to touch my stinging cheek. 'She's not my girl friend,' I said lamely.

We eyed each other and simultaneously burst out laughing. She put her hands on my shoulders and let her head collapse on my right one, still laughing. 'Sam,' she managed to say, 'I'm so sorry. I shouldn't have done it – not to you, Sam. At least I shouldn't have slapped you so hard.'

'The devil you're sorry,' I growled, 'but you shouldn't have put english on it. You damn near took the hide off.'

'Poor Sam!' She touched it; it hurt. 'She's really not your girl friend?'

'No, worse luck. But not from lack of my trying.'

'I'm sure it wasn't. Who is your girl friend, Sam?'

'You are, you vixen!'

'Yes,' she said comfortably, 'I am – if you'll have me. I told you that before. Bought and paid for.'

She was waiting to be kissed; I pushed her away. 'Confound it, woman, I don't want you "bought and paid for".'

It did not faze her. 'I put it badly. Paid for – but not bought. I'm here because I want to be. Now will you kiss me, please?'

She had kissed me once before; this time she *kissed* me. I felt myself sinking into a warm golden haze and I did not ever want to come up. Finally I had to break, and gasped, 'I think I'll sit down for a minute.'

She said, 'Thank you, Sam,' and let me.

'Mary,' I said presently, 'Mary, my dear, there is something you possibly could do for me.'

'Yes?' she said eagerly.

'Tell me how in the name of Ned a person gets breakfast around here? I'm starved.'

She looked startled, but she answered, 'Why, certainly!'

I don't know how she did it; she may have butted into the White House pantry and helped herself. But she returned in a few minutes with sandwiches and two bottles of beer. I was cleaning up my third corned-beef on rye when I said, 'Mary, how long do you figure that meeting will last?'

'Oh, I'd give it a minimum of two hours. Why?'

'In that case,' I said, swallowing the last bite, 'we have time to duck out, find a registry office, get married, and get back before the Old Man misses us.'

She did not answer. Instead she stared at the bubbles in her beer. 'Well?' I insisted.

She raised her eyes. 'I'll do it if you say so. I'm not welshing. But I would rather we didn't.'

'You don't want to marry me?'

'Sam, I don't think you are ready to get married.'

'Speak for yourself!'

'Don't be angry, my dear. You can have me with or without a contract – anywhere, anywhen, any way. But you don't know me yet. Get acquainted with me; you might change your mind.'

'I'm not in the habit of changing my mind.'

She glanced up, then looked away sadly. I felt my face get hot. 'That was a very special circumstance,' I protested. 'It couldn't happen to us again in a hundred years. That wasn't me talking; it was —'

She stopped me. 'I know, Sam. But you don't have to prove anything. I won't run out on you and I don't mistrust you. Take me away on a weekend; better yet, move into my apartment. If I wear well, there's always time to make me what great-grandmother called an "honest woman", heaven knows why.'

I must have looked sullen. She put a hand on mine and said seriously, 'Look at the map, Sam.'

I turned my head. Red as ever, or more so – the danger zone around El Paso had increased. She went on, 'Let's get this cleaned up first, dear. Then, if you still want to, ask me again. In the meantime, you can have the privileges without the responsibilities.'

What could be fairer than that? The trouble was it was not the way I wanted it. Why will a man who has been avoiding marriage like plague suddenly decide that nothing less will suit him?

When the meeting was over, the Old Man collared me and took me for a walk. Yes, a walk, though we went only as far as the Baruch Memorial Bench. There he sat down, fiddled with his pipe, and scowled. The day was as muggy as only Washington can get; the park was almost deserted.

He said, ' "Schedule Counter Blast" starts at midnight.'

Presently he added, 'We swoop down on every relay station, broadcast station, newspaper office, and Western Union office in "Zone Red".'

'Sounds good,' I answered. 'How many men?'

He did not answer; instead he said, 'I don't like it a little bit.'

'Huh?'

'See here, bub – the President went on channels and told everybody to peel off their shirts. We find that the message did not reach the infected territory. What's the next development?'

I shrugged. 'Schedule Counter Blast, I suppose.'

'That hasn't happened yet. Think – it has been more than twenty-four hours: what should have happened and hasn't?'

'Should I know?'

'You should, if you are ever going to amount to anything on your own. Here' – he handed me a combo key – 'scoot out to Kansas City and take a look-see. Stay away from comm stations, cops, and – shucks, you know their ways. Stay away from *them*. Look at everything else. And don't get caught.' He looked at his finger and added, 'Be back here a half hour before midnight. Get going.'

'A lot of time you allow to case a whole city,' I complained. 'It will take three hours just to drive to Kansas City.'

'More than three hours,' he answered. 'Don't attract attention by picking up a ticket.'

'You know darn well I'm a careful driver.'

'Move!'

So I moved. The combo was to the car we had come down in; I picked it up at Rock Creek Park platform. Traffic was light and I commented on it to the dispatcher. 'Freight and commercial carriers are grounded,' he answered. 'The emergency — You got a military clearance?'

I could get one by phoning the Old Man, but bothering him about minutiae does not endear one to him. I said, 'Check the combo.'

He shrugged and slipped it in his machine. My hunch had been right; his eyebrows shot up. 'How you rate!' he commented. 'You must be the President's fair-haired boy.'

Once launched, I set the controls for Kansas City at legal max and tried to think. The transponder beeped as radar beams hit it each time I slid from one control block into the next, but no faces appeared on the screen. Apparently the Old Man's combo was good for the route, emergency or not. I began to wonder what would happen when I slipped over into the red areas – and then realized what he had meant by 'the next development'.

One tends to think of communications as meaning the line-of-sight channels and nothing else. But 'communications' means *all* traffic, even dear old Aunt Mamie, headed for California and stuffed with gossip. The slugs had seized the channels – but news can't be stopped that easily; such measures merely slow it down. Ergo, if the slugs expected to retain control where they were, seizing the channels would be just their first step.

What would they do next? They would do something and I being a part of 'communications' by definition, had better be prepared for evasive action if I wanted to save my pretty pink skin. The Mississippi River and Zone Red were sliding closer by the minute. I wondered what would happen the first time my recognition signal was picked up by a station controlled by masters.

I judged that I was probably safe in the air – but that I

had better not let them spot me landing. Elementary.

'Elementary' in the face of a traffic-control net which was described as the No-Sparrow-Shall-Fall plan. They boasted that a butterfly could not make a forced landing anywhere in the United States without alerting the search and rescue system. Not quite true – but I was no butterfly.

On foot I will make a stab at penetrating any security screen, mechanical, manned, electronic, or mixed. But how can you use misdirection in a car making westing a full degree every seven minutes? Or hang a stupid, innocent look on the nose of a duo? If I went in on foot the Old Man would get his report come next Michaelmas; he wanted it before midnight.

Once, in a rare mellow mood, the Old Man told me that he did not bother agents with detailed instructions – give a man a mission; let him sink or swim. I said his method must use up a lot of agents.

'Some,' he had admitted, 'but not as many as the other way. I believe in the individual and I try to pick individuals who are survivor types.'

'And how in the hell,' I had asked, 'do you pick a "survivor type"?'

He had grinned wickedly. 'A survivor type is one who comes back.'

Elihu, I said to myself, you are about to find out which type you are – and damn his icy heart!

My course would take me towards St Louis, swing me around the city loop, and on to Kansas City. But St Louis was in Zone Red. The map had shown Chicago as green; the amber line had zigzagged west somewhere above Hannibal, Missouri – and I wanted very badly to cross the Mississippi while still in Zone Green. A car crossing that mile-wide river would make a radar blip as sharp as a desert star.

I signalled black control for permission to descend to local-traffic level, then did so without waiting, resuming manual control and cutting my speed. I headed north.

Short of the Springfield loop I headed west, staying low. When I reached the river I crossed slowly, close to the water, with my transponder shut down. Sure, you can't shut off your radar recognition signal in the air – but the Section's cars were not standard. I had hopes, if local traffic were being monitored while I crossed, that my blip would be mistaken for a boat on the river.

I did not know certainly whether the next block-control station across the river was Zone Red or Zone Green. I was about to cut in the transponder again on the assumption that it would be safer to get back into the traffic system when I noticed the shore line opening up ahead. The map did not show a tributary; I judged it to be an inlet, or a new channel not yet mapped. I dropped almost to water level and headed into it. The stream was narrow, meandering, and almost overhung by trees, and I had no more business taking a sky car into it than a bee has of flying down a trombone – but it afforded perfect radar 'shadow'; I could get lost in it.

In a few minutes I *was* lost – lost myself, right off the map. The channel switched and turned and cut back and I was so busy bucking the car by hand that I lost all track of navigation. I swore and wished that the car were a triphib so that I could land on water. The trees suddenly broke; I saw a stretch of level land, kicked her over, and squatted her in with a deceleration that nearly cut me in two against my safety belt. But I was down and no longer trying to play catfish in a muddy stream.

I wondered what to do. No doubt there was a highway close by. I had better find it and stay on the ground.

But that was silly – there was not time for ground travel; I *must* get back into the air. But I did not dare until I knew positively whether traffic here was being controlled by free men, or by slugs.

I had not turned on the stereo since leaving Washington. Now I did so, hunting for a newscast, but not finding one. I got (a) lecture by Myrtle Doolightly, PhD, on *Why Husbands Grow Bored*, sponsored by the Uth-a-gen Hormone Company; (b) a trio of girl hepsters singing 'If You Mean What I Think You Mean, What Are We Waiting For?' (c) an episode in *Lucretia Learns about Life*.

Dear Dr Myrtle was fully dressed. The trio were dressed

the way one would expect, but they did not turn their backs to the camera. Lucretia alternated between having her clothes torn off with taking them off willingly, but the camera always cut or the lights went out just before I could check on whether or not her back was bare – of slugs, that is.

And none of it meant anything. Those programmes could have been taped months before the President announced Schedule Bare Back. I was still switching channels, trying to find a newscast, when I found myself staring at the unctuous smile of an announcer. He was fully dressed.

Shortly I realized that it was one of those silly give-away shows. He was saying: '– and some lucky little woman sitting by her screen right this minute is about to receive, absolutely free, a General Atomics Six-in-One Automatic Home Butler. Who will it be? You? You? Or lucky *you*?' He turned away from scan; I could see his shoulders. They were covered by a jacket and distinctly rounded, almost humped. I was inside Zone Red.

When I switched off I realized that I was being watched – by a male about nine years old. He was wearing only shorts – at his age it meant nothing. I threw back the wind screen. 'Hey, bub, where's the highway?'

He answered, 'Road to Macon's up yonder. Say, mister, that's a Cadillac Zipper, ain't it?'

'Sure thing. Where yonder?'

'Give me a ride, huh, will you?'

'Haven't got time.'

'Take me along and I'll show you.'

I gave in. While he climbed in, I opened my kit, got out shirt, trousers, and jacket. I said, 'Maybe I shouldn't put this on. Do people around here wear shirts?'

He scowled. 'Of course they do. Where do you think you are, mister; Arkansas?'

I asked again about the road. He said, 'Can I punch the button when we take off, huh?'

I explained that we were going to stay on the ground. He was annoyed, but condescended to point a direction. I drove cautiously, as the car was heavy for unpaved countryside.

Presently he said to turn. Quite a bit later I stopped and said, 'Are you going to show me that road, or am I going to wallop you?'

He opened the door and slid out. 'Hey!' I yelled.

He looked back. 'Over that way,' he admitted. I turned the car, not expecting to find a highway, but finding one, nevertheless, fifty yards away. The brat had caused me to drive around three sides of a square.

If you could call it a highway – there was not an ounce of rubber in the paving. Still, it was a road; I followed it to the west. All in all, I had wasted an hour.

Macon, Missouri, seemed too normal to be reassuring; Schedule Bare Back obviously had not been heard of. I gave serious thought to checking this town, then beating back the way I had come, while I could. Pushing farther into country which I knew to be controlled by the masters made me jittery; I wanted to run.

But the Old Man had said 'Kansas City'. I drove the belt around Macon and pulled into a landing flat on the west. There I queued up for local traffic launching and headed for Kansas City in a mess of farmers' 'copters and local craft. I would have to hold local speeds across the state, but that was safer than getting into the hot pattern with my transponder identifying my car to every block control. The field was automatically serviced; it seemed probable that I had managed to enter the Missouri traffic pattern without arousing suspicion.

XVII

Kansas City had not been hurt in the bombings, except on the east where Independence used to be. Consequently it had never been rebuilt. From the southeast you can drive as far as Swope Park before having to choose between parking or paying toll to enter the city proper. Or one can fly in and make another choice : land in the landing flats north of the river and take the tunnels into the city, or land on the downtown platforms south of Memorial Hill.

I decided not to fly in; I did not want to have to pick the car up through a checking system. I do not like tunnels in a pinch – nor launching-platform elevators. A man can be trapped in such. Frankly, I did not want to go into the city at all.

I roaded the car on Route 40 and drove into the Meyer Boulevard tollgate. The line waiting was quite long; I began to feel hemmed in as soon as another car filled in behind me. But the gatekeeper took my toll without glancing at me. I glanced at him, all right, but could not tell whether or not he was being ridden.

I drove through the gate with a sigh of relief – only to be stopped just beyond. A barrier dropped in front of me and I just managed to stop the car, whereupon a cop stuck his head in. 'Safety check,' he said. 'Climb out.'

I protested. 'The city is having a safety drive,' he explained. 'Here's your car check. Pick it up just beyond the barrier. Get out and go in that door.' He pointed to a building near the curb.

'What for?'

'Eyesight and reflexes. You're holding up the line.'

In my mind's eye I saw the map, with Kansas City glowing red. That the city was 'secured' I was sure; therefore this mild-mannered policeman was almost surely hagridden. But, short of shooting him and making an emergency take-off, there was nothing to do but comply. I got out, grumbling, and walked slowly towards the building. It was a temporary job with an old-style unpowered door. I pushed it open with a toe and glanced both sides and up before I entered. There was an empty anteroom with door beyond. Someone inside called, 'Come in.' Still wary, I went in. There were two men in white coats, one with a doctor's speculum strapped to his head. He said briskly, 'This won't take a minute. Step over here.' He closed the door I had entered; I heard the lock click.

It was a sweeter setup than we had worked out for the

Constitution Club. Spread out on a table were transit cells for masters, already opened and warmed. The second man had one ready – for me, I knew – and was holding it towards him, so that I could not see the slug. The transit cells would not arouse alarm in the victims; medical men always have odd things at hand.

As for the rest, I was being invited to place my eyes against the goggles of an ordinary visual acuity tester. The 'doctor' would keep me there, blindfolded without knowing it and reading test figures, while his 'assistant' fitted me with a master. No violence, no slips, no protests.

It was not necessary, as I had learned during my own 'service', to bare the victim's back. Just touch the master to the bare neck, then let the recruit himself adjust his clothing to cover his master.

'Over here,' the 'doctor' repeated. 'Place your eyes against the eyepieces.'

Moving quickly, I went to the bench on which was mounted the acuity tester. Then I turned suddenly around.

The assistant had moved in, the cell ready in his hands. As I turned he tilted it away from me. 'Doctor,' I said, 'I wear contact lenses. Should I take them off?'

'No, no,' he snapped. 'Let's not waste time.'

'But, Doctor,' I protested, 'I want you to see how they fit. I've had a little trouble with this left one —' I lifted both hands and pulled back the lids of my left eye. 'See?'

He said angrily, 'This is not a clinic. Now, if you please —' They were both in reach; lowering my arms in a mighty bear hug, I got them both – and grabbed at the spot between each set of shoulder blades. With each hand I struck something soft under the coats and felt revulsion shake me.

Once I saw a cat struck by a ground car; the poor thing leaped straight up with its back arched the wrong way and all limbs flying. These two unlucky men did the same thing; they contorted every muscle in a grand spasm. I could not hold them; they jerked out of my arms and flopped to the floor. But there was no need; after that first convulsion they went limp, possibly dead.

Someone was knocking. I called out, 'Just a moment. The doctor is busy.' It stopped. I made sure the door was locked, then bent over the 'doctor' and pulled up his coat to see what I had done to his master.

The thing was a ruptured mess. So was the one on the other man – which facts pleased me heartily, as I was determined to burn the slugs if they were not already dead and I was not sure that I could do so without killing the hosts. I left the men, to live or die – or be seized again by titans. I had no way to help them.

The masters waiting in their cells were another matter. With a fan beam and max charge I burned them all. There were two large crates against the wall; I beamed them also until the wood charred.

The knocking resumed. I looked around hastily for somewhere to hide the two men, but there was nowhere, so I decided to run for it. As I was about to go out the exit, I felt that something was missing. I looked around again.

There seemed to be nothing suited to my purpose. I could use clothing from the 'doctor' or his helper, but I did not want to. Then I noticed the dust cover for the acuity tester. I loosened my jacket, snatched up the cover, wadded it and stuffed it under my shirt between my shoulders. With my jacket zipped it made a bulge of the proper size.

Then I went out, '... a stranger and afraid, in a world I never made.'

As a matter of fact, I was feeling pretty cocky.

Another cop took my car check. He glanced sharply at me, then motioned me to climb in. I did and he said, 'Go to police headquarters, under the City Hall.'

' "Police headquarters, the City Hall," ' I repeated and gunned her ahead. I started in that direction and turned on to Nichols Freeway. I came to a stretch where traffic thinned out and punched the button to shift licence plates. It seemed possible that there was already a call out for the plates I had been showing at the gate. I wished that I had been able to change the car's colours and body lines as well.

Before the Freeway reached McGee Traffic Way, I turned down a ramp and stuck thereafter to side streets. It was eighteen hundred, zone six time, and I was due in Washington in four and one-half hours.

XVIII

The city did not look right. It did not have the right flavour, as if it were a clumsily directed play. I tried to put my finger on the fault; it kept slipping away.

Kansas City has many neighbourhoods made up of family units a century old or more. Kids roll on lawns and householders sit on their front porches, just as their great-grandparents did. If there are bomb shelters around, they do not show. The queer old bulky houses, fitted together by guildsmen long since dead, make those neighbourhoods feel like enclaves of security. I cruised through along such streets, dodging dogs and rubber balls and toddlers, and tried to get the feel of the place. It was the slack of the day, time for a drink, for watering lawns, for neighbourly chatting. I saw a woman bending over a flower bed. She was wearing a sun suit and her back was bare; clearly she was not wearing a master, nor were the two kids with her. What could be wrong?

It was a very hot day; I began to look for sun-suited women and men in shorts. Kansas City is in the Bible Belt; people there do not strip to the weather with the unanimity of Laguna Beach or Coral Gables. An adult fully covered up is never conspicuous. So I found people dressed both ways – but the proportions were wrong. Sure, there were plenty of kids dressed for the weather, but in several miles of driving I saw the bare backs of only five women and two men.

I should have seen more like five hundred.

Cipher it out. While some jackets undoubtedly did *not* cover masters, by simple proportion *well over ninety per cent of the population must be possessed.*

This city was not 'secured'; it was saturated. The masters did not simply hold key points and key officials; the masters *were* the city.

I felt a blind urge to blast off and streak out of Zone Red at emergency maximum. They knew that I had escaped the gate trap; they would be looking for me. I might be the only free man driving a car in the entire city – and they were all around me!

I fought it down. An agent who gets the wind up is no use and is not likely to get out of a tight spot. But I had not recovered from what it had done to me to be possessed; it was hard to be calm.

I counted ten and tried to figure it. It seemed that I must be wrong; there could not possibly be enough masters to saturate a city with a million population. I remembered my own experiences, recalling how we picked our recruits and made each new host count. Of course that had been a secondary invasion depending on shipments, whereas Kansas City almost certainly had had a saucer land near by. Still it did not make sense; it would take a dozen saucers or more to carry enough masters to saturate Kansas City. If there had been that many, surely the space stations would have radar-tracked their landing orbits.

Could it be that they had no trajectories to track? We did not know what the masters were capable of in engineering and it was not safe to judge their limitations by our own.

But the data I had led to a conclusion which contradicted common logic; therefore I must check before I reported. One thing seemed sure: if the masters had in fact almost saturated this city, they were nevertheless still keeping up the masquerade, permitting the city to look like a city of free human beings. Perhaps I was not as conspicuous as I feared.

I moseyed along another mile or so, going nowhere. I found myself heading into the retail district around the Plaza. I swung away; where there are crowds, there are cops. In so doing, I passed a public swimming pool. I observed it and filed what I had seen. I was several blocks away before I reviewed the swimming pool datum; it had not been much: it carried a sign – CLOSED FOR THE SEASON.

A swimming pool closed down during the hottest part of the summer? It meant nothing; swimming pools have gone out of business before and will again. But it was contrary to the logic of economics to close such an enterprise during the season of greatest profit except through utter necessity. The odds against it were long. But a swimming pool was one place where the masquerade could not possibly be maintained. A closed pool was less conspicuous than a pool unpatronized in hot weather. The masters always noted and followed the human point of view in their manoeuvres. Shucks, I had been there!

Item: a trap at the city's tollgates; item: too few sun suits; item: a closed swimming pool.

Conclusion: the slugs were incredibly more numerous than anyone had dreamed.

Corollary: Schedule Counter Blast was based on a mistaken estimate; it would work as well as hunting rhinoceroses with a slingshot.

Counter argument: what I thought I saw was impossible. I could hear Secretary Martinez's restrained sarcasm tearing my report to shreds. I needed proof strong enough to convince the President over the reasonable objections of his official advisers – and I had to have it *now*. Breaking all traffic laws, I could not clip much off two and a half hours' running time back to Washington.

What should I do? Go downtown, mingle with crowds, and then tell Martinez that I was sure that almost every man I passed was possessed? How could I prove it? For that matter, how could I myself be certain? As long as the titans kept up the farce of 'business as usual' the telltales would be subtle, a super-abundance of round shoulders, a paucity of bare ones.

I had some notion of how the city had been saturated, granting a large enough supply of slugs. I felt sure that I would encounter another tollgate trap on the way out and that there would be others on launching platforms and at every entrance and exit to the city proper. Every person leaving would be a new agent; every person entering would be a new slave.

I had noticed a vendo-printer for the Kansas City *Star* on the last corner I had passed. Now I swung around the block, pulled up to it and got out. I shoved a dime in the slot and waited nervously for my paper to be printed.

The *Star*'s format had its usual dull respectability – no excitement, no mention of an emergency, no reference to Schedule Bare Back. The lead story was headed PHONE SERVICE DISRUPTED BY SUNSPOT STORM, with a subhead: *City Semi-isolated by Solar Static*. There was a three-column, semi-stereo trukolor of the sun, its face disfigured by cosmic acne. It was a convincing and unexciting explanation of why Mamie Schultz, herself free of parasites, could not get her call through to Grandma in Pittsburgh.

I tucked the paper under my arm to study later and turned back to my car – just as a police car glided silently up and cramped in across the nose of it. A police car seems to condense a crowd out of air. A moment before the corner had been deserted. Now there were people all around and the cop was coming towards me. My hand crept towards my gun; I would have dropped him had I not been sure that most of those around me were equally dangerous.

He stopped in front of me. 'Let me see your licence,' he said pleasantly.

'Certainly, Officer,' I agreed. 'It's clipped to the instrument board of my car.' I stepped past him, letting it be assumed that he would follow. I could feel him hesitate, then take the bait. I led him around between my car and his. This let me see that he did not have a mate in his car, a most welcome variation from human practice. More important, it placed my car between me and the too-innocent bystanders.

'There,' I said, pointing inside, 'it's fastened down.' Again he hesitated, then looked – long enough for me to use the technique I had developed through necessity. My left hand slapped his shoulders and I clutched with all my strength.

His body seemed to explode, so violent was the spasm. I was in the car and gunning it almost before he hit the pavement.

None too soon. The masquerade broke as it had in Barnes's outer office; the crowd closed in. One woman clung by her nails to the outside of the car for fifty feet or more before she fell off. By then I was making speed and still accelerating. I cut in and out of traffic, ready to take to the air but lacking space.

A street showed up on the left; I slammed into it. It was a mistake; trees arched over it and I could not take off. The next turn was even worse. Of necessity I slowed down. Now I was cruising at conservative city speed, still watching for some boulevard wide enough for an illegal take-off. My thoughts began to catch up and I realized that there was no sign of pursuit.

My knowledge of the masters came to my aid. Except for 'direct conference', a titan lives in and through his host; he sees what the host sees; receives and passes on information through whatever organs and by whatever means are available to the host. It was unlikely that any of the slugs at the corner had been looking for that particular car other than the one possessing the body of a policeman – and I had settled with it! Now, of course, the other parasites present would be on the lookout for me, too – but they had only the bodily abilities and facilities of their hosts. I decided that I need treat them with no more respect than I would give to any casual crowd of witnesses, i.e. ignore them; change neighbourhoods and forget it.

For I had barely thirty minutes left and I had decided on what I needed as proof – a prisoner, a man who had been possessed and could tell what had happened to the city. I had to rescue a host.

I had to capture one without hurting him, kill or remove his rider, and kidnap him back to Washington. I had no time to make plans; I must act *now*. Even as I decided, I saw a man walking in the block ahead, stepping along like a man who sees home and supper. I pulled alongside him and said, 'Hey!'

He stopped. 'Eh?'

I said, 'I've just come from City Hall. No time to explain – slide in and we'll have a direct conference.'

He answered, 'City Hall? What are you talking about?'

I said, 'Change in plans. Don't waste time. Get in!'

He backed away. I jumped out and grabbed at his hunched shoulders.

Nothing happened – save that my hand struck bony human flesh, and the man began to yell.

I jumped into the car and got out of there fast. When I was blocks away I slowed and thought it over. Could it be that my nerves were so overwrought that I saw signs of titans where there were none?

No! For the moment I had the Old Man's indomitable will to face facts. The tollgate, the sun suits, the swimming pool, the cop at the vendo-printer – those facts I *knew*, and this last fact simply meant that I had picked the one man in ten, or whatever the odds were, who was not yet recruited. I speeded up, looking for a new victim.

He was a middle-aged man watering his lawn, a figure so normal looking that I was half a mind to pass him by. But I had no time left – and he wore a sweater which bulged suspiciously. Had I seen his wife on the veranda I would have gone past, for she was dressed in halter and skirt and so could not have been possessed.

He looked up as I stopped. 'I've just come from City Hall,' I repeated. 'You and I need a direct conference right away. Get in.'

He said quietly, 'Come in the house. That car is too public.'

I wanted to refuse but he was already heading for the house. As I came up he whispered, 'Careful. The woman is not of us.'

'Your wife?'

'Yes.'

We stopped on the porch and he said, 'My dear, this is Mr O'Keefe. We have business to discuss. We'll be in the study.'

She smiled and answered, 'Certainly, my love. Good evening, Mr O'Keefe. Sultry, isn't it?'

I agreed and she went back to her knitting. We went inside and the man ushered me into his study. Since we were keeping the masquerade, I went in first, as befitted an escorted visitor. I did not like turning my back on him. For that reason I was half expecting it; he hit me near the base of the neck. I rolled with it and went down almost unhurt. I continued to roll and fetched up on my back.

In training school they used to slap us with sandbags for trying to get up, once down. So I stayed down and was threatening him with my heels as soon as I hit. He danced out of range. Apparently he did not have a gun and I could not get at mine. But there was a real fireplace in the room, complete with poker, shovel, and tongs; he circled towards it. There was a small table just out of my reach. I lunged, grabbed a leg and threw it. It caught him in the face as he grabbed the poker. Then I was on him.

His master was dying in my fingers and he himself was convulsing under its last, terrible command when I became aware of his wife, screaming in the doorway. I bounced up and let her have one. She went down in mid-scream and I returned to her husband.

A limp man is amazingly hard to lift, and he was heavy. Fortunately I am a big husky; I managed a lumbering dog trot towards the car. I doubt if our fight disturbed anyone but his wife, but her screams must have aroused half that end of town. There were people popping out of doors on both sides of the street. So far, none of them was near, but I was glad that I had left the car door open.

Then I was sorry; a brat like the one who had given me trouble earlier was inside fiddling with the controls. Cursing, I dumped my prisoner in the lounge circle and grabbed the kid. He struggled, but I tore him loose and threw him out – into the arms of the first of my pursuers. He was still untangling himself as I slammed into the seat and shot forward without bothering with door or safety belt. As I took the first corner the door swung shut and I almost went out of my seat; I then held a straight course long enough to fasten the belt. I cut sharp another corner, nearly ran down a ground car, and went on.

I found a wide boulevard – the Paseo, I think – and jabbed the take-off key. Possibly I caused several wrecks; I had no time to worry. Without waiting to reach altitude I wrestled her to course east and continued to climb as I made easting. I kept her on manual across Missouri and expended every launching unit in her racks to give more speed. That reckless, illegal action may have saved my neck; somewhere over Columbia, just as I fired the last one, I felt the car shake to concussion. Someone had launched an interceptor and the pesky thing had fused where I had just been.

There were no more shots, which was good, as I would have been a duck on water from then on. My starboard impeller began to run hot, possibly from the near miss or perhaps simply from abuse. I let it heat, praying that it would not fly apart, for another ten minutes. Then, with the Mississippi behind me and the indicator 'way up into 'danger' I cut it out and let the car limp along on the port unit. Three hundred was the best she would do – but I was out of Zone Red.

I had not had time to give my passenger more than a glance. He lay sprawled on the floor pads, unconscious or dead. Now that I was back among men and no longer had power for illegal speeds there was no reason not to go automatic. I flipped the transponder, signalled a request for a block assignment, and put the controls on automatic without waiting for permission. I then swung around into the lounge and looked my man over.

He was still breathing. There was a welt on his face, but no bones seemed broken. I slapped his face and dug thumb-nails into his ear lobes, but I could not rouse him. The dead slug was beginning to stink, but had no way to dispose of it. I left him and went back to the control seat.

The chronometer read twenty-one thirty-seven Washington time – and I still had better than six hundred miles to go. Allowing nothing for landing, for tearing over to the

White House, and finding the Old Man, I would reach Washington a few minutes after midnight. So I was already late and the Old Man was sure as the devil going to make me stay in after school for it.

I tried to start the starboard impeller. No dice – it was probably frozen solid. Perhaps just as well, as anything that goes that fast can be explosively dangerous if it gets out of balance – so I desisted and tried to raise the Old Man by phone.

The phone would not work. Perhaps I had jiggered it in one of the spots of exercise I had been forced to take. I put it back, feeling that this was one of those days when it was just not worth while to get out of bed. I turned to the car's communicator and punched the emergency tab. 'Control,' I called out. 'Control!'

The screen lighted up and I was looking at a young man. He was, I saw with relief, bare to the waist. 'Control answering – Block Fox Eleven. What are you doing in the air? I've been trying to raise you ever since you entered my block.'

'Never mind!' I snapped. 'Patch me into the nearest military circuit. This is crash priority!'

He looked uncertain, but the screen flickered and shortly another picture built up showing a military message centre – and that did my heart good, as everyone in sight was stripped to the waist. In the foreground was a young watch officer; I could have kissed him. Instead I said, 'Military emergency – patch me through the Pentagon and there to the White House.'

'Who are you?'

'No time, no time! I'm a civil agent and you wouldn't recognize my ID. Hurry!'

I might have talked him into it but he was shouldered out of scan by a wing commander. 'Land at once!' was all that he said.

'Look, Skipper,' I said. 'This is a military emergency; you've got to put me through. I —'

'*This* is a military emergency,' he interrupted. 'Civil craft have been grounded the past three hours. Land at once.'

'But I've got to —'

'Land or be shot down. We are tracking; I am about to launch an interceptor to burst a half mile ahead of you. Make any manoeuvre but landing, and the next will burst on you.'

'Will you *listen*, please? I'll land, but I've got to get —' He switched off, leaving me pumping air.

The first burst seemed short of a half mile ahead; I landed.

I cracked up, but without hurting myself or my passenger. I did not have long to wait. They had me flare-lighted and were swooping down before I had satisfied myself that the boat wouldn't move. They took me in and I met the wing commander personally. He even put my message through after his psych squad got through giving me the antidote for the sleep test. By then it was one-thirteen, zone five – and Schedule Counter Blast had been underway one hour and thirteen minutes.

The Old Man listened to a summary, grunted, then told me to see him in the morning.

XIX

Schedule Counter Blast was the worst wet firecracker in military history. The drops were made just at midnight, zone five, on over ninety-six hundred communication points – newspaper offices, block controls, relay stations, and so forth. The raiding squads were the cream of our sky-borne forces, plus technicians to put each communication point back into service.

Whereupon the President's speech was to go out from each local station; Schedule Bare Back would take effect all through the infected territory; and the war would be over, save for mopping up.

By twenty-five minutes after midnight reports started coming in that such-and-such points were secured. A little later there were calls for help from other points. By one in the morning most of the reserves had been committed, but the operation seemed to be going well – so well, indeed, that unit commanders were landing and reporting from the ground.

That was the last anybody ever heard of them.

Zone Red swallowed up the task force as if it had never existed – over eleven thousand craft, more than a hundred and sixty thousand fighting men and technicians, seventy-one group commanders and – why go on? The United States had received its worst military setback since Black Sunday. I am not criticizing Martinez, Rexton, and the General Staff, nor those poor devils who made the drop. The programme was based on what appeared to be a true picture, and the situation called for fast action with the best we had.

It was nearly daylight, so I understand, before Martinez and Rexton got it through their heads that the messages they had gotten back about successes were actually faked, fakes sent by their own men – *our* own men – but hag-ridden, possessed, and brought into the masquerade. After my report, more than an hour too late to stop the raids, the Old Man had tried to get them not to send in any more men, but they were flushed with success and anxious to make a clean sweep.

The Old Man asked the President to insist on visual checks, but the operation was being controlled by relay through Space Station Alpha and there just aren't enough channels to parallel audio with video through a space station. Rexton had said, 'Quit worrying. As fast as we get local stations back in our hands, our boys will patch into the ground-relay net and you will have all the visual evidence you want.'

The Old Man had pointed out that by then it would be too late. Rexton had burst out, 'Confound it, man! Do you want a thousand men to be killed just to quiet your jitters?'

The President had backed him up.

By morning they had their visual evidence. Stations in the central valley were giving out with the same old pap: *Rise and Shine with Mary Sunshine, Breakfast with the Browns,* and such junk. There was not a station with the President's stereocast, not one that conceded that anything had happened. The military dispatches tapered off around four o'clock and Rexton's frantic calls were not answered. Task Force Redemption ceased to exist – *spurlos versenkt.*

I did not get to see the Old Man until nearly eleven the next morning. He let me report without comment, and without bawling me out, which was worse.

He was about to dismiss me when I put in, 'How about my prisoner? Didn't he confirm my conclusions?'

'Oh, him? Still unconscious. They don't expect him to live.'

'I'd like to see him.'

'You stick to things you understand.'

'Well – have you got something for me to do?'

'I think you had better – no, do this: trot down to the zoo. You'll see things that put a different light on what you picked up in Kansas City.'

'Huh?'

'Look up Dr Horace, the assistant director. Tell him I sent you.'

Horace was a nice little guy who looked like one of his own baboons; he turned me over to a Dr Vargas, who was a specialist in exotic biologies – the same Vargas who was on the second Venus Expedition. He showed me what had happened. If the Old Man and I had gone to the National Zoological Gardens instead of sitting around in the park, it would not have been necessary for me to go to Kansas City. The ten titans we had captured in Congress, plus two the next day, had been sent to the zoo to be placed on anthropoids – chimps and orang-utans, mostly. No gorillas.

The director had had the apes locked up in the zoo's hospital. Two chimpanzees, Abélard and Héloise, were caged together; they had always been mates and there seemed no reason to separate them. That sums up our psychological difficulty in dealing with the titans; even the men who transplanted the slugs still thought of the result as apes, rather than as titans.

The next treatment cage held a family of tuberculous gibbons. They were not used as hosts, since they were sick, and there was no communication between cages. They were shut one from another by sliding panels, and each cage had its own air-conditioning. The next morning the panel had been slid back and the gibbons and the chimps were together. Abélard or Héloïse had found some way to pick the lock. The lock was supposed to be monkey-proof, but it was not ape-*cum*-titan proof.

Five gibbons, plus two chimps plus two titans – but the next morning there were seven apes ridden by *seven* titans.

This was discovered two hours before I left for Kansas City, but the Old Man had not been notified. Had he been, he would have *known* that Kansas City was saturated. I might have figured it out myself. Had the Old Man known about the gibbons, Schedule Counter Blast would not have taken place.

'I saw the President's stereocast,' Dr Vargas said to me. 'Weren't you the man who – I mean, weren't you the —'

'Yes, I was "the man who",' I agreed shortly.

'Then you can tell us a great deal about these phenomena.'

'Perhaps I should be able to,' I admitted slowly, 'but I can't.'

'Do you mean that no cases of fission reproduction took place while you were, uh, their prisoner?'

'That's right.' I thought about it. 'At least I think that's right.'

'I was given to understand that, uh, victims have full memory of their experiences?'

'Well, they do and they don't.' I tried to explain the odd detached frame of mind of a servant of the masters.

'I suppose it could happen while you sleep.'

'Maybe. Besides sleep, there is another time, or rather times, which are difficult to remember. During conference.'

'Conference?'

So I explained. His eyes lit up, 'Oh, you mean "conjugation".'

'No, I mean "conference".'

'We mean the same thing. Don't you see? Conjugation and fission – they reproduce at will, whenever the supply of hosts permits. Probably one contact for each fission; then, when opportunity exists, fission – two adult daughter parasites in a matter of hours . . . less, possibly.'

If that were true – and, looking at the gibbons, I could not doubt it – then why had we depended on shipments at the Constitution Club? Or had we? I did not know; I did what my master wanted done and saw only what came under my eyes. But it was clear how Kansas City had been saturated. With plenty of 'live stock' at hand and a space ship loaded with transit cells to draw from, the titans had reproduced to match the human population.

Assume a thousand slugs in that space ship, the one we believed to have landed near Kansas City; suppose that they could reproduce when given opportunity every twenty-four hours.

First day, one thousand slugs.

Second day, two thousand.

Third day, four thousand.

At the end of the first week, the eighth day, that is – a *hundred and twenty-eight thousand* slugs.

After two weeks, *more than sixteen million slugs.*

But we did not know that they were limited to spawning once a day. Nor did we know that a flying saucer could lift only a thousand transit cells; it might be ten thousand – or more – or less. Assume ten thousand as breeding stock with fission every twelve hours. In two weeks the answer comes out —

MORE THAN TWO AND A HALF TRILLION!!!!

The figure did not mean anything; it was cosmic. There aren't anything like that many people on the whole globe, not even counting in apes.

We were going to be knee-deep in slugs – and that before long. I felt worse than I had in Kansas City.

Dr Vargas introduced me to a Dr McIlvaine of the Smithsonian Institution; McIlvaine was a comparative psychologist, the author, so Vargas told me, of *Mars, Venus, and Earth: A Study in Motivating Purposes*. Vargas seemed to expect me to be impressed, but I had not read it. Anyhow, how can anyone study the motives of Martians when they were all dead before we swung down out of trees?

They started swapping trade talk; I continued to watch the gibbons. Presently McIlvaine asked me, 'Mr Nivens, how long does a conference last?'

'Conjugation,' Vargas corrected him.

'Conference,' McIlvaine repeated. 'It's the more important aspect.'

'But, Doctor,' Vargas insisted, 'conjugation is the means of gene exchange whereby mutation is spread through —'

'Anthropocentricism, Doctor! You do not know that this life form has genes.'

Vargas turned red. 'You will allow me gene equivalents?' he said stiffly.

'Why should I? I repeat, sir, that you are reasoning by uncertain analogy. There is only one characteristic common to all life forms and that is the drive to survive.'

'And to reproduce,' insisted Vargas.

'Suppose the organism is immortal and has no need to reproduce?'

'But —' Vargas shrugged. 'We know that they reproduce.' He gestured at the apes.

'And I am suggesting,' McIlvaine came back, 'that this is not reproduction, but a single organism availing itself of more space. No, Doctor, it is possible to get so immersed in the idea of the zygote-gamete cycle that one forgets that there may be other patterns.'

Vargas started out, 'But throughout the entire system —'

McIlvaine cut him short, 'Anthropocentric, terrocentric, solocentric – it is a provincial approach. These creatures may be from outside the solar system entirely.'

I said, 'Oh no!' I had had a sudden flash picture of the planet Titan and with it a choking sensation.

Neither one noticed. McIlvaine continued, 'Take the amoeba – a more basic, and much more successful life form than ours. The motivational psychology of the amoeba —'

I switched off my ears; free speech gives a man the right to talk about the 'psychology' of an amoeba, but I don't have to listen.

They did some direct experimentation, which raised my opinion of them a little. Vargas had a baboon wearing a slug placed in the cage with the gibbons and chimps. As soon as the newcomer was dumped in they gathered in a ring facing outwards and went into direct conference, slug to slug. McIlvaine jabbed his finger at them. 'You see? Conference is *not* for reproduction, but for exchange of memory. The organism, temporarily divided, has now re-identified itself.'

I could have told him the same thing without the double talk; a master who has been out of touch always gets into direct conference as soon as possible.

'Hypothesizing!' Vargas snorted. 'They have no opportunity to reproduce just now. George!' He ordered the boss of the handling crew to bring in another ape.

'Little Abe?' asked the crew boss.

'No, I want one without a parasite. Let me see – make it Old Red.'

The crew boss said, 'Cripes, Doc, don't pick on Old Red.'

'This won't hurt him.'

'How about Satan? He's a mean bastard anyway.'

'All right, but hurry it up.'

So they brought in Satan, a coal-black chimp. He may have been aggressive elsewhere; he was not so here. They dumped him inside; he shrank back against the door and began to whine. It was like watching an execution. I had had my nerves under control – a man can get used to anything – but the ape's hysteria was contagious. I wanted to run.

At first the hagridden apes simply stared at him like a jury. This went on for a long while. Satan's whines changed to low moans and he covered his face. Presently Vargas said, 'Doctor! Look!'

'Where?'

'Lucy – the old female. There.' He pointed.

It was the matriarch of consumptive gibbons. Her back was towards us; the slug thereon had humped itself together. An iridescent line ran down the centre of it.

It began to split as an egg splits. In a few minutes only, the division was complete. One new slug centred itself over her spine; the other flowed down her back. She was squatting almost to the floor; it slithered off and plopped gently on the concrete. It crept slowly towards Satan. The ape screamed hoarsely – and swarmed up into the top of the cage.

So help me, they sent a squad to arrest him – two gibbons, a chimp, and the baboon. They tore him loose and hauled him down and held him face down on the floor.

The slug slithered closer.

It was a good two feet away when it grew a pseudopod – slowly, at first – a stalk that weaved around like a cobra. Then it lashed out and struck the ape on a foot. The others promptly let go of him, but Satan did not move.

The titan seemed to pull itself in by the extension it had formed, and attached itself to Satan's foot. From there it crawled up; when it reached the base of his spine Satan sat up. He shook himself and joined the others.

Vargas and McIlvaine started talking excitedly, apparently unmoved. I wanted to smash something – for me, for Satan, for the whole simian race.

McIlvaine maintained that we were seeing something new to our concepts, an intelligent creature so organized as to be immortal and continuous in its personal identity – or its group identity; the argument grew confused. He theorized that it would have continuous memory back to its racial beginning. He described the slugs as a four-dimensional worm in spacetime, intertwined as a single organism, and the talk grew so esoteric as to be silly.

As for me, I did not know and did not care; the only way I cared about slugs was to kill them.

XX

For a wonder, when I got back the Old Man was available – the President had left to address a secret session of the United Nations. I told the Old Man what I had seen and added my opinion of Vargas and McIlvaine. 'Boy scouts,' I complained, 'comparing stamp collections. They don't realize it's serious.'

The Old Man shook his head. 'Don't sell them short, son,' he advised me. 'They are more likely to come up with the answer than are you and I.'

'Humph!' I said, or something stronger. 'They are more likely to let those slugs escape.'

'Did they tell you about the elephant?'

'What elephant? They damn near didn't tell me anything; they got interested in each other and ignored me.'

'You don't understand scientific detachment. About the elephant: an ape with a rider got out, somehow. Its body was found trampled to death in the elephant house. And one of the elephants was gone.'

'You mean there is an elephant loose *with a slug on him*?' I had a horrid vision – something like a tank with a cybernetic brain.

'Her,' the Old Man corrected me. 'They found her over in Maryland, quietly pulling up cabbages. No parasite.'

'Where did the slug get to?' Involuntarily I glanced around.

'A duo was stolen in the adjoining village. I'd say the slug is somewhere west of the Mississippi.'

'Anybody missing?'

He shrugged again. 'How can you tell, in a free country? At least, the titan can't hide on a human host anywhere short of Zone Red.'

His comment made me think of something I had seen at the zoo and had not reasoned through. Whatever it was, it eluded me. The Old Man went on, 'It's taken drastic action to make the bare-shoulders order stick, though. The President has had protests on moral grounds, not to mention the National Association of Haberdashers.'

'Huh?'

'You would think we were trying to sell their daughters down to Rio. There was a delegation in, called themselves the Mothers of the Republic, or some such nonsense.'

'The President's time is being wasted like *that*, at a time like *this*?'

'McDonough handled them. But he roped me in on it.' The Old Man looked pained. 'We told them that they could not see the President unless they stripped naked. That stopped 'em.'

The thought that had been bothering me came to the surface. 'Say, Boss, you might have to.'

'Have to what?'

'Make people strip naked.'

He chewed his lip. 'What are you driving at?'

'Do we know, as a certainty, that a slug can attach itself only near the base of the brain?'

'You should know.'

'I thought I did, but now I'm not sure. That's the way we always did it, when I was, uh, with them.' I recounted in more detail what I had seen when Vargas had had poor old Satan exposed to a slug. 'That ape moved as soon as the thing reached the base of his spine. I'm sure they prefer to ride up near the brain. But maybe they could ride down inside a man's pants and just put out an extension to the end of his spinal cord.'

'Hmm ... you'll remember, son, that the first time I had a crowd searched I made everybody peel to the buff. That was not accidental.'

'I think you were justified. They might be able to conceal themselves anywhere on the body. Take those droopy drawers you've got on. One could hide in them and it would just make you look a bit satchel-fannied.'

'Want me to take 'em off?'

'I can do better than that; I'll give you the Kansas City

Clutch.' My words were joking but I was not; I grabbed at the bunchiness of his pants and made sure he was clean. He submitted with good grace; then gave me the same treatment.

'But we can't,' he complained as he sat down, 'go around slapping women on the rump. It won't do.'

'You may have to,' I pointed out, 'or make everybody strip.'

'We'll run some experiments.'

'How?' I asked.

'You know that head-and-spine armour deal? It's not worth much, except to give the wearer a feeling of security. I'll tell Dr Horace to take an ape, fit such an armour so that a slug can't reach anything but his legs, say – and see what happens. We'll vary the areas too.'

'Uh, yes. But don't use an ape, Boss.'

'Why not?'

'Well – they're too human.'

'Damn it, bub, you can't make an omelet —'

'– without breaking eggs. Okay, but I don't have to like it.'

XXI

I spent the next several days lecturing to brass, answering fool questions about what titans ate for lunch, explaining how to tackle a man who was possessed. I was billed as an 'expert', but half the time my pupils seemed sure that they knew more about slugs than I did.

The titans continued to hold Zone Red, but they could not break out without being spotted – we hoped. And we did not try to break in again because every slug held one of our own people as hostage. The United Nations were no help. The President wanted a Schedule Bare Back on a global scale, but they hemmed and hawed and sent the matter to committee for investigation. The truth was they did not believe us; that was the enemy's great advantage – only the burned believed in the fire.

Some nations were safe through their own customs. A Finn who did not climb into a steam bath in company every day or so would have been conspicuous. The Japanese too were casual about undressing. The South Seas were relatively safe, as were large parts of Africa. France had gone enthusiastically nudist, on weekends at least, right after World War III – a slug would have a tough time hiding. But in countries where the body-modesty taboo meant something, a slug could stay hidden until his host began to stink. The United States itself, Canada, England – most particularly England.

They flew three slugs (with apes) to London; I understand that the King wanted to set an example as the President had, but the Prime Minister, egged on by the Archbishop of Canterbury, would not let him. The Archbishop had not even bothered to look; moral behaviour was more important than mundane peril. Nothing about this appeared in the news, and the story may not be true, but English skin was not exposed to the cold stares of neighbours.

The Russian propaganda system began to blast us as soon as they had worked out a new line. The whole thing was an 'American Imperialist fantasy'. I wondered why the titans had not attacked Russia first; the place seemed tailor-made for them. On second thought, I wondered if they had. On third thought, I wondered what difference it would make.

I did not see the Old Man during this period; I got my assignments from Oldfield, his deputy. Consequently I did not know it when Mary was relieved from special duty with the President. I ran into her in the lounge of the Section offices. 'Mary!' I yelped and fell over my feet.

She gave me that slow, sweet smile and moved over. 'Hello, darling!' she whispered. She did not ask what I had been doing, nor scold me that I had not been in touch with her, nor even comment on how long it had been. Mary let water over the dam take care of itself.

Not me – I babbled. 'This is wonderful! I thought you were still tucking the President into his beddy-bye. How long have you been here? When do you have to go back? Say, can I dial you a drink? No, you've got one.' I started to dial one for myself; it popped out into my hand. 'Huh? How'd this get here?'

'I ordered it when you came in the door.'

'Mary, did I tell you that you are wonderful?'

'No.'

'Very well, then, I will: You're wonderful.'

'Thank you.'

I went on, 'How long are you free? Say, couldn't you possibly get some leave? They can't expect you to be on duty twenty-four hours a day, week after week, with no time off. I'm going straight to the Old Man and tell him —'

'I'm on leave, Sam.'

' – just what I think of — Huh?'

'I'm on leave now.'

'You *are*? For how long?'

'Subject to call. All leaves read that way now.'

'But – how long have you been on leave?'

'Since yesterday. I've been sitting here, waiting for you.'

'Yesterday!' I had spent yesterday giving kindergarten lectures to brass hats who did not want them. I stood up. 'Don't move. I'll be right back.'

I rushed over to the operations office. Oldfield looked up when I came in and said in a surly tone, 'What do *you* want?'

'Chief, that series of bedtime stories I'm scheduled to tell: better cancel them.'

'Why?'

'I'm a sick man; I've rated sick leave for a long time. Now I've got to take it.'

'You're sick in the head.'

'That's right; I'm sick in the head. I hear voices. People have been following me around. I keep dreaming I'm back with the titans.' That last point was true.

'But since when has being crazy been any handicap in this Section?' He waited for me to argue the point.

'Look – do I get leave or don't I?'

He fumbled through papers, found one and tore it up. 'Okay. Keep your phone handy; you're subject to recall. Get out.'

I got. Mary looked up when I came in and gave me the soft warm treatment again. I said, 'Grab your things; we're leaving.'

She did not ask where; she simply stood up. I snatched my drink, gulped some, and spilled the rest. We were up on the pedestrian level of the city before we spoke. Then I asked, 'Now – where do you want to get married?'

'Sam, we discussed that before.'

'Sure we did and now we are going to do it. Where?'

'Sam, my very dear – I will do what you say. But I am still opposed to it.'

'Why?'

'Sam, let's go to my apartment. I'd like to cook dinner for you.'

'Okay, you can cook dinner – but not there. And we get married first.'

'Please, Sam!'

Somebody said, 'Keep pitching, kid. She's weakening.' I looked around and found that we were playing to a gallery.

I swept an arm wide and shouted irritably, 'Haven't you people got anything to do? Go get drunk!'

Somebody else said, 'I'd say he ought to take her offer.'

I grabbed Mary's arm and did not say another word until I had gotten her into a cab. 'All right,' I said gruffly, 'why not? Let's have your reasons.'

'Why get married, Sam? I'm yours; you don't need a contract.'

'Why? Because I love you, damn it!'

She did not answer for quite a while; I thought I had offended her. When she did I could hardly hear her. 'You hadn't mentioned that before, Sam.'

'Hadn't I? Oh, I must have.'

'No, I'm quite sure that you haven't. Why didn't you?'

'Uh, I don't know. An oversight, I guess. I'm not right sure what the word "love" means.'

'Neither am I,' she said softly, 'but I love to hear you say it. Say it again, please.'

'Huh? Okay. I love you. I love you, Mary.'

'Oh, Sam!'

She snuggled against me and began to tremble. I shook her a little. 'How about *you*?'

'Me? Oh, I do love you, Sam. I've loved you ever since —'

'Ever since what?'

I expected her to say that she had loved me ever since I took her place in Project Interview; what she said was, 'I've loved you ever since you slapped me.'

Is that logic?

The driver was cruising slowly along the Connecticut coast; I had to wake him before I could get him to land in Westport. We went to the city hall. I stepped up to a counter in the bureau of sanctions and licences and said to a clerk, 'Is this where we get married?'

'That's up to you,' he answered. 'Hunting licences on the left, dog licences on the right. This is the happy medium – I hope.'

'Good,' I said stiffly. 'Will you oblige by issuing a licence?'

'Sure. Everybody ought to get married at least once; that's what I tell my old lady.' He got out a form. 'Let's have your serial numbers.'

We gave them to him. 'Now – are either of you married in any other state?' We said we weren't; he went on, 'You're sure? If you don't tell me, so I can put on a rider showing other contracts, this contract ain't valid.'

We told him again that we weren't married anywhere. He went on, 'Term, renewable, or lifetime? If it's over ten years, the fee is the same as for lifetime; if it's under six months, you don't need this; you get the short form from that vendo machine over there.'

Mary said in a small voice, 'Lifetime.'

The clerk looked surprised. 'Lady, are you sure you know what you're doing? The renewable contract, with the automatic option clause, is just as permanent and you don't have to go through the courts if you change your mind.'

I said, 'You heard the lady!'

'Okay, okay – either party, mutual consent, or binding?'

'Binding,' I answered, and Mary nodded.

'Binding it is,' he agreed, stroking the typer. 'Now the meat of the matter: who pays and how much? Salary or endowment?'

I said, 'Salary'; I didn't own enough to set up a fund.

In a firm voice Mary said, 'Neither.'

The clerk said, 'Huh?'

'Neither,' Mary repeated. 'This is not a financial contract.'

The clerk stopped completely. 'Lady, don't be foolish,' he said reasonably. 'You heard the gentleman say that he was willing to do the right thing.'

'No.'

'Hadn't you better talk with your lawyer before you go ahead? There's a public communicator in the hall.'

'No!'

'Well, I'm darned if I see what you need a licence for.'

'Neither do I,' Mary told him.

'You mean you don't want this?'

'No! Put it down the way I told you to. "No salary." '

The clerk looked helpless but bent over the typer. 'I guess that's all,' he said finally. 'You've kept it simple, I'll say that. "Do - you - both - solemnly - swear - that - the - above - facts - are - true - to - the - best - of - your - knowledge - and - belief - that - you - are - entering - into - this - agreement - uninfluenced - by - drugs - or - other - illegal - inducements - and - that - there - exists - no - undisclosed - covenants - nor - other - legal - impediments - to - the - execution - and - registration - of - the - above - contract?" '

We both said that we did and we were and it was and there weren't. He pulled it out of the typer. 'Let's have your thumb-prints. Okay, that'll be ten dollars, including federal tax.' I paid him and he shoved the form into the copier and threw the switch. 'Copies will be mailed to you,' he announced, 'at your serial-number addresses. Now – what type of ceremony are you looking for? Maybe I can help.'

'We don't want a religious ceremony,' Mary told him.

'Then I've got just what you want. Old Dr Chamleigh. Nonsectarian, best stereo accompaniment in town, all four walls and full orchestra. He gives you the works, fertility rites and everything, but dignified. And he tops it off with a fatherly straight-from-the-shoulder word of advice. Makes you feel *married*.'

'No.' This time I said it.

'Oh, come now!' the clerk said to me. 'Think of the little lady. If she sticks by what she just swore to, she'll never have another chance. Every girl is entitled to a formal wedding. Honest – I don't get much of a commission.'

I said, 'You can marry us, can't you? Go ahead. Get it over with!'

He looked surprised. 'Didn't you know? In this state you marry yourself. You've *been* married, ever since you thumb-printed the licence.'

I said, 'Oh.' Mary didn't say anything. We left.

I hired a duo at the landing flat north of town; the heap was ten years old but it had full automatic and that was all that mattered. I looped around the city, cut across Manhattan Crater, and set the controls. I was happy but terribly nervous – and then Mary put her arms around me. After a long time I heard the *BEEEEP! beeb-beep BEEEEP!* of the beacon at my shack, whereupon I unwound myself and landed. Mary said sleepily, 'Where are we?'

'At my cabin in the mountains,' I told her.

'I didn't know you had a cabin in the mountains. I thought you were headed for my apartment.'

'What, and risk those bear traps? Anyhow, it's not mine; it's ours.'

She kissed me again and I loused up the landing. She slid out ahead of me while I was securing the board; I found her staring at the shack. 'Sweetheart, it's beautiful!'

'You can't beat the Adirondacks,' I agreed. There was a slight haze with the sun low in the west, giving that wonderful, depth upon depth, stereo look.

She glanced at it and said, 'Yes, yes – but I didn't mean that. I meant your – our cabin. Let's go inside, right now.'

'Suits,' I agreed, 'but it's really just a simple shack.' Which it was – not even an indoor pool. I had kept it that way; when I came up here I didn't want to feel that I had brought the city with me. The shell was conventional steel-and-fibre-glass, but I had had it veneered in duroslabs which looked like real logs. The inside was just as simple – a big living room with a real fireplace, deep rugs and plenty of low chairs. The services were in a Kompacto special, buried under the foundation – air-conditioner, power pack, cleansing system, sound equipment, plumbing, radiation alarm, servos – everything but deep-freeze and the other kitchen equipment, out of sight and mind. Even the stereo screens would not be noticed unless in use. It was about as near as a man could get to a real log cabin and still have inside plumbing.

'*I* think it's lovely,' Mary said seriously. 'I wouldn't want an ostentatious place.'

'You and me both.' I worked the combo and the door dilated; Mary was inside at once. 'Hey! Come back!' I yelled.

She did so. 'What's the matter, Sam? Did I do something wrong?'

'You sure did.' I dragged her out, then swung her up in my arms, and carried her across the threshold, kissing her as I put her down. 'There. Now you are in your own house, properly.'

The lights came on as we entered. She looked around, then turned and threw her arms around my neck. 'Oh, darling, darling!'

We took time out. Then she started wandering around, touching things. 'Sam, if I had planned it myself, it would have been just this way.'

'It hasn't but one bathroom,' I apologized. 'We'll have to rough it.'

'I don't mind. I'm glad; now I know you didn't bring any of those women of yours up here.'

'What women?'

'You know darn well. If you had been planning this as a nest, you would have included a woman's bathroom.'

'You know too much.'

She did not answer but wandered out into the kitchen. I heard her squeal. 'What's the matter?' I asked, following her out.

'I never expected to find a real kitchen in a bachelor's lodge.'

'I'm not a bad cook. I wanted a kitchen so I bought one.'

'I'm so glad. Now I *will* cook you dinner.'

'It's your kitchen; suit yourself. But don't you want to wash up? You can have first crack at the shower. Tomorrow we'll get a catalogue and you can pick out a bathroom of your own. We'll have it flown in.'

'You take the first shower,' she said. 'I want to start dinner.'

Mary and I slipped into domesticity as if we had been married for years. Oh, not that our honeymoon was humdrum, nor that there weren't a thousand things we still had to learn about each other – the point was that we already seemed to know the necessary things about each other that made us married. Especially Mary.

I don't remember those days too clearly. I was happy; I had forgotten what it was like, had not known that I was not happy. Interested, I used to be – yes. Diverted, entertained, amused – but not happy.

We did not turn on a stereo, we did not read a book. We saw no one and spoke to no one – except that on the second day we walked down to the village; I wanted to show Mary off. On the way back we passed the shack of John the Goat, our local hermit. John did what little caretaking I required. Seeing him, I waved.

He waved back. He was dressed as usual, stocking cap, an old army blouse, shorts, and sandals. I thought of warning him about the bare-to-the-waist order, but decided against it. Instead I cupped my hands and shouted, 'Send up the Pirate!'

'Who's the Pirate, darling?' Mary asked.

'You'll see.'

Which she did; as soon as we got back the Pirate came in,

for I had his little door keyed to his own *meeow* – the Pirate being a large and rakish tomcat. He strutted in, told me what he thought of people who stayed away so long, then head-bumped my ankle in forgiveness. I roughed him up, then he inspected Mary. She dropped to her knees and made the sounds used by people who understand cat protocol, but the Pirate looked her over suspiciously. Suddenly he jumped into her arms and commenced to buzz, while bumping her under the chin.

'That's a relief,' I announced. 'For a moment I didn't think I was going to be allowed to keep you.'

Mary looked up and smiled. 'You need not have worried. I'm two-thirds cat myself.'

'What's the other third?'

'You'll find out.'

From then on the cat was with us – or with Mary – almost all the time, except when I shut him out of our bedroom. That I would not stand for, though both Mary and the Pirate thought it small of me.

Mary never borrowed trouble. She did not like digging into the past. Oh, she would let me talk about mine but not about her own. Once when I started quizzing her she changed the subject by saying, 'Let's go look at the sunset.'

'Sunset?' I answered. 'Can't be – we just finished breakfast.' The mix-up about the time of day jerked me back to reality. 'Mary, how long have we been up here?'

'Does it matter?'

'You're darn right it matters. It's been more than a week, I'm sure. One of these days our phones will start screaming and then it's back to the treadmill.'

'In the meantime what difference does it make?'

I still wanted to know what day it was. I could have found out by switching on a stereo, but I would probably have bumped into a newscast – and I did not want that; I was still pretending that Mary and I were away in a different world, where titans did not exist. 'Mary,' I said fretfully, 'how many tempus pills have you?'

'None.'

'Well, I've got enough for us both. Let's stretch it out. Suppose we have just twenty-four more hours; we could fine it down into a month, subjective time.'

'No.'

'Why not? Let's *carpe* that old *diem*.'

She put a hand on my arm and looked up into my eyes. 'No, darling, it's not for me. I must live each moment and not let it be spoiled by worrying about the moment ahead.' I looked stubborn; she went on, 'If you want to take them, I won't mind, but please don't ask me to.'

'Confound it, I'm not going on a joy ride alone.' She did not answer, which is the damnedest way of winning an argument I know of.

Not that we argued. If I tried to start one Mary would give in and somehow it would work out that I was mistaken. I did try several times to find out more about her; it seemed to me that I ought to know *something* about the woman I was married to. To one question she looked thoughtful and answered, 'I sometimes wonder whether I ever did have a childhood – or was it something I dreamed last night?'

I asked her point-blank what her name was. 'Mary,' she said tranquilly.

'Mary really is your name?' I had long since told her my right name, but we went on using 'Sam'.

'Certainly it's my name, dear. I've been "Mary" since you first called me that.'

'Oh. All right, you are my beloved Mary. But what was your name before?'

Her eyes held an odd hurt look, but she answered steadily, 'I was once known as "Allucquere".'

' "Allucquere",' I repeated, savouring it, 'Allucquere. What a strange and beautiful name. Allucquere. It has a rolling majesty. My darling Allucquere.'

'My name is Mary now.' And that was that. Somewhere, somewhen, I was convinced, Mary had been hurt, badly hurt. But it seemed unlikely that I was ever going to know about it. Presently I ceased to worry about it. She was what she was, now and forever, and I was content to bask in the warm light of her presence.

I went on calling her 'Mary', but the name that she had once had kept running through my mind. Allucquere ... Allucquere. ... I wondered how it was spelled.

Then suddenly I knew. My pesky pack-rat memory was pawing away at the shelves in the back of my mind where I keep the useless junk that I am helpless to get rid of. There had been a community, a colony that used an artificial language, even to given names ...

The Whitmanites, that was it – the anarchist-pacifist cult that got kicked out of Canada, then failed to make a go of it in Little America. There was a book, written by their prophet, *The Entropy of Joy* – I had skimmed it once; it was full of pseudo-mathematical formulas for achieving happiness.

Everybody is for 'happiness', just as they are against 'sin', but the cult's practices got them in hot water. They had a curious and very ancient solution to their sexual problems, a solution which produced explosive results when the Whitmanite culture touched any other pattern of behaviour. Even Little America had not been far enough away. I had heard somewhere that the remnants had emigrated to Venus – in which case they must all be dead by now.

I put it out of my mind. If Mary were a Whitmanite, or had been reared that way, that was her business. I certainly was not going to let the cult's philosophy cause a crisis now or ever; marriage is not ownership and wives are not property.

XXII

The next time I mentioned tempus pills, she did not argue but suggested that we hold it down to a minimum dose. It was a fair compromise – we could always take more.

I prepared it as injections so that it would take hold faster. Ordinarily I watch a clock after I've taken tempus; when the second hand stops I know that I'm loaded. But my shack has no clocks and neither of us was wearing ring watches. It was sunrise and we had been awake all night, cuddled up on a big low couch by the fireplace.

We continued to lie there, feeling good and dreamy, and I was considering the idea that the drug had not worked. Then I realized that the sun had stopped rising. I watched a bird fluttering past the window. If I stared at him long enough, I could see his wings move.

I looked back from it to my wife. The Pirate was curled up on her stomach, his paws tucked in as a muff. They seemed asleep. 'How about breakfast?' I said. 'I'm starved.'

'You get it,' she answered. 'If I move, I'll disturb Pirate.'

'You promised to love, honour, and fix me breakfast,' I replied and tickled her feet. She gasped and drew up her legs; the cat squawked and landed on the floor.

'Oh dear!' she said. 'You made me move too fast. I've offended him.'

'Never mind the cat, woman; you're married to me.' But I knew that I had made a mistake. In the presence of those not under the drug, one should move with great care. I simply hadn't thought about the cat; no doubt he thought we were behaving like drunken jumping jacks. I intentionally slowed down and tried to woo him.

No use – he was streaking towards his door. I could have stopped him, for to me his movement was a molasses crawl, but had I done so I would simply have frightened him more. I let him go and went to the kitchen.

Do you know, Mary was right; tempus-fugit drug is no good for honeymoons. The ecstatic happiness I had felt before was masked by the euphoria of the drug. The drug's euphoria is compelling, but the loss was real; I had substituted for the true magic a chemical fake. Nevertheless it was a good day – or month. But I wished that I had stuck to the real thing.

Late that evening we came out of it. I felt the slight irritability which marks the loosening hold of the drug, found my ring watch and timed my reflexes. When they were back to normal I timed Mary's, whereupon she informed me that she had been out of it for twenty minutes or so – pretty accurate matching of dosage.

'Do you want to go under again?' she asked.

I kissed her. 'No; frankly, I'm glad to be back.'

'I'm so glad.'

I had the usual ravenous appetite that one has afterwards; I mentioned it. 'In a minute,' she said. 'I want to call Pirate.'

I had not missed him that day – or 'month' – just past; the euphoria is like that. 'Don't worry,' I told her. 'He often stays out all day.'

'He hasn't before.'

'He has with me,' I answered.

'I think I offended him – I know I did.'

'He is probably down at Old John's. That is his usual way of punishing me. He'll be all right.'

'But it's late at night – I'm afraid a fox might get him. Do you mind, darling? I'll just step out and call him.' She headed for the door.

'Put something on,' I ordered. 'It will be nippy out.'

She went back to the bedroom and got a négligé I had bought for her the day we had gone to the village. She went out; I put wood on the fire and went into the kitchen. While I was trying to make up my mind about a menu, I heard her saying, 'Bad, bad cat! You worried Mama,' in that cooing voice suitable for babies and felines.

I called out, 'Fetch him in and close the door – and mind the penguins!' She did not answer and I did not hear the door relax, so I went back into the living room. She was just coming in and did not have the cat with her. I started to speak and then caught sight of her eyes. They were staring, filled with unspeakable horror. I said, 'Mary!' and started towards her. She seemed to see me and turned back towards the door; her movements were jerky, spasmodic. As she turned I saw her shoulders.

Under the négligé was a hump.

I don't know how long I stood there. Probably a split second, but it is burned into me as endless. I jumped and grabbed her by the arms. She looked at me and her eyes were no longer wells of horror but merely dead.

She gave me the knee.

I squeezed and managed to avoid the worst of it. Look – you don't tackle a dangerous opponent by grabbing his arms, but this was my *wife*. I couldn't come at Mary with a feint-shift-and-kill.

But the slug had no compunctions about me. Mary – or *it* – was giving me everything she had, and I had all I could do to keep from killing her. I had to keep her from killing me – and I had to kill the slug – and I had to keep the slug from getting at me or I would not be able to save her.

I let go with one hand and jabbed her chin. The blow did not even slow her down. I grabbed again, with both arms and legs, trying to encase her in a bear hug to immobilize her without injuring her. We went down, Mary on top. I shoved my head into her face to stop her biting me.

I held her so, curbing her strong body by sheer muscle. Then I tried to paralyse her with nerve pressure, but she knew the key spots as well as I did – and I was lucky that I was not myself paralysed.

There was one thing left that I could do: clutch the slug itself – but I knew the shattering effect that had on the host. It might kill her; it was sure to hurt her horribly. I wanted to make her unconscious, then remove the slug gently before I killed it ... drive it off with heat or force it to turn loose with mild shocks.

Drive it off with heat ...

I was given no time to develop the idea; she got her teeth

147

in my ear. I shifted my right arm and grabbed at the slug.

Nothing happened. Instead of sinking my fingers into it I found that this slug had a leathery covering; it was as if I had clutched a football. Mary jerked when I touched it and took away part of my ear, but there was no bone-crushing spasm; the slug was still alive and in control.

I tried to get my fingers under it; it clung like a suction cup. My fingers would not go under.

In the meantime I was suffering damages other places. I rolled over and got to my knees, still hugging her. I had to let her legs free and that was bad, but I bent her across a knee and struggled to my feet. I dragged and carried her to the fireplace.

She almost got away from me; it was like wrestling a mountain lion. But I got her there, grabbed her mop of hair and slowly forced her shoulders over the fire.

I meant only to singe it, force it to drop off to escape that heat. But she struggled so hard that I slipped, banging my own head against the arch of the opening and dropping her shoulders against the coals.

She screamed and bounded out of the fire, carrying me with her. I struggled to my feet, still dazed by the wallop. and saw her collapsed on the floor. Her hair, her beautiful hair, was burning.

So was her négligé. I slapped at them both with my hands. The slug was no longer on her. Still crushing the flames with my hands I glanced around and saw it lying on the floor by the fireplace – and the Pirate was sniffing at it.

'Get away from there!' I yelled. 'Pirate! Stop that!' The cat looked up inquiringly. I went on doing what I had to do, making certain that the fire was out. When I was sure, I left her; there was not even time to make certain that she was still alive. What I wanted was the fireplace shovel; I did not dare risk touching the thing with my hands. I turned to get it.

But the slug was no longer on the floor; it had gotten Pirate. The cat was standing rigid, feet wide apart, and the slug was settling into place. I dived at Pirate and got him by his hind legs just as he made his first controlled movement.

Handling a frenzied cat with bare hands is reckless at best; controlling one which is already controlled by a titan is impossible. Hands and arms being slashed by claws and teeth at every step, I hurried to the fireplace again. Despite Pirate's wails and struggles I forced the slug against the coals and held it there, cat fur and my hands alike burning, until the slug dropped off directly into the flames. Then I took Pirate out and laid him on the floor. He was no longer struggling. I made sure that he was no longer burning anywhere and went back to Mary.

She was still unconscious. I squatted down beside her and sobbed.

An hour later I had done what I could for Mary. Her hair was gone from the left side of her head and there were burns on shoulders and neck. But her pulse was strong, her respiration steady though fast and light, and I did not judge that she would lose much body fluid. I dressed her burns – I keep a full stock out there in the country – and gave her an injection to make her sleep. Then I had time for Pirate.

He was still where I had left him and he did not look good. He had gotten it much worse than Mary and probably flame in his lungs as well. I thought he was dead, but he lifted his head when I touched him. 'I'm sorry, old fellow,' I whispered. I think I heard him mew.

I did for him what I had done for Mary, except that I was afraid to give him a soporific. After that I went into the bathroom and looked myself over.

The ear had stopped bleeding; I decided to ignore it. My hands were what bothered me. I stuck them under hot water and yelped, then dried them in the air blast and that hurt too. I couldn't figure out how I could dress them, and, besides, I needed to use them.

Finally I dumped about an ounce of the jelly for burns into each of a pair of plastic gloves and put them on. The stuff included a local anaesthetic; I could get by. Then I went to the stereophone and called the village medical man. I explained what had happened and what I had done about it and asked him to come up at once.

'At *night*?' he said. 'You must be joking.'

I said that I decidedly was not.

He answered, 'Don't ask the impossible, man. Yours makes the fourth alarm in this county; nobody goes out at night. I'll stop in and see your wife first thing in the morning.'

I told him to go straight to the devil first thing in the morning and switched off.

Pirate died a little after midnight. I buried him at once so that Mary would not see him. Digging hurt my hands, but he did not take a very big hole. I said goodbye to him and came back in. Mary was resting quietly; I brought a chair to the bed and watched over her. Probably I dozed from time to time; I can't be sure.

XXIII

About dawn Mary began to struggle and moan. I put a hand on her. 'There, baby, there. It's all right. Sam's here.'

Her eyes opened and for a moment held the same horror. Then she saw me and relaxed. 'Sam! Oh, darling, I've had the most terrible dream.'

'It's all right,' I repeated.

'Why are you wearing gloves?' She became aware of her own dressings; she looked dismayed and said, 'It wasn't a dream!'

'No, dearest, it wasn't a dream. But it's all right; I killed it.'

'You killed it? You're sure it's dead?'

'Quite sure.'

'Oh. Come here, Sam. Hold me tight.'

'I'll hurt your shoulders.'

'Hold me!' So I did, while trying to be careful of her burns. Presently her trembling stopped. 'Forgive me, darling. I'm weak and womanish.'

'You should have seen the shape I was in when they got me back.'

'I did see. Now tell me what happened. The last I remember you were trying to force me into the fireplace.'

'Look, Mary, I couldn't help it; I had to – I couldn't get it off!'

'I know, darling, I know – and thank you for doing it! Thank you from the bottom of my heart. Again I owe you everything.'

We both cried and I blew my nose and went on, 'You didn't answer when I called, so I went into the living room and there you were.'

'I remember. Oh, darling, I tried so hard!'

I stared at her. 'I know you did – you tried to leave. But how? Once a slug gets you, that's it. There's no way to fight it.'

'Well, I lost – but I tried.' Somehow, Mary had forced her will against that of a parasite, and that can't be done. I *know*. I had a sneaking hunch that had Mary not been able to resist the slug by some amount, however slight, I would have lost the struggle, handicapped as I was by what I could not do.

'I should have used a light, Sam,' she went on, 'but it never occurred to me to be afraid *here*.' I nodded; this was the safe place, like crawling into bed or into sheltering arms.

'Pirate came at once. I didn't see the thing until I had touched him. Then it was too late.' She sat up. 'Where is he, Sam? Is he all right? Call him.'

So I had to tell her about Pirate. She listened without expression, nodded, and never referred to him again. I changed the subject by saying, 'Now that you are awake I had better fix you some breakfast.'

'*Don't go!*' I stopped. 'Don't go out of my sight at all,' she went on, 'not for any reason. I'll get breakfast.'

'The hell you will. You'll stay in that bed, like a good girl.'

'Come here and take off those gloves. I want to see your hands.' I did not take them off – could not bear to think about it; the anaesthesia had worn off. She said grimly, 'Just as I thought. You were burned worse than I was.'

So she got breakfast. Furthermore, she ate – I wanted nothing but coffee. I did insist that she drink a lot too; large-area burns are no joke. Presently she pushed aside her plate and said, 'Darling, I'm not sorry it happened. Now I know. Now we've both been there.' I nodded dumbly. Sharing happiness is not enough. She stood up and said, 'Now we must go.'

'Yes,' I agreed, 'I want to get you to a doctor as soon as possible.'

'I didn't mean that.'

'I know you didn't.' There was no need to discuss it; we both knew that the music had stopped and that now it was time to go back to work. The heap we had arrived in was still sitting on my landing flat, piling up rental charges. It took about three minutes to burn the dishes, switch off everything, and get ready.

Mary drove, because of my hands. Once in the air she said, 'Let's go straight to the Section offices. We'll get treatment there and find out what has been going on – or are your hands hurting too badly?'

'Suits,' I agreed. I wanted to learn the situation, and I wanted to get back to work. I asked Mary to switch on the squawk screen to catch a newscast. But the car's communication equipment was as junky as the rest of it; we could not even pick up audio. Fortunately the remote-control circuits were okay, or Mary would have had to buck traffic by hand.

A thought had been fretting me; I mentioned it to Mary. 'A slug would not mount a cat just for the hell of it, would it?'

'I suppose not.'

'But why? But it has to make sense; everything they do makes sense, grisly sense, from their viewpoint.'

'But it did make sense. They caught a human that way.'

'Yes, I know. But how could they plan it? Surely there aren't enough of them that they can afford to place themselves on cats on the off chance that the cat might catch a human. Or are there?' I remembered Kansas City, saturated, and shivered.

'Why ask me, darling? I don't have an analytical brain.'

'Drop the modest little girl act and try this for size: Where did the slug come from? It had to get to the Pirate on the back of another host. What host? I'd say it was Old John – John the Goat. Pirate would not let any other human get close to him.'

'Old John?' Mary closed her eyes, then opened them. 'I can't get any feeling about it. I was never close to him.'

'By elimination I think it must be true. Old John wore a coat when everyone else was complying with the bare-back order. Ergo, he was hagridden before Schedule Bare Back. But why would a slug single out a hermit way up in the mountains?'

'To capture you.'

'Me?'

'To *recapture* you.'

It made some sense. Possibly any host that ever escaped them was a marked man; in that case the dozen-odd congressmen we had rescued were in special danger. I'd mark that down to report for analysis.

On the other hand, they might want me in particular. What was special about me? I was a secret agent. More important, the slug that had ridden me must have known what I knew about the Old Man and known that I had access to him. I held an emotional certainty that the Old Man was their principal antagonist; the slug must have known that I thought so; he had full use of my mind.

That slug had even met the Old Man, talked with him. Wait a minute. *That* slug was dead. My theory came tumbling down.

And built up again at once. 'Mary,' I asked, 'have you

used your apartment since the morning you and I had breakfast there?'

'No. Why?'

'Don't go back there for any purpose. I recall thinking, while I was with *them*, that I would have to booby-trap it.'

'Well, you didn't, did you?'

'No. But it may have been booby-trapped since then. There may be the equivalent of Old John waiting, spider fashion, for you – or me – to return there.' I explained to her McIlvaine's 'group memory' idea. 'I thought at the time he was spinning the dream stuff scientists are so fond of. But now it's the only hypothesis I can think of that covers everything – unless we assume that the titans are so stupid that they would as soon fish in a bathtub as in a brook. Which they aren't.'

'Just a moment, dear. By Dr McIlvaine's theory each slug is really every other slug; is that it? In other words, that *thing* that caught me last night was just as much the one that rode you when you were with them as was the one that actually did ride you — Oh, dear, I'm getting confused. I mean —'

'That's the general idea. Apart, they are individuals; in direct conference they merge memories and Tweedledum becomes exactly like Tweedledee. If that is true, this one last night remembers everything learned from me, provided it has had direct conference with the slug that rode me, or a slug that had been linked through any number of slugs by direct conference to the slug that had ridden me, after the time it did – which you can bet it did, from what I know of their habits. It would have – the first one, I mean — Wait a minute. Take three slugs; Joe, Moe, and, uh, Herbert. Herbert is the one last night; Moe is the one which —'

'Why give them names if they are not individuals?' Mary asked.

'Just to keep them — No reason; let it lie that if McIlvaine is right there are hundreds of thousands, maybe millions, of slugs who know exactly who we are, by name and sight and everything; know where your apartment is, where mine is, and where our cabin is. They've got us on a list.'

'But —' She frowned. 'That's a horrid thought, Sam. How would they know when to find us at the cabin? We didn't tell anybody. Would they simply stake it out and wait?'

'They must have. We don't know that waiting matters to a slug; time may mean something different to them.'

'Like Venerians,' she suggested. I nodded; a Venerian is as likely as not to 'marry' his own great-great-grand-daughter – and be younger than she is. It depends on how they estivate, of course.

'In any case,' I went on, 'I've got to report this, including our guesses, for the boys in the analytical group to play with.'

I was about to go on to say that the Old Man would have to be especially careful, as it was he they were really after. But my phone sounded for the first time since leave had started. I answered and the Old Man's voice cut in ahead of the talker's: 'Report in person.'

'On our way,' I acknowledged. 'About thirty minutes.'

'Make it sooner. You use Kay Five; tell Mary to come in by Ell One. Move.' He switched off before I could ask him how he had known that Mary was with me.

'Did you get it?' I asked Mary.

'Yes, I was in the circuit.'

'Sounds as if the party was about to start.'

It was not until we had landed that I began to realize how wildly the situation had changed. We were complying with Schedule Bare Back; we had not heard of 'Schedule Sun Tan'. Two cops stopped us as we got out. 'Stand still!' one of them ordered. 'Don't make any sudden moves.'

You would not have known they were cops, except for the manner and the drawn guns. They were dressed in gun belts, shoes, and skimpy breech clouts – little more than straps. A second glance showed their shields clipped to their belts. 'Now,' the same one went on, 'off with those pants, buddy.'

I did not move quickly enough. He barked, 'Make it

snappy! Two have been shot trying to escape already to-day; you may be the third.'

'Do it, Sam,' Mary said quietly. I did it. It left me dressed in shoes and gloves, feeling like a fool – but I managed to keep my phone and my gun covered as I took off my shorts.

The cop made me turn around. His mate said, 'He's clean. Now the other one.' I started to put on my shorts; the first cop stopped me.

'Hey! Looking for trouble? Leave 'em off.'

I said reasonably, 'I don't want to get picked up for in-decent exposure.'

He looked surprised, then guffawed, and turned to his mate. 'You hear that, Ski?'

The second one said patiently, 'Listen, you got to co-operate. You know the rules. You can wear a fur coat for all of me – but you won't get picked up for indecent exposure; you'll get picked up DOA. The vigilantes are a lot quicker to shoot than we are.' He turned to Mary. 'Now, lady, if you please.'

Without argument Mary started to remove her shorts. The second cop said kindly, 'That isn't necessary, lady; not the way those things are built. Just turn around slowly.'

'Thank you,' Mary said and complied. The policeman's point was well taken; Mary's briefies appeared to have been sprayed on, and her halter too.

'How about those bandages?' the first one commented.

I answered, 'She's been badly burned. Can't you see that?'

He looked doubtfully at the sloppy, bulky job I had done on the dressings. 'Mmmm . . .' he said, '*if* she was burned.'

'Of course she was burned!' I felt my judgement slipping; I was the perfect heavy husband, unreasonable where my wife was concerned. 'Damn it, look at her hair! Would she ruin a head of hair like that just to fool you?'

The first cop said darkly, 'One of *them* would.'

The more patient one said, 'Carl is right. I'm sorry, lady; we'll have to disturb those bandages.'

I said excitedly, 'You can't do that! We're on our way to a doctor. You'll just —'

Mary said, 'Help me, Sam.'

I shut up and started to peel up one corner of the dressing, my hands trembling with rage. Presently the older one whistled and said, 'I'm satisfied. How about you, Carl?'

'Me, too, Ski. Cripes, girlie, what happened?'

'Tell them, Sam.'

So I did. The older cop finally commented, 'You got off easy – no offence, madam. So it's cats now, eh? Dogs I knew about. Horses, yes. But you wouldn't think the ordinary cat could carry one.' His face clouded. 'We got a cat and now we'll have to get rid of it. My kids won't like that.'

'I'm sorry,' Mary told him.

'It's a bad time for everybody. Okay, folks, you can go.'

'Wait a minute,' the first one said. 'Ski, if she goes through the streets with that thing on her back somebody is likely to burn her.'

The older one scratched his chin. 'That's true,' he said. 'We'll just have to dig up a prowl car for you.'

Which they did. I had to pay the charges on the rented wreck, then I went along as far as Mary's entrance. It was in a hotel through a private elevator; I got in with her to avoid explanations, then went back up after she got out at a level lower than the obvious controls of the car provided for. I was tempted to go in with her, but the Old Man had ordered me to come in by Kay Five.

I was tempted, too, to put my shorts on. In the prowl car and during a quick march through a side door of the hotel, with police around us to keep Mary from being shot, I had not minded much – but it took nerve to face the world without pants.

I need not have worried. The short distance I had to go was enough to show me that a fundamental custom had gone with last year's frost. Most men were wearing straps as the cops had been, but I was not the only man naked to his shoes. One in particular I remember; he was leaning against a street-roof stanchion and searching every passer-by with cold eyes. He was wearing nothing but slippers and a brassard lettered 'VIG' – and he was cradling an Owens mob gun. I saw three more like him; I was glad that I was carrying my shorts.

Few women were naked, but the rest might as well have been – string brassières, translucent trunks – nothing that could hide a slug. Most of the women would have looked better in togas. That was my first impression, but before long even that had worn off. Ugly bodies weren't any more noticeable than ugly taxicabs; the eye ignored them. And so it appeared to be with everybody; those on the streets seemed to have acquired utter indifference. Skin was skin and what of it?

I was let in to see the Old Man at once. He looked up and growled, 'You're late.'

I answered, 'Where's Mary?'

'In the infirmary, getting treated and dictating her report. Let's see your hands.'

'I'll show them to the doctor, thanks,' I replied. 'What's up?'

'If you would ever bother to listen to a newscast,' he grumbled, 'you would know what was up.'

XXIV

I'm glad I had not looked at a newscast; our honeymoon would never have gotten to first base. While we had been telling each other how wonderful the other one was the war had almost been lost. My suspicion that the slugs could hide themselves on any part of the body and still control hosts had been correct; it had been proved by experiment before Mary and I had holed up on the mountain, although I had not seen the report. I suppose the Old Man knew it; certainly the President did and the other top V.I.P.s.

So Schedule Sun Tan replaced Schedule Bare Back, and

everybody skinned down to the buff.

Like hell they did! The matter was still 'top secret' at the time of the Scranton Riot. Don't ask me why; our government has gotten the habit of classifying anything as secret which the all-wise statesmen and bureaucrats decide we are not big enough to know, a Mother-Knows-Best-Dear policy. The Scranton Riot should have convinced anybody that the slugs were loose in Zone Green, but even that did not bring on Schedule Sun Tan.

The fake air-raid alarm on the east coast took place, as I figure it, the third day of our honeymoon; afterwards it took a while to figure out what had happened, even though it was obvious that lighting could not fail by accident in so many different shelters. It gives me horrors to think about it – all those people crouching in the darkness, waiting for the all-clear, while zombies moved among them, slapping slugs on them. Apparently in some air-raid bunkers the recruitment was one hundred per cent.

So there were more riots the next day and we were well into the Terror. Technically, the start of vigilantism came the first time a desperate citizen pulled a gun on a cop – Maurice T. Kaufman of Albany, and the cop was Sergeant Malcolm MacDonald. Kaufman was dead a half second later and MacDonald followed him, torn to pieces by the mob, along with his titan master. But the vigilantes did not really get going until the air-raid wardens put organization into the movement.

The wardens, being stationed aboveground during raids, largely escaped – but they felt responsible. Not that all vigilantes were wardens – but a stark-naked, armed man on the street was as likely to be wearing a warden's armband as the 'VIG' brassard. Either way, you could count on him shooting at any unexplained excrescence on a human body – shoot and investigate afterwards.

While my hands were dressed I was brought up to date. The doctor gave me a short shot of tempus and I spent the time – subjective, about three days; objective, less than an hour – studying stereo tapes through an over-speed scanner. This gadget has never been released to the public, though it is bootlegged at some of the colleges around examination week. You adjust the speed to match your subjective rate and use an audio frequency step-down to let you hear what is being said. It is hard on the eyes but it is a big help in my profession.

It was hard to believe that so much could have happened. Take dogs. A vigilante would kill a dog on sight, even though it was not wearing a slug – because it was even money that it would be wearing one before sunrise, that it would attack a man, and that the titan would change riders in the dark.

A hell of a world where you could not trust dogs!

Apparently cats were hardly ever used; poor old Pirate was an exception. But in Zone Green dogs were rarely seen now by day. They filtered out of Zone Red at night, travelled in the dark, and hid out at dawn. They kept showing up even on the coasts. It made one think of werewolf legends.

I scanned dozens of tapes which had been monitored from Zone Red; they fell into three time groups: the masquerade period, when the slugs had been continuing the 'normal' broadcasts; a short period of counterpropaganda during which the slugs had tried to convince citizens in Zone Green that the government had gone crazy; and the current period in which pretence had been dropped.

According to Dr McIlvaine, the titans have no true culture; they are parasitic even in that and merely adapt the culture they find. Maybe he assumes too much, but that is what they did in Zone Red. The slugs would have to maintain the basic economic activity of their victims, since the slugs would starve if the hosts starved. They continued that economy with variations that we would not use – that business of processing damaged and excess people in fertilizer plants, for example – but in general farmers stayed farmers, mechanics went on being mechanics, and bankers were still bankers. That last seems silly, but experts claim that any 'division-of-labour' economy requires an accounting system.

But why did they continue human recreations? Is the desire to be amused a universal need? What they picked from human ideas of fun to keep and 'improve on' does not speak well for us, although some of their variations may have merit – that stunt they pulled in Mexico, for example, of giving the bull an even break with the matador.

But most of it just makes one sick and I won't elaborate. I am one of the few who saw even transcriptions on such things; I saw them professionally. I hope that Mary, in her briefing, did not have to look at such, but Mary would never say so if she had.

There was one thing which I saw in the tapes so outrageous, so damnably disgusting that I hesitate to mention it, though I feel I must: there were men and women here and there among the slaves, humans (if you could call them that) without slugs – trusties – renegades ...

I hate slugs, but I would turn from killing a slug to kill one such.

We were losing ground everywhere; our methods were effective only in stopping their spread, and not fully effective in that. To fight them directly we would have to bomb our own cities, with no certainty of killing the humps. What we needed was a weapon that would kill slugs but not men, or something that would disable humans or render them unconscious without killing and thereby permit us to rescue our compatriots. No such weapon was available, though the scientists were all busy on the problem. A 'sleep' gas would have been perfect, but it is lucky that no such gas was known before the invasion, or the slugs could have used it against us. It must be remembered that the slugs then had as much, or more, of the military potential of the United States at their disposal as had the free men.

Stalemate – with time on their side. There were fools who wanted to H-bomb the cities of the Mississippi Valley out of existence, like curing a lip cancer by cutting off the head, but they were offset by their twins who had not seen slugs, did not believe in slugs, and felt that the whole matter was a tyrannical Washington plot. These second sort were fewer each day, not because they changed their minds but because the vigilantes were awfully eager.

Then there was the *tertium quid*, the flexible mind, the 'reasonable' man – he favoured negotiation; he thought we could 'do business' with the titans. One such committee, a delegation from the caucus of the opposition party in Congress, actually tried it. Bypassing the State Department, they got in touch with the Governor of Missouri via a linkage rigged across Zone Amber, and were assured of safe conduct and diplomatic immunity – 'guarantees' from a titan, but they accepted them. They went to St Louis – and never came back. They sent messages back; I saw one such, a rousing speech adding up to, 'Come on in; the water is fine!'

Do steers sign treaties with meat packers?

North America was still the only known centre of infection. The only action by the United Nations, other than placing the space stations at our disposal, was to move to Geneva. It was voted, with twenty-three nations abstaining, to define our plight as 'civil disorder' and to urge each member nation to give such aid as it saw fit to the legitimate governments of the United States, Mexico, and Canada.

It remained a creeping war, a silent war, with battles lost before we knew they were joined. Conventional weapons were hardly useful except in policing Zone Amber – now a double no man's land from the Canadian forests to the Mexican deserts. It was deserted in the daytime, save for our own patrols. At night our scouts drew back and the dogs came through – and other things.

Only one atom bomb had been used in the entire war and that against a saucer which landed near San Francisco south of Burlingame. Its destruction was according to doctrine, but the doctrine was under criticism; it should have been captured for study. I found my sympathies with those who wanted to shoot first and study later.

By the time the dose of tempus was wearing off I had a picture of the United States in a shape that I had not imagined even when I was in Kansas City – a country undergoing Terror. Friend might shoot friend; wife denounce husband. Rumour of a titan could drum up a mob on any street, with Judge Lynch baying in the van. To rap on a door at night was to invite a blast through the door. Honest folk stayed home; at night the dogs were out.

The fact that most of the rumoured discoveries of slugs were baseless made them no less dangerous. It was not exhibitionism which caused many people to prefer outright nudity to the tight and scanty clothing permitted under Schedule Sun Tan; even the skimpiest clothing invited a doubtful second look, a suspicion that might be decided too abruptly. The head-and-spine armour was never worn now; the slugs had faked it and used it almost at once. And there had been the case of a girl in Seattle; she had been dressed in sandals and a big purse, nothing else – but a vigilante who apparently had developed a nose for the enemy followed her and noticed that she never moved the purse from her right hand, even when she opened it to make change.

She lived, for he burned her arm off at the wrist, and I suppose that she had a new one grafted on; the supply of such spare parts was a glut. The slug was alive, too, when the vigilante opened the purse – but not for long.

The drug had worn off by the time I scanned this incident and I mentioned the matter to the nurse. 'Mustn't worry,' she told me. 'It does no good. Now flex the fingers of your right hand, please.'

I flexed them, while she helped the doctor spray on surrogate skin. 'Wear gloves for rough work,' the doctor cautioned, 'and come back next week.' I thanked them and went to the operations office. I looked for Mary first, but she was busy in Cosmetics.

XXV

'Hands all right?' the Old Man asked.

'They'll do. False skin for a week. They do a graft job on my ear tomorrow.'

He looked vexed. 'There's no time for a graft to heal; Cosmetics will have to fake one.'

'The ear doesn't matter,' I told him, 'but why bother to fake it? Impersonation job?'

'Not exactly. Now that you've been briefed, what do you think of the situation?'

I wondered what answer he was fishing for. 'Not good,' I conceded. 'Everybody watching everybody else. Might as well be in Russia.'

'Hmmm ... speaking of Russia, would you say that it was easier to penetrate and maintain surveillance in Russia or in Zone Red? Which would you rather tackle?'

I eyed him suspiciously. 'What's the catch? You don't let a man pick his assignment.'

'I asked your professional opinion.'

'Mmmm ... I don't have enough data. Have the slugs infested Russia?'

'That,' he answered, 'is what I must find out.'

I realized suddenly that Mary had been right; agents should not marry. 'This time of year,' I said, 'I think I'd want to enter through Canton. Unless you were figuring on a drop?'

'What makes you think I want you to go there?' he asked. 'We might find out quicker and easier in Zone Red.'

'Huh?'

'Certainly. If there is infection anywhere but in this continent, the titans in Zone Red must know it. Why go half around the globe to find out?'

I put aside the plans I had been forming to be a Hindu

164

merchant, travelling with his wife, and thought about what he was saying. Could be ... could be. 'How in the devil can Zone Red be penetrated now?' I asked. 'Do I wear a plastic imitation slug on my shoulders? They'd catch me the first time I was called on for direct conference.'

'Don't be a defeatist. Four agents have gone in already.'

'And come back?'

'Well, no, not exactly.'

'Have you decided that I've cluttered up the pay roll long enough?'

'I think the others used the wrong tactics —'

'Obviously!'

'The trick is to convince them that you are a renegade. Got any ideas?'

The idea was so overwhelming that I did not answer at once. Finally I burst out, 'Why not start me easy? Can't I impersonate a Panama pimp for a while? Or practice being an axe murderer? I have to get in the mood for this.'

'Easy,' he said. 'It may not be practical —'

'Hmmph!'

'But you might bring it off. You've had more experience with their ways than any agent I've got. You must be rested up, aside from that little singe on your fingers. Or maybe we should drop you near Moscow and let you take a direct look. Think it over. Don't get into a fret about it for a day or so.'

'Thanks. Thank you too much.' I changed the subject. 'What have you got planned for Mary?'

'Why don't you stick to your own business?'

'I'm married to her.'

'Yes.'

'Well, for the love of Pete! Don't you even want to wish me luck?'

'It strikes me,' he said slowly, 'that you have had all the luck one man could ask for. You have my blessing for whatever it's worth.'

'Oh. Well, thanks.' I am slow. Up to that moment it had not occurred to me that the Old Man might have had something to do with Mary's leave and mine falling together so conveniently. I said, 'Look here, Dad—'

'*Huh?*' It was the second time I had called him that in a month; it put him on the defensive.

'You meant for Mary and me to marry all along. You planned it that way.'

'Eh? Don't be ridiculous. I believe in free will, son – and free choices. Both of you were entitled to leave; the rest was accidental.'

'Hmm! Accidents don't happen; not around you. Never mind; I'm satisfied with the outcome. Now about the job; give me a bit longer to size up the possibilities. Meanwhile, I'll see Cosmetics about a rubber ear.'

XXVI

We finally decided to attempt to penetrate Zone Red. The evaluation group had advised that there was no chance of impersonating a renegade; the question hinged on, 'How does a man get to be a renegade? Why do the titans trust him?' It answers itself: a slug knows its host's mind. If a titan, through possessing a man's mind, *knows* that he is a natural renegade, a man who can be had, then it may suit the slug's purposes to let him be renegade rather than host. But first the slug had to plumb the vileness in the man's mind and be sure of its quality.

We concluded this from logical necessity – human logic, but it had to be slug logic, too, since it fitted what the slugs could and could not do. As for me, it was not possible even under deep hypnotic instruction to pass myself off as a candidate for renegade. So the psycho lads decided – and to which I said, 'Amen!'

It may seem illogical that titans would 'free' a host even though they knew that the host was the sort who could be owned. But in the renegades the slugs had a supply of 'trustworthy' fifth columnists. 'Trustworthy' is not the right word, but English has no word for this form of villainy. That Zone Green was being penetrated by renegades was certain, but it is often hard to tell a fifth columnist from a custard head; it made them hard to catch.

So I got ready. I took under hypnosis a refresher in the languages I would need, with emphasis on the latest shibboleth phrases; I was provided with a personality and given much money. The reporting equipment was a new model and a joy to have, ultramicrowave stuff hardly larger than a loaf of bread and the power pack so well shielded that it would not make a Geiger counter even nervous.

I had to drop through their screen, but it would be under a blanket of anti-radar 'window' to give their search technicians fits. Once inside I had to make up my mind whether or not the Russian axis was slug infested, then dictate a report to whatever space station was in sight – in line-of-sight, that is; I can't pick out a space station by eye and I doubt those who say they can. Report made, I was free to walk, ride, crawl, sneak and/or bribe my way out if I could.

But I never had a chance to use these preparations; the Pass Christian saucer landed.

It was only the third to be seen after landing. The Grinnell saucer had been concealed by the slugs and the Burlingame saucer was a radioactive memory. But the Pass Christian saucer was both tracked and seen on the ground.

It was tracked by Space Station Alpha and recorded as an 'extremely large meteorite'. The mistake was caused by its extreme speed. The primitive radar of sixty-odd years ago had picked up saucers many times, especially when cruising at atmospheric speeds while scouting this planet. But our modern radar has been 'improved' to the point where saucers cannot be seen; our instruments are too specialized. Traffic block control sees atmospheric traffic only; the defence screen and fire-control radars see only what they are supposed to see. The fine screen 'sees' a range from atmospheric speeds up to orbiting missiles at five miles a second; the coarse screen overlaps the fine screen, starting down at the lowest missile speed and carrying on up to about ten miles per second.

There are other selectivities, but none of them sees objects at speeds over ten miles per second – with the single exception of space station meteor-count radars – which are not military. Consequently, the 'giant meteor' was not associated with flying saucers until later.

But the Pass Christian saucer was seen to land. The submersible cruiser UNS *Robert Fulton*, on patron of Zone Red out of Mobile, was ten miles off Gulfport with only her receptors showing when the saucer landed. The space ship popped up on the screens of the cruiser as it dropped from outer space speed (around fifty-three miles per second by the space station record) to a speed the cruiser's radars would accept.

It came out of nothing, slowed to zero, and disappeared – but the operator had a fix on the last blip, a few miles away on the Mississippi coast. The cruiser's skipper was puzzled. The track surely could not be a ship; ships don't decelerate at fifty gravities! It did not occur to him that g's might not matter to a slug. He swung his ship over and took a look.

His first dispatch read: SPACE SHIP LANDED BEACH WEST OF PASS CHRISTIAN MISSISSIPPI. His second was: LANDING FORCE BEACHING TO CAPTURE.

If I had not been in the Section offices preparing for my drop I might have been left out of the party. As it was, my phone shrilled; I bumped my head on the study machine and swore. The Old Man said, 'Come at once. Move!'

It was the same party we had started with so many weeks – or years? – before, the Old Man, Mary, and myself. We were heading south at emergency maximum before the Old Man told us why.

When he did, I said, 'Why the family group? You need a full-scale air task force.'

'It will be there,' he answered grimly. Then he grinned his old wicked grin. 'What do you care? The "Cavanaughs" are riding again. Eh, Mary?'

I snorted. 'If you want that sister-and-brother routine, you had better get another boy.'

'Just the part where you protect her from dogs and strange men,' he answered soberly. 'And I do mean dogs, and I do mean very strange men. This may be the payoff, son.'

He went into the operator's compartment, closed the panel, and got busy at the communicator. I turned to Mary. She snuggled up and said, 'Howdy, Bud.'

I grabbed her. 'Don't give me that "Bud" stuff or somebody's going to get a paddling.'

XXVII

We were almost shot down by our own boys, then we picked up an escort of two Black Angels, who turned us over to the command ship from which Air Marshal Rexton was watching the action. The command ship matched speeds and took us inboard with an anchor loop. I found the manoeuvre disconcerting.

Rexton wanted to spank us and send us home – but spanking the Old Man is a chore. They finally unloaded us and I squatted our car down on the sea-wall roadway west of Pass Christian – scared silly, I should add; we were buffeted by A.A. on the way down. There was fighting all around and above us, but there was a curious calm near the saucer itself.

The outlander ship loomed up almost over us, not fifty yards away. It was as convincing and as ominous as the plastic-board fake in Iowa had been phoney. It was a discus of great size, tilted slightly towards us; it had grounded partly on one of the high-stilted old mansions which line that coast. The saucer was partly supported by the wreckage and by the thick trunk of a tree that had shaded the house.

The ship's canted attitude let us see the upper surface and what was surely its air lock – a metal hemisphere, a dozen feet across, at its centre. This hemisphere was lifted out or up from the body of the ship some six or eight feet. I could not see what held it out but I assumed that there must be a central shaft or piston; it came out like a poppet valve. It was easy to see why the saucer had not closed up again and taken off; the air lock was fouled, held open by a 'mud turtle', one of those little amphibious tanks – part of the landing force of the *Fulton*.

Let me place this on record: the tank had been commanded by Ensign Gilbert Calhoun of Knoxville; with him was Powerman 2/C Florence Berzowski and a gunner named Booker T. W. Johnson. They were all dead, of course, before we got there.

The car, as soon as I roaded it, was surrounded by a landing-force squad commanded by a pink-cheeked lad who seemed anxious to shoot somebody or anybody. He was less anxious when he got a look at Mary, but he still refused to let us approach the saucer until he had checked with his tactical commander – who in turn consulted the skipper of the *Fulton*. We got an answer back in a short time, considering that it was probably referred clear back to Washington.

While waiting, I watched the battle and was pleased to have no part of it. Somebody was going to get hurt – a good many had already. There was a male body just behind the car – a boy not more than fourteen. He was still clutching a rocket launcher, and across his shoulders was the mark of the beast. I wondered whether the slug had crawled away and was dying, or whether, perhaps, it had managed to transfer to the person who had bayoneted the boy.

Mary had walked west on the highway with the downy young naval officer while I was examining the corpse. The notion of a slug, possibly still alive, being around caused me to hurry to her. 'Get back into the car,' I said.

She continued to look west along the road. 'I thought I might get in a shot or two,' she answered, her eyes bright.

'She's safe here,' the youngster assured me. 'We're holding them, well down the road.'

I ignored him. 'Listen, you bloodthirsty little hellion,' I snapped, 'get back in that car before I break every bone in your body!'

'Yes, Sam.' She turned and did so.

I looked back at the young salt. 'What are you staring at?' I demanded. The place smelled of slugs and the wait was making me nervous.

'Nothing much,' he said, looking me over. 'In my part of the country we don't speak to ladies that way.'

'Then why in the hell don't you go back where you come from?' I answered and stalked away. The Old Man was missing too; I did not like it.

An ambulance, coming back from the west, ground to a halt beside me. 'Has the road to Pascagoula been opened?' the driver called out.

The Pascagoula River, thirty miles east of where the saucer had landed, was roughly Zone Amber for that area; the town of that name was east of the river's mouth and in Zone Green – while sixty or seventy miles west of us on the same road was New Orleans, the heaviest concentration of titans south of St Louis. Our opposition came from New Orleans, while our nearest base was in Mobile.

'I haven't heard,' I told the driver.

He chewed a knuckle. 'Well – I made it through; maybe I'll make it back.' His turbines whined and he was away. I continued to look for the Old Man.

Although the ground fighting had moved away from the site, the air fighting was all around us. I was watching vapour trails and trying to figure out who was what and how they could tell, when a big transport streaked into the area, put on the brakes with a burst of rato units, and spilled a platoon of sky boys. Again I wondered; it was too far away to tell whether they wore slugs or not. At least it came in from the east.

I spotted the Old Man talking with the landing-force commander. I went up and interrupted. 'We ought to get out of here, Boss. This place is due to be atom-bombed ten minutes ago.'

The commander answered. 'Relax,' he said blandly, 'the concentration does not merit even a pony bomb.'

I was about to ask him sharply how he knew that the slugs would figure it that way, when the Old Man interrupted. 'He's right, son.' He took my arm and walked me back towards the car. 'He's right, but for the wrong reasons.'

'Huh?'

'Why haven't *we* bombed the cities *they* hold? They don't want to damage that ship; they want it back. Go on back to Mary. Dogs and strange men – remember?'

I shut up, unconvinced. I expected us all to be clicks in a Geiger counter any second. Slugs fought with gamecock recklessness – perhaps because they were really not individuals. Why should they be more cautious about one of their ships? They might be more anxious to keep it out of our hands than to save it.

We had just reached the car and spoken to Mary when the still-damp snottie came trotting up. He saluted the Old Man. 'The commander says that you are to have anything you want, sir – anything at all!'

From his manner I gathered that the answering dispatch had been spelled out in flaming letters, accompanied by ruffles and flourishes. 'Thank you, sir,' the Old Man said mildly. 'We merely want to inspect the captured ship.'

'Yes, sir. Come with me, sir.' He came with us instead, having difficulty deciding whether to escort the Old Man or Mary. Mary won. I followed, keeping my mind on watching out and ignoring the presence of the youngster. The country on that coast, unless gardened, is practically jungle; the saucer lapped over into a brake of that sort and the Old Man took a short cut through it. The kid said, 'Watch out, sir. Mind where you step.'

I said, 'Slugs?'

He shook his head. 'Coral snakes.'

At that point a poisonous snake would have seemed as pleasant as a honey bee, but I must have been paying some attention to his warning for I was looking down when the next thing happened.

I first heard a shout. Then, so help me, a Bengal tiger was charging us.

Probably Mary got in the first shot. Mine was not behind that of the young officer; it might even have been ahead. The Old Man shot last. Between us we cut that beast so many ways that it would never make a rug. And yet the slug on it was untouched; I fried it with my second bolt. The young fellow looked at it without surprise. 'Well,' he said, 'I thought we had cleaned up that load.'

'What do you mean?'

'One of the first transport tanks they sent out. Regular Noah's Ark. We were shooting everything from gorillas to polar bears. Say, did you ever have a water buffalo come at you?'

'No, and I don't want to.'

'Not as bad as the dogs, really. If you ask me, those things don't have much sense.' He looked at the slug, quite unmoved.

We got out of there fast and on to the titan ship – which did not make me less nervous, but more. Not that there was anything frightening in the appearance of the ship itself.

But its appearance wasn't *right*. While it was artificial, one knew without being told that it was not made by men. Why? I don't know. Its surface was dull mirror, not a mark on it – not any sort of a mark; there was no way to tell how it had been put together. It was as smooth as a Jo block.

I could not tell of what it was made. Metal? Of course, it *had* to be metal. But was it? You would expect it to be either bitterly cold – or possibly intensely hot from its landing. I touched it and it was not anything at all, neither cold nor hot. I noticed another thing presently: a ship that size, landing at high speed, should have blasted a couple of acres. There was no blast area at all; the brake around it was green and rank.

We went up to the parasol business, the air lock, if that is what it was. The edge was jammed down on the little mud turtle; the armour of the tank was crushed in, as one might crush a pasteboard box with the hand. Those 'mud turtles' are built to launch five hundred feet deep in water; they are *strong*.

Well, I suppose this one was strong. The parasol arrangement had damaged it, but the air lock had not closed. On the other hand, the metal, or whatever the space-ship's door was made of, was unmarked by the exchange.

The Old Man turned to me. 'Wait here with Mary.'

'You're not going in there by yourself?'

'Yes. There may be very little time.'

The kid spoke up. 'I'm to stay with you, sir. That's what the commander said.'

'Very well, sir,' the Old Man agreed. 'Come along.' He peered over the edge, then knelt and lowered himself by his hands. The kid followed him. I felt burned up, but had no desire to argue the arrangements.

They disappeared into the hole. Mary turned to me and said, 'Sam, I don't like this. I'm afraid.'

She startled me. I was afraid myself – but I had not expected her to be. 'I'll take care of you.'

'Do we have to stay? He did not say so, quite.'

I considered it. 'If you want to go back to the car I'll take you back.'

'Well – no, Sam, I guess we have to stay. Come closer to me.' She was trembling.

I don't know how long it was before they stuck their heads over the rim. The youngster climbed out and the Old Man told him to stand guard. 'Come on,' he said to us, 'it's safe – I think.'

'The hell it is,' I told him, but I went because Mary was already starting. The Old Man helped her down.

'Mind your head,' he said. 'Low bridge all the way.'

It is a platitude that unhuman races produce unhuman works, but very few humans have ever been inside a Venerian labyrinth, and still fewer have seen the Martian ruins – and I was not one of the few. I don't know what I expected. Superficially the inside of the saucer was not, I suppose, too startling, but it was strange. It had been thought out by unhuman brains, which did not depend on human ideas in fabricating, brains which had never heard of the right angle and the straight line or which regarded them as unnecessary or undesirable. We found ourselves in a small oblate chamber, and from there we crawled through a tube about four feet thick, a tube which seemed to wind down into the ship and which glowed from all its surface with a reddish light.

The tube held an odd and somewhat distressing odour, as if of marsh gas, and mixed with it faintly was the reek of dead slugs. That and the reddish glow and the total lack of heat response from the wall of the tube as my palms pressed against it gave me the unpleasant fancy that I was crawling through the gut of some unearthly behemoth rather than exploring a strange machine.

The tube branched like an artery and there we came across our first Titanian androgyne. He – let me call it 'he' – was sprawled on his back, like a child sleeping, his head pillowed on his slug. There was a suggestion of a smile on the little rosebud mouth; at first I did not realize that he was dead.

At first sight the similarities between the Titanian people and ourselves are more noticeable than the differences; we impress what we expect to see on what we do see. Take the pretty little 'mouth', for example; how was I to know that it was an organ for breathing solely?

But despite the casual similarities of four limbs and a head-like protuberance, we are less like them than is a bullfrog like a bull pup. Nevertheless, the general effect is pleasing and faintly human. 'Elfin' I should say – the elves of Saturn's moons.

When I saw the little fellow I managed to draw my gun. The Old Man turned and said, 'Take it easy. It's dead. They're all dead, smothered in oxygen when the tank ruined their air seal.'

I still had my gun out. 'I want to burn the slug,' I insisted. 'It may still be alive.' It was not covered by the shell we had lately come to expect, but was naked and ugly.

He shrugged. 'Suit yourself. It can't possibly hurt you.

175

That slug can't live on an oxygen breather.' He crawled across the little body, giving me no chance to shoot had I decided to. Mary had not drawn but had shrunk against my side and was breathing in sharp sobbing gasps. The Old Man stopped and said patiently, 'Coming, Mary?'

She choked and then gasped, 'Let's go back! Let's get out of here!'

I said, 'She's right. This is no job for three people; this is something for a research team and proper equipment.'

He paid no attention to me. 'It has to be done, Mary. You know that. And you have to be the one to do it.'

'Why does she have to do it?' I demanded angrily.

Again he ignored me. 'Well, Mary?'

From somewhere inside she called on reserves. Her breathing became normal, her features relaxed, and she crawled across the slug-ridden elfin body with the serenity of a queen going to the gallows. I lumbered after, still hampered by my gun and trying not to touch the body.

We came at last to a large chamber which may have been the control room; there were many of the dead little elfin creatures in it. Its inner surface was cavitated and picked out with lights much brighter than the reddish illumination, and the space was festooned with processes as meaningless to me as the convolutions of a brain. I was troubled again with the thought – completely wrong – that the ship itself was a living organism.

The Old Man paid no mind but crawled through and into another ruddy-glowing tube. We followed its contortions to where it widened out to ten feet or more with a 'ceiling' almost tall enough to let us stand erect. But that was not what caught our eyes; the walls were no longer opaque.

On each side of us, beyond transparent membranes, were thousands on thousands of slugs, swimming, floating, writhing in some fluid which sustained them. Each tank had an inner diffuse light of its own, and I could see back into the palpitating mass. I wanted to scream.

I still had my gun out. The Old Man placed his hand over the bell of it. 'Don't,' he warned me. 'You don't want to let *that* loose in *here*. Those are for us.'

Mary looked at them with a face too calm. I doubt that she was fully conscious in the ordinary sense. I looked at her, glanced back at the walls of that ghoulish aquarium, and said urgently, 'Let's get out of here if we can – then just bomb it out of existence.'

'No,' he said quietly, 'there is more. Come.' The tube narrowed in again, then enlarged and we were in a somewhat smaller chamber. Again there were transparent walls; again there were things floating beyond them.

I had to look twice before I could believe what I saw.

Floating just beyond the wall, face down, was the body of a man – a human, Earth-born man – about forty or fifty years old. His arms were curved across his chest and his knees were drawn up, as if he were sleeping.

I watched him, thinking terrible thoughts. He was not alone; there were more beyond him, male and female, young and old, but he got my attention. I was sure that he was dead; it did not occur to me to think otherwise. Then I saw his mouth working – and I wished he were dead.

Mary was wandering around as if she were drunk – no, not drunk but preoccupied and dazed. She went from one wall to the other, peering into the crowded, half-seen depths. The Old Man looked only at her. 'Well, Mary?' he said softly.

'I can't find them!' she said piteously in a voice like a little girl's. She ran back to the other side.

The Old Man grasped her arm. 'You're not looking for them in the right place,' he said firmly. 'Go back where they are. Remember?'

Her voice was a wail. '*I can't remember!*'

'You must remember. This is what you can do for them. You must return to where they are and look for them.'

Her eyes closed and tears started leaking from them. She gasped and choked. I pushed myself between them and said, 'Stop this! What are you doing to her?'

He pushed me away. 'No, son,' he whispered fiercely. 'Keep out of this – you *must* keep out.'

'But —'

'No!' He let go of Mary and led me to the entrance. 'Stay there. And, as you love your wife, as you hate the titans, do not interfere. I shan't hurt her – I promise.'

'What are you going to do?' But he had turned away. I stayed, unwilling but afraid to tamper with what I did not understand.

Mary had sunk to the floor and now squatted on it like a child, face covered with hands. The Old Man knelt down and touched her arm. 'Go back,' I heard him say. 'Back to where it started.'

I could barely hear her answer. 'No – no.'

'How old were you? You seemed to be about seven or eight when you were found. It was before that?'

'Yes – yes, it was before that.' She sobbed and collapsed to the floor. 'Mama! Mama!'

'What is your mama saying?' he asked gently.

'She doesn't say anything. She's looking at me so queerly. There's something on her back. I'm afraid, I'm afraid!'

I hurried towards them, crouching to keep from hitting the low ceiling. Without taking his eyes off Mary the Old Man motioned me back. I stopped, hesitated. 'Go back,' he ordered. ' 'Way back.'

The words were directed at me and I obeyed them – but so did Mary. 'There was a ship,' she muttered, 'a big shiny ship —' He said something; if she answered I could not hear it. I stayed back this time. Despite my vastly disturbed emotions, I realized that something important was going on, something big enough to absorb the Old Man's full attention in the presence of the enemy.

He continued to talk soothingly but insistently. Mary quieted, seemed to sink into lethargy, but I could hear that she answered him. After a while she was talking in the monotonous logorrhea of emotional release. Only occasionally did he prompt her.

I heard something crawling along the passage behind me, turned and drew my gun, with a wild feeling that we were trapped. I almost shot him before I recognized the ubiquitous young officer we had left outside. 'Come out!' he said urgently. He pushed past me into the chamber and repeated the demand to the Old Man.

The Old Man looked exasperated beyond endurance. 'Shut up and don't bother me,' he said.

'You've *got* to, sir,' the youngster insisted. 'The commander says that you must come out at once. We're falling back; the commander says he may have to use demolition at any moment. If we are still inside – *blooie!* That's it.'

'Very well,' the Old Man agreed calmly. 'Go tell your commander that he must hold off until we get out; I have vitally important information. Son, help me with Mary.'

'Aye aye, sir!' the youngster acknowledged. 'But hurry!' He scrambled away. I picked up Mary and carried her to where the chamber narrowed into a tube; she seemed almost unconscious. I put her down.

'We'll have to drag her,' the Old Man said. 'She may not come out of this soon. Here – let me get her up on your back; you can crawl with her.'

I paid no attention but shook her. 'Mary!' I shouted. 'Mary! Can you hear me?'

Her eyes opened. 'Yes, Sam?'

'Darling, we've got to get out of here – *fast!* Can you crawl?'

'Yes, Sam.' She closed her eyes again.

I shook her again. 'Mary!'

'Yes, darling? What is it? I'm so tired.'

'Listen, Mary, you've got to crawl out of here. If you don't the slugs will get us. Do you understand?'

'All right, darling.' Her eyes stayed open but were vacant. I got her headed up the tube and came after her. Whenever she faltered I slapped at her. I lifted and dragged her through the chamber of slugs and again through the control room, if such it was. When we came to where the tube was partly blocked by the dead elfin creature she stopped; I wormed past her and stuffed it into the branching tube. There was no doubt, this time, that its slug was dead. Again I had to slap her into co-operation.

After an endless nightmare of leaden-limbed striving we reached the outer door; the young officer was there and helped us lift her out, him pulling and the Old Man and me lifting and pushing. I gave the Old Man a leg up, jumped out myself, and took her away from the youngster. It was quite dark.

We went back past the crushed house, avoiding the brake, and thence down to the road. Our car was no longer there. We were hurried into a 'mud turtle' tank – none too soon, for the fighting was almost on top of us. The tank commander buttoned up and the craft lumbered into the water. Fifteen minutes later we were inside the *Fulton*.

And an hour later we disembarked at the Mobile base. The Old Man and I had had coffee and sandwiches in the wardroom of the *Fulton*; some of the Wave officers had cared for Mary in the women's quarters. She joined us as we left and seemed normal. I said, 'Mary, are you all right?'

She smiled. 'Of course, darling. Why shouldn't I be?'

A command ship and escort took us out of there. I had supposed that we were headed back to the Section offices, or to Washington. The pilot put us into a mountainside hangar in one of those egg-on-a-plate manoeuvres that no civilian craft can accomplish – in the sky at high speed, then in a cave and stationary. 'Where are we?' I asked.

The Old Man did not answer but got out; Mary and I followed. The hangar was small, just parking space for a dozen craft, an arresting platform, and a single launching rack. Guards directed us on back to a door set in living rock; we went through and found ourselves in an anteroom. A loudspeaker told us to strip. I hated to part with my gun and phone.

We went on in and were met by a young fellow whose clothing was an armband showing three chevrons and crossed retorts. He turned us over to a girl who was wearing less, only two chevrons. Both of them noticed Mary, each with typical response. I think the corporal was glad to pass us on to the captain who received us.

'We got your message,' the captain said. 'Dr Steelton is waiting.'

'Thank you, ma'am,' the Old Man answered. 'Where?'

'Just a moment,' she said, went to Mary and felt through her hair. 'We have to be sure,' she said apologetically. If she was aware of the falseness of much of Mary's hair, she did not mention it. 'All right,' she decided, 'let's go.' Her own hair was cut mannishly short.

'Right,' agreed the Old Man. 'No, son, this is as far as you go.'

'Why?' I asked.

'Because you darn near loused up the first try,' he explained briefly. 'Now pipe down.'

The captain said, 'The officers' mess is down the first passageway to the left. Why not wait there?'

So I did. I passed a door decorated primly in red skull-and-crossbones and stencilled with: WARNING – LIVE PARASITES BEYOND THIS DOOR; *Qualified Personnel only – Use Procedure 'A'.* I gave it a wide berth.

The officers' mess had three or four men and two women lounging in it. I found an unoccupied chair, sat down, and wondered who you had to be to get a drink around there. After a time I was joined by a large male extrovert wearing a colonel's insignia on a neck chain. 'Newcomer?' he asked.

I admitted it. 'Civilian expert?' he went on.

'I don't know about "expert",' I replied. 'I'm a field operative.'

'Name? Sorry to be officious,' he apologized, 'but I'm the security officer around here. My name's Kelly.'

I told him mine. He nodded. 'Matter of fact, I saw you coming in. Now, Mr Nivens, how about a drink?'

I stood up. 'Whom do I have to kill to get it?'

' – though as far as I can see,' Kelly went on later, 'this place needs a security officer the way a horse needs roller skates. We should publish our results as fast as we get them.'

I commented that he did not sound like a brass hat. He laughed. 'Believe me, son, not all brass hats are as they are pictured – they just seem to be.'

I remarked that Air Marshal Rexton struck me as a pretty sharp citizen.

'You know him?' the colonel asked.

'Not exactly, but my work has thrown me in his company a bit. I last saw him earlier today.'

'Hmm —' said the colonel. 'I've never met the gentleman. You move in more rarefied strata than I do, sir.'

I explained that it was mere happenstance, but from then on he showed me more respect. Presently he was telling me about the work the laboratory did. 'By now we know more about those foul creatures than does Old Nick himself. But do we know how to kill them without killing their hosts? We do not.

'Of course,' he went on, 'if we could lure them one at a time into a room and douse them with anaesthetics, we could save the hosts – but that is like the old saw about how to catch a bird: it's no trouble if you can sneak up close enough to put salt on its tail. I'm not a scientist – just a cop under a different tag – but I've talked to the scientists here. This is a biological war. We need a bug, one that will bite the slug and not the host. Doesn't sound too hard, does it? We know a hundred things that will kill the slug – smallpox, typhus, syphilis, encephalitis lethargica, Obermayer's virus, plague, yellow fever, and so on. They all kill the host.'

'Couldn't they use something that everyone is immune to?' I asked. 'Everybody has typhoid shots. And almost everybody is vaccinated for smallpox.'

'No good. If the host is immune, the parasite doesn't get exposed to it. Now that the slugs have developed this outer cuticle the parasite's environment is the host. No, we need something the host will catch and that will kill the slug, but won't give the host more than a mild fever.'

I started to answer when I saw the Old Man in the doorway. I exused myself and went to him. 'What was Kelly grilling you about?' he asked.

'He wasn't grilling me,' I answered.

'That's what you think. You know what Kelly that is?'

'Should I?'

'You should. Or perhaps not; he never lets his picture be taken. That's B. J. Kelly, the greatest scientific criminologist of our generation.'

'*That* Kelly! But he's not in the Army.'

'Reserve, probably. But you can guess how important this lab is. Come on.'

'Where's Mary?'

'You can't see her now. She's recuperating.'

'Is she – hurt?'

'I promised you she would not be. Steelton is the best in his line. But we had to go down deep, against great resistance. That's always rough on the subject.'

I thought about it. 'Did you get what you were after?'

'Yes and no. We aren't through.'

'What were you after?'

We had been walking along one of the place's endless underground passageways. Now he turned us into a small office and sat down. The Old Man touched the desk communicator and said, 'Private conference.'

'Yes, sir,' a voice answered. 'We will not record.' A green light came on in the ceiling.

'Not that I believe them,' the Old Man complained, 'but it may keep anyone but Kelly from playing it back. Now, son, about what you want to know; I'm not sure you are entitled to it. You are married to the girl, but you don't own her soul – and this stuff comes from down so deep that she did not know she had it.'

I said nothing; he went on in worried tones, 'It might be better to tell you enough to make you understand. Otherwise you would bother her to find out. I don't ever want that to happen. You might throw her into a bad wingding. I doubt if she'll remember anything – Steelton is a very gentle operator – but you could stir up things.'

I took a deep breath. 'You'll have to judge.'

'Well, I'll tell you a bit and answer your questions – some of them – in exchange for a solemn promise never to bother your wife with it. You don't have the skill.'

'Very well, sir. I promise.'

'Well, there was a group of people, a cult, you might call them, that got into disrepute.'

'I know – the Whitmanites.'

'Eh? How did you know? From Mary? No, she couldn't

have; she didn't know herself.'

'No, not from Mary. I figured it out.'

He looked at me with odd respect. 'Maybe I've under-estimated you, son. As you say, the Whitmanites. Mary was one, as a kid in Antarctica.'

'Wait a minute!' I said. 'They left Antarctica in' – the wheels buzzed and the number came up – 'in 1974.'

'Surely.'

'But that would make Mary around forty years old!'

'Do you care?'

'Huh? Why, no – but she can't be.'

'She is and she isn't. Chronologically her age is about forty. Biologically she is in her middle twenties. Subjec-tively she is even younger, because she doesn't consciously remember anything earlier than about 1990.'

'What do you mean? That she doesn't remember, I can understand – she never *wants* to remember. But what do you mean by the rest?'

'What I said. She is no older than she is because – you know that room where she started to remember? She spent ten years or more in suspended animation in just such a tank as that.'

XXVIII

As I get older, I don't get tougher; I get softer. The thought of my beloved Mary swimming in that artificial womb, neither dead nor alive but preserved like a pickled grass-hopper, was too much for me.

I heard the Old Man saying, 'Take it easy, son. She's all right.'

I said, 'Go ahead.'

Mary's overt history was simple, though mystifying. She had been found in the swamps near Kaiserville at the north pole of Venus – a little girl who could give no account of herself and who knew only her name – Allucquere. Nobody spotted the significance of the name, and a child of her apparent age could not be associated with the Whitmanite debacle in any case; the 1980 supply ship had not been able to find any survivor of their 'New Zion' colony. Ten years of time and more than two hundred miles of jungle separated the little waif of Kaiserville from the God-struck colonists of New Zion.

In 1990 an unaccounted-for earth child on Venus was incredible, but there was no one around with the intellectual curiosity to push the matter. Kaiserville was made up of miners, doxies, company representatives of Two Planets Corporation – and nothing else. Shovelling radioactive mud in the swamps would not leave much energy for wonder.

She grew up using poker chips for toys and calling every woman in crib row 'mother' or 'auntie'. They shortened her name to 'Lucky'. The Old Man did not say who paid her way back to Earth; the real question was where she had been from the time New Zion was eaten up by the jungle, and just what had happened to the colony.

But the only record was buried in Mary's mind, locked tight with terror and despair.

Some time before 1980 – about the time of the flying-saucer reports from Russo-Siberia, or a year or so earlier – the titans had discovered New Zion colony. If you place it one Saturn year earlier than the invasion of Earth, the times fit fairly well. The titans probably were not looking for earthmen on Venus; more likely they were scouting Venus as they had long scouted Earth. Or they may have known where to look; we know that they kidnapped earthmen over the course of two or more centuries; they may have captured someone whose brain could tell them where to find New Zion. Mary's dark memories could contain no clue to that.

Mary saw the colony captured, saw her parents turned into zombies who no longer cared for her. Apparently she herself was not possessed, or she may have been possessed and turned loose, the titans finding a weak and ignorant young girl an unsuitable slave. In any case, for what was to her baby mind an endless time, she hung around, unwanted, uncared for, but unmolested, scavenging like a mouse. The slugs were moving in to stay; their principal slaves were Venerians, and the colonists were only incidental. It is sure that Mary saw her parents being placed in suspended animation – for later use in the invasion of Earth? Possible.

In due course she herself was placed in the tanks. Inside a titan ship? At a base on Venus? More probably the latter, as when she woke, she was still on Venus. There are many gaps. Were the slugs that rode the Venerians identical with the slugs which rode the colonists? Possible – both Earth and Venus have oxy-carbon economy. The slugs seem endlessly protean, but they have to adapt themselves to the biochemistry of their hosts. Had Venus an oxy-silicon economy like Mars, or a fluorine economy, the same parasite type could not have fed on both.

But the gist of the matter lay in the situation as it was when Mary was removed from the artificial incubator. The titan invasion of Venus had failed, or was failing. She was possessed as soon as they removed her from the tank – but Mary had outlived the slug that possessed her.

Why had the slugs died? Why had the invasion of Venus failed? It was for clues to these questions that the Old Man and Dr Steelton had gone fishing in Mary's brain.

I said, 'Is that all?'

He answered, 'Isn't that enough?'

'It raises as many questions as it answers,' I complained.

'There is a great deal more,' he told me. 'But you aren't a Venerian expert, nor a psychologist. I've told you what I have so that you will know why we have to work on Mary and won't question her about it. Be good to her, boy; she's had more than her share of grief.'

I ignored the advice; I can get along or not get along with my own wife without help, thank you. 'What I can't see,' I answered, 'is why you had Mary linked up with flying saucers in the first place? I can see now that you took her along on that first trip on purpose. You were right – but why? And don't give me any malarky.'

The Old Man looked puzzled. 'Son, do you ever have hunches?'

'Lord, yes!'

'What is a "hunch"?'

'Eh? It's a belief that something is so, or isn't so, without evidence.'

'I'd call a hunch the result of automatic reasoning below the conscious level on data you did not know you possessed.'

'Sounds like the black cat in the coal cellar at midnight. You didn't have any data. Don't tell me that your unconscious mind works on data you are going to get next week.'

'Ah, but I did have data.'

'Huh?'

'What's the last thing that happens to a candidate before he is certified as an agent?'

'The personal interview with you.'

'No, no!'

'Oh – the trance analysis.' I had forgotten hypno-analysis for the simple reason that the subject never remembers it. 'You mean you had this data on Mary then. It wasn't a hunch at all.'

'No again. I had a very little of it – Mary's defences are strong. And I had forgotten what little I knew. But I knew that Mary was the agent for this job. Later I played back her hypno interview; then I *knew* that there must be more. We tried for it – and did not get it. But I knew that there had to be more.'

I thought it over. 'You sure put her over the bumps to get it.'

'I had to. I'm sorry.'

'Okay, okay.' I waited a moment, then said, 'Look – what was there in *my* hypno record?'

'That's not a proper question.'

'Nuts.'

'And I couldn't tell you if I would. I have never listened to your analysis, son.'

'Huh?'

'I had my deputy play it. He said there wasn't anything I needed to know, so I never played it.'

'So? Well – thanks.'

He merely grunted. Dad and I have always managed to embarrass each other.

XXIX

The slugs had died from something they contracted on Venus; that much we thought we knew. We weren't likely to get another chance in a hurry to collect direct information, as a dispatch came in while the Old Man and I were talking, saying that the Pass Christian saucer had been bombed to keep it from being recaptured. The Old Man had hoped to get at those human prisoners in that ship, revive them, and question them.

That chance was gone. What they could dig out of Mary had better be the answer. If some infection peculiar to Venus was fatal to slugs but not fatal to humans – at least Mary had lived through it – then the next step was to test them all and determine which one. Just dandy! It was like examining every grain of sand on a beach. The list of diseases native to Venus which are not fatal but merely nastily annoying is very long. From the standpoint of a Venerian bug we must be too strange a diet to suit his taste. If a Venerian bug has a viewpoint, which I doubt, McIlvaine's silly ideas notwithstanding.

The problem was made harder by the fact that diseases native to Venus which were represented by living cultures on Earth were strictly limited in number. Such an omission could be repaired – in a century or so of exploration and research on a strange planet.

In the meantime there was a breath of frost in the air; Schedule Sun Tan could not go on for ever.

They had to go back where they hoped the answer was – into Mary's brain. I did not like it, but I could not stop it. She did not appear to know why she was being asked to submit, over and over again, to hypnotics. She seemed serene, but the strain showed – circles under her eyes, things like that. Finally I told the Old Man that it had to stop. 'You know better than that, son,' he said mildly.

'The hell I do! If you haven't gotten what you want by now, you'll never get it.'

'Do you know how long it takes to search *all* a person's memories, even if you limit it to a particular period? Exactly as long as the period itself. What we need – if it's there at all – may be subtle.'

' "If it's there at all," ' I repeated. 'You don't know that it is. See here – if Mary miscarries as a result of this, I'll break your neck personally.'

'If we don't succeed,' he answered gently, 'you'll wish to heaven that she had. Or do you want to raise up kids to be hosts to titans?'

I chewed my lip. 'Why didn't you send me to Russia, instead of keeping me here?'

'Oh, that. I want you here, with Mary, keeping her morale up, instead of acting like a spoiled brat! In the second place, it isn't necessary.'

'Huh? What happened? Some other agent report in?'

'If you would ever show a grown-up interest in the news, you would know.'

I hurried out and brought myself up to date. This time I had managed to miss the first news of the Asiatic plague, the second biggest news story of the century, the only continent-wide epidemic of Black Death since the seventeenth century.

I could not understand it. Russians are crazy, granted. But their public-health measures were fairly good; they were carried out 'by the numbers' and no nonsense tolerated. A country has to be literally lousy to spread plagues – rats, lice, and fleas, the historical vectors. The Russian bureaucrats had even cleaned up China to the point where bubonic plague and typhus were endemic rather than epidemic.

Now both plagues were spreading across the whole Sino-Russo-Siberian axis, to the point where the government had broken down and pleas were being sent out for UN help. What had happened?

I put the pieces together and looked up at the Old Man again. 'Boss – there *were* slugs in Russia.'

'Yes.'

'You know? Well, for cripes sake, we'd better move fast, or the whole Mississippi Valley will be in the shape that Asia is in. Just one little rat —' The titans did not bother about human sanitation. I doubted if there had been a bath taken between the Canadian border and New Orleans since the slugs dropped the masquerade. Lice ... Fleas ...

'You might as well bomb them, if that's the best we have to offer. It's a cleaner way to die.'

'So it is.' The Old Man sighed. 'Maybe that's the best solution. Maybe it's the only one. But you know we won't. As long as there is a chance we'll keep on trying.'

I mulled it over at length. We were in still another race against time. Fundamentally the slugs must be too stupid to keep slaves; perhaps that was why they moved from planet to planet – they spoiled what they touched. After a while their hosts would die and then they needed new hosts.

Theory, just theory. But one thing was sure: Zone Red would be plague-ridden unless we found a way to kill the slugs, and that mighty soon! I made up my mind to do something I had considered before – force myself into the mind-searching sessions. If there were something in Mary's hidden memories which could be used to kill slugs, I might see it where others had failed. In any case I was going in, whether Steelton and the Old Man liked it or not. I was tired of being treated like a cross between a prince consort and an unwelcome child.

XXX

Mary and I had been living in a cubicle intended for one officer; we were as crowded as a plate of *smörgåsbord*, but we did not care. I woke up first the next morning and made my usual quick check to be sure that a slug had not gotten to her. While I was doing so, she opened her eyes and smiled drowsily. 'Go back to sleep,' I said.

'I'm awake now.'

'Mary, do you know the incubation period for bubonic plague?'

She answered, 'Should I know? One of your eyes is slightly darker than the other.'

I shook her. 'Pay attention, wench. I was in the lab library last night, doing some figuring. As I get it, the slugs must have moved in on the Russians at least three months before they invaded us.'

'Yes, of course.'

'You know? Why didn't you say so?'

'Nobody asked me.'

'Oh, for heaven's sake! Let's get up; I'm hungry.'

Before we left I said, 'Guessing games at the usual time?'

'Yes.'

'Mary, you never talk about what they ask you.'

She looked surprised. 'But I never know.'

'That's what I gathered. Deep trance with a "forgetter" order, eh?'

'I suppose so.'

'Hmm ... well, there'll be some changes made. Today I am going with you.'

All she said was, 'Yes, dear.'

They were gathered as usual in Dr Steelton's office, the Old Man, Steelton himself, a Colonel Gibsy who was chief of staff, a lieutenant-colonel, and an odd lot of sergeant technicians, j.o.s, and flunkies. In the Army it takes an eight-man working party to help a brass hat blow his nose.

The Old Man's eyebrows shot up when he saw me but he said nothing. A sergeant tried to stop me. 'Good morning, Mrs Nivens,' he said to Mary, then added, 'I don't have you on the list.'

'I'm putting myself on the list,' I announced, and pushed on past him.

Colonel Gibsy glared and turned to the Old Man with a Hrrumph-hrrumph-what's-all-this? noise. The rest looked frozen-faced – except one Wac sergeant who could not keep from grinning.

The Old Man said to Gibsy, 'Just a moment, Colonel,' and limped over to me. In a voice that reached me alone he said, 'Son, you promised me.'

'And I withdraw it. You had no business exacting a promise from a man about his wife.'

'You've no business here, son. You are not skilled in these matters. For Mary's sake, get out.'

Up to that moment it had not occurred to me to question the Old Man's right to stay, but I found myself announcing my decision as I made it. 'You are the one with no business here. *You* are not an analyst. So get out.'

The Old Man glanced at Mary. Nothing showed in her face. The Old Man said slowly, 'You been eating raw meat, son?'

I answered, 'It's my wife who is being experimented on; from here on I make the rules.'

Colonel Gibsy butted in with, 'Young man, are you out of your mind?'

I said, 'What's your status?' I glanced at his hands and added, 'That's a VMI ring, isn't it? Have you any other qualifications? Are you an MD? Or a psychologist?'

He drew himself up. 'You seem to forget that this is a military reservation.'

'You forget that my wife and I aren't military personnel!' I added, 'Come, Mary. We're leaving.'

'Yes, Sam.'

I added to the Old Man, 'I'll tell the offices where to send our mail.' I started for the door with Mary following.

The Old Man said, 'Just a moment, as a favour to me.' I stopped and he went on to Gibsy, 'Colonel, will you step outside with me? I'd like a word in private.'

Colonel Gibsy gave me a general court-martial look but he went. We all waited. The juniors continued to be poker-faced, the lieutenant-colonel looked perturbed, and the little sergeant seemed about to burst. Steelton was the only one who appeared unconcerned. He took papers out of his 'incoming' basket and commenced to work quietly.

Ten or fifteen minutes later a sergeant came in. 'Dr Steelton, the commanding officer says to go ahead.'

'Very well, Sergeant,' he acknowledged, then looked at me and said, 'Let's go into the operating room.'

I said, 'Not so fast. Who are these others? How about him?' I indicated the lieutenant-colonel.

'Eh? He's Dr Hazelhurst – two years on Venus.'

'Okay, he stays.' I caught the eye of the sergeant with the grin and said, 'What's your job, sister?'

'Me? Oh, I'm sort of chaperon.'

'I'm taking over the chaperon business. Now, Doctor, suppose you sort out the spare wheels from the people you actually need.'

'Certainly, sir.'

It turned out that he really wanted no one but Colonel Hazelhurst. We went inside – Mary, myself, and the two specialists.

The operating room contained a psychiatrists' couch surrounded by chairs. The double snout of a tri-dim camera poked out of the overhead. Mary went to the couch and lay down; Dr Steelton got out an injector. 'We'll try to pick up where we left off, Mrs Nivens.'

I said, 'Just a moment. You have records of the earlier attempts?'

'Of course.'

'Let's play them over first. I want to come up to date.'

He hesitated, then answered, 'If you wish. Mrs Nivens, I

suggest that you wait in my office. Or suppose I send for you later?'

It was probably the contrary mood that I was in; bucking the Old Man had gotten me hiked up. 'Let's find out first if she *wants* to leave.'

Steelton looked surprised. 'You don't know what you are suggesting. These records would be emotionally disturbing to your wife – even harmful.'

Hazelhurst put in, 'Very questionable therapy, young man.'

I said, 'This isn't therapy and you know it. If therapy had been your object you would have used eidetic recall techniques instead of drugs.'

Steelton looked worried. 'There was not time. We had to use rough methods for quick results. I'm not sure that I can authorize the subject to see the records.'

Hazelhurst put in, 'I agree with you, Doctor.'

I exploded. 'Damn it, nobody asked you and you haven't got any authority in the matter. Those records were snitched out of my wife's head and they belong to *her*. I'm sick of you people trying to play God. I don't like it in a slug and I don't like it any better in a human being. She'll make up her own mind. Now *ask her*!'

Steelton said, 'Mrs Nivens, do you wish to see your records?'

Mary answered, 'Yes, Doctor, I'd like to very much.'

He seemed surprised. 'Uh, to be sure. Do you wish to see them by yourself?'

'My husband and I will see them. You and Dr Hazelhurst are welcome to remain.'

Which they did. A stack of tape spools were brought in, each labelled with attributed dates and ages. It would have taken hours to go through them all, so I discarded those which concerned Mary's life after 1991, as they could hardly affect the problem.

We began with her very early life. Each record started with the subject – Mary – choking and groaning and struggling the way people always do when they are being forced back on a memory track which they would rather not follow; then would come the reconstruction, both in her voice and in others'. What surprised me most was Mary's face – in the tank, I mean. We had the magnification stepped up so that the stereo image was practically in our laps and we could follow every expression.

First her face became that of a little girl. Oh, her features were the same grown-up features, but I knew that I was seeing my darling as she must have been when she was very small. It made me hope that we would have a little girl ourselves.

Then her expression would change to match when other actors out of her memory took over. It was like watching an incredibly able monologist playing many parts.

Mary took it calmly, but her hand stole into mine. When we came to the terrible part when her parents changed, became not her parents but slaves of slugs, she clamped down hard on my fingers. But she controlled herself.

I skipped over the spools marked 'period of suspended animation' and proceeded to the group concerned with the time from her resuscitation to the group concerned with her rescue from the swamps.

One thing was certain: she had been possessed by a slug as soon as she was revived. The dead expression was that of a slug not bothering to keep up a masquerade; the stereo-casts from Zone Red were full of that look. The barrenness of her memories from that period confirmed it.

Then, rather suddenly, she was no longer hagridden but was again a little girl, very sick and frightened. There was a delirious quality to her remembered thoughts, but, at the last, a new voice came out loud and clear: 'Well, skin me alive! Look, Pete – it's a little girl!'

Another voice answered, 'Alive?' and the first voice answered, 'I don't know.'

That tape carried on into Kaiserville, her recovery, and many new voices and memories; presently it ended.

'I suggest,' Dr Steelton said as he took the tape out of the projector, 'that we play another of the same period. They are all slightly different and this period is the key to the whole matter.'

'Why, Doctor?' Mary wanted to know.

'Eh? Of course you need not if you don't want to, but this period is the one which we are investigating. We must build up a picture of what happened to the parasites, why they died. If we could tell what killed the titan which, uh, possessed you before you were found – what killed it and left you alive – we might have the weapon we need.'

'But don't you *know*?' Mary asked wonderingly.

'Eh? Not yet, but we'll get it. The human memory is an amazingly complete record.'

'But I thought you knew. It was "nine-day fever".'

'*What?*' Hazelhurst bounced out of his chair.

'Couldn't you tell from my face? It was utterly characteristic – the mask, I mean. I used to nurse it back ho – back in Kaiserville, because I had had it once and was immune.'

Steelton said, 'How about it, Doctor? Have you ever seen a case of it?'

'Seen a case? No, by the time of the second expedition they had the vaccine. I'm acquainted with its clinical characteristics, of course.'

'But can't you tell from this record?'

'Well,' Hazelhurst answered carefully, 'I would say that what we have seen is consistent with it, but not conclusive.'

'What's not conclusive?' Mary said sharply. 'I told you it was "nine-day fever".'

'We must be sure,' Steelton said apologetically.

'How sure can you get? There is no question about it. I was told that I had been sick with it when Pete and Frisco found me. I nursed other cases later and I never caught it. I remember their faces when they were ready to die – just like my own face in the record. Anyone who has ever seen a case could not possibly mistake it for anything else. What more do you want? Fiery letters in the sky?'

I had never seen Mary so close to losing her temper – except once. I said to myself: Look out, gentlemen, better duck!

Steelton said, 'I think you have proved your point, dear lady. But tell me: you were believed to have no conscious memory of this period, and my own examination of you confirmed it. Now you speak as if you had.'

Mary looked puzzled. 'I remember it now – quite clearly. I haven't thought about it in many years.'

'I think I understand.' He turned to Hazelhurst. 'Well, Doctor? Do we have a culture of it? Have your boys done any work on it?'

Hazelhurst seemed stunned. 'Work on it? Of course not! It's out of the question – nine-day fever! We might as well use polio – or typhus. I'd rather treat a hangnail with an axe!'

I touched Mary's arm. 'Let's go, darling. I think we have done all the damage we can.' She was trembling and her eyes were full of tears. I took her into the messroom for systemic treatment – distilled.

Later on I bedded Mary down for a nap and sat with her until she was asleep. Then I looked up my father in the office they had assigned to him. 'Howdy,' I said.

He looked at me speculatively. 'Well, Elihu, I hear you hit the jackpot.'

'I prefer to be called "Sam",' I answered.

'Very well, Sam. Success is its own excuse; nevertheless the jackpot appears to be disappointingly small. Nine-day fever – no wonder the colony died out and the slugs as well. I don't see how we can use it. We can't expect everyone to have Mary's indomitable will to live.'

I understood him; the fever carried a ninety-eight per cent plus death rate among unprotected earthmen. With those who had taken the shots the rate was an effective zero – but that did not figure. We needed a bug that would just make a man sick – but would kill his slug. 'I can't see that it matters,' I pointed out. 'It's odds-on that you will have typhus or plague – or both – throughout the Mississippi Valley in the next six weeks.'

'Or the slugs may have learned a lesson in Asia and will start taking drastic sanitary measures,' he answered. The idea startled me so that I almost missed the next thing he said, which was: 'No, Sam, you'll have to devise a better plan.'

'*I'll* have to? I just work here.'

'You did once, but now you've taken charge of this job.'

'Huh? What the devil are you talking about? I'm not in charge of anything – and don't want to be. You're the boss.'

He shook his head. 'A boss is the man who does the bossing. Titles and insignia come later. Tell me – do you think Oldfield could ever replace me?'

I shook my head; Dad's chief deputy was the executive officer type, a 'carry-outer', not a 'think-upper'. 'I've never promoted you,' he went on, 'because I knew that when the time came you would promote yourself. Now you've done it – by bucking my judgement on an important matter, forcing your own on me, and by being justified in the outcome.'

'Oh, rats! I got bullheaded and forced one issue. It never occurred to you big brains that you were failing to consult the one real Venus expert you had on tap – Mary, I mean. But I didn't expect to find out anything; I had a lucky break.'

He shook his head. 'I don't believe in luck, Sam. Luck is a tag given by the mediocre to account for the accomplishments of genius.'

I placed my hands on the desk and leaned towards him. 'Okay, so I'm a genius – but you're not going to make me hold the sack. When this is over Mary and I are going up in the mountains and raise kittens and kids. I don't intend to boss screwball agents.'

He smiled gently.

I went on, 'I don't *want* your job – understand me?'

'That is what the devil said to the Deity after he displaced Him. Don't take it so hard, Sam. I'll keep the title for the present. In the meantime, what are your plans, sir?'

XXXI

The worst of it was, he meant it. I tried to go limp on him, but it did not work. A top-level conference was called that afternoon; I was notified but stayed away. Shortly a polite little Wac came to tell me that the commanding officer was waiting and would I please come at once?

So I went – and tried to stay out of the discussion. But my father has a way of conducting a meeting, even if he is not in the chair, by looking expectantly at the one he wants to hear from. It's a subtle trick, as the group does not know that it is being led.

But *I* knew. With every eye in the room on you, it is easier to voice an opinion than to keep quiet. Particularly as I found that I had opinions.

There was much moaning and groaning about the utter impossibility of using nine-day fever. Admitted that it would kill slugs. It would even kill Venerians, who can be chopped in two and survive. But it was sure death to any human – almost any human; I was married to one who *had* survived – death to the enormous majority. Seven to ten days after exposure, then curtains.

'Yes, Mr Nivens?' It was the commanding general, addressing me. I hadn't said anything, but Dad's eyes were on me, waiting.

'I think there has been a lot of despair voiced at this session,' I said, 'and a lot of opinions given that were based on assumptions. The assumptions may not be correct.'

'Yes?'

I did not have an instance in mind; I had been shooting from the hip. 'Well, I hear constant reference to nine-day fever as if the 'nine-day' part were an absolute fact. It's not.'

The boss brass shrugged impatiently. 'It's a convenient tag – it averages nine days.'

'Yes, but how do you know it lasts nine days – for a slug?'

By the murmur with which it was received I knew that I had hit the jackpot again.

I was invited to explain why I thought the fever might run a different time in slugs, and why it mattered. I bulled on ahead. 'As to the first,' I said, 'in the only case we know about the slug did die in less than nine days – a lot less. Those of you who have seen the records on my wife – and I gather that entirely too many of you have – are aware that her parasite left her, presumably dropped off and died, long before the eighth-day crisis. If experiments confirm this, then the problem is different. A man infected with the fever might be rid of his slug in – oh, call it four days. That gives you five days to catch him and cure him.'

The general whistled. 'That's a pretty heroic solution, Mr Nivens. How do you propose to cure him? Or even catch him? I mean to say, suppose we plant an epidemic in Zone Red, it would take incredibly fast footwork – in the face of stubborn resistance, remember – to locate and treat more than fifty million people before they died.'

I slung the hot potato right back – and wondered how many 'experts' had made their names by passing the buck. 'The second question is a logistical and tactical problem – *your* problem. As to the first, there is your expert.' I pointed to Dr Hazelhurst.

Hazelhurst huffed and puffed and I knew how he felt. Insufficient former art … more research needed … experiments would be required. … He seemed to recall that work had been done towards an antitoxin but the vaccine for immunizing had proven so successful that he was not sure the antitoxin had ever been perfected. He concluded lamely by saying that the study of the exotic diseases of Venus was still in its infancy.

The general interrupted him. 'This antitoxin business – how soon can you find out about it?'

Hazelhurst said that there was a man at the Sorbonne he wanted to phone.

'Do so,' his commanding officer said. 'You are excused.'

Hazelhurst came buzzing at our door before breakfast the next morning. I stepped out into the passage to see him. 'Sorry to wake you,' he said, 'but you were right about that antitoxin matter.'

'Huh?'

'They are sending me some from Paris; it should arrive any minute. I do hope it's still potent.'

'And if it isn't?'

'Well, we have the means to make it. We'll have to, of course, if this wild scheme is used – millions of units of it.'

'Thanks for telling me,' I said. I started to turn away; he stopped me.

'Uh, Mr Nivens. About the matter of vectors —'

'Vectors?'

'Disease vectors. We can't use rats or mice or anything like that. Do you know how the fever is transmitted on Venus? By a little flying rotifer, the Venerian equivalent of an insect. But we don't have any such, and that is the *only* way it can be carried.'

'Do you mean to say you couldn't give it to me if you tried?'

'Oh, yes – I could inject you. But I can't picture a million paratroopers dropping into Zone Red and asking the parasite-ridden population to hold still while they gave them injections.' He spread his hands helplessly.

Something started turning over slowly in my brain. A million men, in a single drop . . . 'Why ask me?' I said. 'It's a medical problem.'

'Uh, yes, of course. I just thought — Well, you seemed to have a ready grasp —' He paused.

'Thanks.' My mind was struggling with two problems at once and having traffic trouble. How many people were there in Zone Red? 'Let me get this straight: suppose you had the fever; I could not catch it from you?' The drop could not be medical men; there weren't that many.

'Not easily. If I took a smear and placed it in your throat, you might contract it. If I made a trace transfusion from my veins to yours, you would be sure to be infected.'

'Direct contact, eh?' How many people could one para-

201

trooper service? Twenty? Thirty? Or more? 'If that is what it takes, you don't have any problem.'

'Eh?'

'What's the first thing a slug does when he runs across another he hasn't seen lately?'

'*Conjugation!*'

' "Direct conference" I've always called it – but I use the sloppy old slug language for it. Do you think that would pass on the disease?'

'Think so? I'm sure of it! We have demonstrated, right in this laboratory, that there is exchange of living protein during conjugation. They could not possibly escape transmission; we can infect the whole colony as if it were one body. Now why didn't I think of that?'

'Don't go off half cocked,' I said. 'But I suspect that it will work.'

'It will, it will!' He started to go, then stopped. 'Oh, Mr Nivens, would you mind very much – I know it's a lot to ask —'

'What is? Speak up.' I was anxious to work out the rest of the other problem.

'Well, would you permit me to announce this method of vectoring? I'll give you full credit, but the general expects so much and this is just what I need to make my report complete.' He looked so anxious that I almost laughed.

'Not at all,' I said. 'It's your department.'

'That's decent of you. I'll try to return the favour.' He went away happy and so was I; I was beginning to like being a 'genius'.

I stopped to straighten out in my mind the main features of the big drop. Then I went in. Mary opened her eyes and gave me that long heavenly smile. I reached down and smoothed her hair. 'Howdy, flame top. Did you know that your husband is a genius?'

'Yes.'

'You did? You never said so.'

'You never asked me.'

Hazelhurst referred to it as the 'Nivens vector'. Then I

was asked to comment, though Dad looked my way first.

'I agree with Dr Hazelhurst,' I started out, 'subject to experimental confirmation. However, he has left for discussion aspects which are tactical rather than medical. Important considerations of timing – crucial, I should say —' I had worked out my opening speech, even to the hesitations, while eating breakfast. Mary does not chatter at breakfast, thank goodness!

'– require vectoring from many focal points. If we are to save a nominal hundred per cent of the population of Zone Red, it is necessary that all parasites be infected at nearly the same time in order that rescue squads may enter *after* the slugs are no longer dangerous and *before* any host has passed the point where antitoxin can save him. The problem is susceptible to mathematical analysis —' Sam boy, I said to myself, you old phoney, you could not solve it with an electronic integrator and twenty years of sweat. '– and should be turned over to your analytical section. However, let me sketch out the factors. Call the number of vector origins "X"; call the number of rescue workers "Y". There will be an indefinitely large number of simultaneous solutions, with optimum solution depending on logistic factors. Speaking in advance of rigorous mathematical treatment' – I had done my damnedest with a slipstick, but I did not mention that – 'and basing my opinions on my own unfortunately-too-intimate knowledge of their habits, I would estimate —'

You could have heard a pin drop, if anybody in that bare-skinned crew had had a pin. The general interrupted once when I placed a low estimate on 'X'; 'Mr Nivens, I think we can assure you of my number of volunteers for vectoring.'

I shook my head. 'You can't accept volunteers, General.'

'I think I see your objection. The disease would have to be given time to establish in the volunteer and the timing might be dangerously close. But I think we could get around that – a gelatine capsule of antitoxin embedded in tissue, or something of the sort. I'm sure the staff could work it out.'

I thought they could, too, but my real objection was a

deep-rooted aversion to any human soul having to be possessed by a slug. 'You *must not* use human volunteers, sir. The slug will know everything that his host knows – and he simply will not go into direct conference; he'll warn the others by word of mouth instead. No, sir, we will use animals – apes, dogs, anything large enough to carry a slug but incapable of speech, and in quantities to infect the whole group before any slug knows that it is sick.'

I gave a fast sketch of the final drop, 'Schedule Mercy', as I saw it. 'The first drop – "Schedule Fever" – can start as soon as we have enough antitoxin for the second drop. In less than a week thereafter there should be no slug left alive on this continent.'

They did not applaud, but it felt that way. The general hurried away to call Air Marshal Rexton, then sent his aide back to invite me to lunch. I sent word that I would be pleased provided the invitation included my wife.

Dad waited for me outside the conference room. 'Well, how did I do?' I asked him, more anxious than I tried to sound.

He shook his head. 'Sam, you wowed 'em. I think I'll sign you up for twenty-six weeks of stereo.'

I tried not to show how pleased I was. I had gotten through the whole performance without once stammering; I felt like a new man.

XXXII

.

That ape Satan which had wrung my heart at the National Zoo turned out to be as mean as he was billed, once he was free of his slug. Dad had volunteered to be the test case for the Nivens–Hazelhurst theories, but I put my foot down and Satan drew the short straw. It was neither filial affection nor its neo-Freudian antithesis that caused me to balk him; I was afraid of the combination Dad-*cum*-slug. I did not want him on their side even under laboratory conditions. Not with his shrewd, tricky mind! People who have never experienced possession cannot appreciate that the host is utterly *against* us – with all his abilities intact.

So we used apes for the experiments. We had on hand not only apes from the National Zoological Gardens but simian citizens from half a dozen zoos and circuses.

Satan was injected with nine-day fever on Wednesday the twelfth. By Friday the fever had taken hold; another chimp-*cum*-slug was put in with him; the slugs immediately went into direct conference, after which the second ape was removed.

On Sunday the sixteenth Satan's master shrivelled up and fell off. Satan was immediately injected with antitoxin. Late Monday the other slug died and its host was dosed.

By Wednesday the nineteenth Satan was well though a bit thin, and the second ape, Lord Fauntleroy, was recovering. To celebrate, I gave Satan a banana, and he took off the first joint of my left index finger and me with no time for a repair job. It was no accident; that ape was nasty.

But a minor injury could not depress me. After I had it dressed I looked for Mary, failed to find her, and ended up in the messroom, wanting someone with whom to share a toast.

The place was empty; everyone in the labs was working, mounting Schedule Fever and Schedule Mercy. By order of the President all possible preparations were confined to this one lab in the Smoky Mountains. The apes for vectoring, some two hundred of them were there; the culture and antitoxin were being 'cooked' here; the horses for serum were stalled in an underground handball court.

The million-plus men for Schedule Mercy could not be here, but they would know nothing until alerted just before the drop, at which time each would be issued a hand gun and bandoleers of individual antitoxin injectors. Those who had never parachuted would be pushed, if necessary, by some sergeant with a large foot. Everything was being done to keep the secret close; the only way I could see that we could lose would be for the titans to find out our plans, through a renegade or by some other means. Too many plans have failed because some fool told his wife.

If we failed to keep this secret, our ape vectors would be shot on sight wherever they appeared in the titan nation. Nevertheless, I relaxed over my drink, happy and reasonably sure that the secret would not leak. Traffic was 'incoming only' until after Drop Day, and Colonel Kelly censored or monitored all communication outward.

As for a leak outside, the chances were slight. The general, Dad, Colonel Gibsy, and myself had gone to the White House the week before. There Dad put on an exhibition of belligerence and exasperation that got us what we wanted; in the end even Secretary Martinez was kept in the dark. If the President and Rexton could keep from talking in their sleep for another week, I did not see how we could miss.

A week would be none too soon: Zone Red was spreading. After the battle of Pass Christian the slugs had pushed on and now held the Gulf Coast past Pensacola; there were signs of more to come. Perhaps the slugs were growing tired of our resistance and might decide to waste raw material by A-bombing the cities we still held. If so – well, a radar screen can alert your defences; it won't stop a determined attack.

But I refused to worry. One more week . . .

Colonel Kelly came in and sat down beside me. 'How about a drink?' I suggested. 'I feel like celebrating.'

He examined the paunch bulging in front of him and said, 'I suppose one more beer wouldn't put me in any worse shape.'

'Have two beers. Have a dozen.' I dialled for him, and told him about the success of the experiments with the apes.

He nodded. 'Yes, I had heard. Sounds good.'

' "Good", the man says! Colonel, we are on the one-yard line and goal to go. A week from now we'll have won.'

'So?'

'Oh, come now!' I answered, irritated. 'Then you'll be able to put your clothes back on and lead a normal life. Or don't you think our plans will work?'

'Yes, I think they will work.'

'Then why the crêpe-hanging?'

He said, 'Mr Nivens, you don't think that a man with my potbelly enjoys running around without his clothes, do you?'

'I suppose not. As for myself, I may hate to give it up. It saves time and it's comfortable.'

'Don't worry about it. This is a permanent change.'

'Huh? I don't get you. You said our plans would work and now you talk as if Schedule Sun Tan would go on forever.'

'In a modified way, it will.'

I said, 'Pardon me? I'm stupid today.'

He dialled for another beer. 'Mr Nivens, I never expected to see a military reservation turned into a ruddy nudist camp. Having seen it, I never expect to see us change back – because we *can't*. Pandora's box has a one-way lid. All the king's horses and all the king's men —'

'Conceded,' I answered. 'Things never go back quite to what they were before. But you are exaggerating. The day the President rescinds Schedule Sun Tan the blue laws will go back into effect and a man without pants will be liable to arrest.'

'I hope not.'

'Huh? Make up your mind.'

'It's made up for me. Mr Nivens, as long as there exists a possibility that a slug is alive the polite man must be willing to bare his body on request – or risk getting shot. Not just this week and next, but twenty years from now, or a hundred. No, no!' he added, 'I am not disparaging your plans – but you have been too busy to notice that they are strictly local and temporary. For example, have you made any plans for combing the Amazonian jungles, tree by tree?'

He went on, 'Just a rhetorical inquiry. This globe has nearly sixty million square miles of land; we can't begin to search it for slugs. Shucks, man, we haven't even made a dent in rats, and we've been at that a long time.'

'Are you trying to tell me it's hopeless?' I demanded.

'Hopeless? Not at all. Have another drink. I'm trying to say that we are going to have to learn to *live* with this horror, the way we had to learn to live with the atom bomb.'

XXXIII

We were gathered in the same room in the White House; it put me in mind of the night after the President's message many weeks before. Dad and Mary, Rexton and Martinez were there, as well as our own lab general, Dr Hazelhurst, and Colonel Gibsy. Our eyes were on the big map still mounted across one wall; it had been four and a half days since the drop of Schedule Fever, but the Mississippi Valley still glowed in ruby lights.

I was getting jittery, even though the drop had been an apparent success and we had lost only three craft. According to the equations, every slug within reach of direct conference should have been infected three days ago, with an estimated twenty-three per cent overlap. The operation had been computed to contact about eighty per cent in the first twelve hours, mostly in cities.

Soon, slugs should start dying a darn sight faster than flies ever did – *if* we were right.

I tried to sit still while I wondered whether those ruby lights covered a few million very sick slugs – or merely two hundred dead apes. Had somebody skipped a decimal point? Or blabbed? Or had there been an error in our reasoning so colossal that we could not see it?

Suddenly a light blinked green; everybody sat up. A voice began to come out of the stereo gear, though no picture built up. 'This is Station Dixie, Little Rock,' a very tired southern voice said. 'We need help very badly. Anyone who is listening, please pass on this message: Little Rock, Arkansas, is in the grip of a terrible epidemic. Notify the Red Cross. We have been in the hands of —' The voice trailed off, either from weakness or transmission failure.

I remembered to breathe. Mary patted my hand and I sat back, relaxing consciously. It was joy too great to be pleasure. I saw now that the green light had not been Little Rock, but farther west, in Oklahoma. Two more lights blinked green, one in Nebraska and one north of the Canadian line. Another voice came over, a twangy New England voice; I wondered how he had gotten into Zone Red.

'A little like election night, eh, Chief?' Martinez said heartily.

'A little,' the President agreed, 'but we do not usually get returns from Old Mexico.' He pointed to the board; green lights were showing in Chihuahua.

'By George, you're right. Well, I guess "State" will have some incidents to straighten out when this is over, eh?'

The President did not answer and he shut up, to my relief. The President seemed to be talking to himself; he noticed me, smiled, and spoke out loud:

> *Great fleas have little fleas*
> *Upon their backs to bite 'em,*
> *And little fleas lesser fleas,*
> *And so*, ad infinitum.'

I smiled to be polite, though I thought the notion was gruesome, under the circumstances. The President looked away and said, 'Would anyone like supper? I find that I am hungry, for the first time in days.'

By late next afternoon the board was more green than red. Rexton had caused to be set up two annunciators keyed into the command centre in the New Pentagon; one showed percentage of completion of the complicated score deemed necessary before the big drop; the other showed projected time of drop. The figures on it changed from time to time. For the past two hours they had been hovering around 17:43, east-coast time.

Rexton stood up. 'I'm going to freeze it at seventeen forty-five,' he announced. 'Mr President, will you excuse me?'

'Certainly, sir.'

Rexton turned to Dad and myself. 'If you Don Quixotes are still determined to go, now is the time.'

I stood up. 'Mary, you wait for me.'

She asked, 'Where?' It had been settled – and not peacefully! – that she was not to go.

The President interrupted. 'I suggest that Mrs Nivens stay here. After all, she is a member of the family.'

I said, 'Thank you, sir.' Colonel Gibsy got a very odd look.

Two hours later we were coming in on our target and the jump door was open. Dad and I were last in line, after the kids who would do the real work. My hands were sweaty and I stunk with the old curtain-going-up stink. I was scared as hell – I never like to jump.

XXXIV

Gun in my left hand, antitoxin injector ready in my right, I went from door to door in my assigned block. It was an older section of Jefferson City, slums almost, consisting of apartment houses built fifty years ago. I had given two dozen injections and had three dozen to go before it would be time for me to rendezvous at the State House. I was getting sick of it.

I knew why I had come – it was not just curiosity; I wanted to see them *die*! I wanted to watch them die, see them dead, with a weary hate that passed all other needs.

But now I had seen them dead and I wanted no more of it; I wanted to go home, take a bath, and forget it.

It was not hard work, just monotonous and nauseating. So far I had not seen one live slug, though I had seen many dead ones. I had burned one skulking dog that appeared to have a hump; I was not sure, as the light had been bad. We had hit shortly before sundown and now it was almost dark.

I finished checking the apartment building I was in, shouted to make sure, and went out into the street. It was almost deserted; with the whole population sick with the fever, we found few on the streets. The lone exception was a man who came weaving towards me, eyes vacant. I yelled, 'Hey!'

He stopped. I said, 'I've got what you need to get well. Hold out your arm.'

He struck at me feebly. I hit him carefully and he went face down. Across his back was the red rash of the slug; I picked a reasonably clean and healthy patch over his kidney and stuck in the injector, bending it to break the point after it was in. The units were gas-loaded; nothing more was needed.

The first floor of the next house held seven people, most of them so far gone that I did not speak but simply gave them their shots and hurried on. I had no trouble. The second floor was like the first.

The top floor had three empty apartments, at one of which I had to burn out the lock to enter. The fourth flat was occupied, in a manner of speaking. There was a dead woman on the floor of the kitchen, her head bashed in. Her slug was still on her shoulders, but merely resting there, for it was dead too. I left them quickly and looked around.

In the bathroom, sitting in an old-fashioned tub, was a middle-aged man. His head slumped on his chest and his wrist veins were open. I thought he was dead, but he looked up as I bent over him. 'You're too late,' he said dully. 'I killed my wife.'

Or too soon, I thought. From the appearance of the bottom of the tub, and judging by his grey face, five minutes later would have been better. I looked at him, wondering whether or not to waste an injection.

He spoke again. 'My little girl —'

'You have a daughter?' I said loudly. 'Where is she?'

His eyes flickered, but he did not speak. His head slumped forward again. I shouted at him, then felt his jaw line, and dug my thumb into his neck, but could find no pulse.

The child was in bed in one of the rooms, a girl of eight or so who would have been pretty had she been well. She roused and cried and called me daddy. 'Yes, yes,' I said soothingly, 'Daddy's going to take care of you.' I gave her the injection in her leg; I don't think she noticed it.

I turned to go, but she called out again, 'I'm thirsty. Want a drink of water.' So I had to go back into that bathroom again.

As I was giving it to her my phone shrilled and I spilled some of it. 'Son! Can you hear me?'

I reached for my belt and switched on my phone. 'Yes. What's up?'

'I'm in that little park just north of you. I'm in trouble.'

'Coming!' I put down the glass and started to leave – then, caught by indecision, I turned back. I could not leave my new friend to wake up with a parent dead in each room. I gathered her up and stumbled down to the second floor. I entered the first door I came to and laid her on a sofa. There were people in the flat, too sick to bother with her, but it was all I could do.

'Hurry, son!'

'On my way!' I dashed out and wasted no more breath talking, but made speed. Dad's assignment was directly north of mine, paralleling it and fronting on one of those pint-sized downtown parks. When I got around the block I did not see him at first and ran on past him.

'Here, son, over here – at the car!' This time I could hear him both through the phone and by bare ear. I swung around and spotted the car, a big Cadillac duo much like the Section often used. There was someone inside but it was too dark for me to see. I approached cautiously until I heard him say, 'Thank God! I thought you would never come,' and knew that it was he.

I had to duck to get in through the door. It was then that he clipped me.

I came to, to find my hands tied and my ankles as well. I was in the second driver's seat of the car, and the Old Man was in the other at the controls. The wheel on my side was latched up out of the way. The realization that the car was in the air brought me fully awake.

He turned and said cheerfully, 'Feeling better?' I could see his slug, riding high on his shoulders.

'Some better,' I admitted.

'Sorry I had to hit you,' he went on, 'but there was no other way.'

'I suppose not.'

'I'll have to leave you tied up for the present. Later on we can make better arrangements.' He grinned, his old wicked grin. Most amazingly his own personality came through with every word the slug said.

I did not ask what 'better arrangements' were possible; I did not want to know. I concentrated on checking my bonds – but the Old Man had given them his personal attention.

'Where are we going?' I asked.

'South.' He fiddled with the controls. ' 'Way south. Give me a moment to lay this heap in the groove and I will explain what's in store for us.' He was busy for a few seconds, then said, 'There – that will hold her until she levels off at thirty thousand.'

The mention of that much altitude caused me to look at the control board. The duo did not merely look like one of the Section's cars; it actually *was* one of our souped-up jobs. 'Where did you get this car?' I asked.

'The Section had it cached in Jefferson City. I looked and, sure enough, nobody had found it. Fortunate, wasn't it?'

There could be a second opinion, I thought, but I did not argue. I was still checking the possibilities – and finding them between slim and hopeless. My own gun was gone. He was probably carrying his on the side away from me; it was not in sight.

'But that was not the best of it,' he went on; 'I had the good luck to be captured by what was almost certainly the only healthy master in the whole of Jefferson City – not that I believe in luck. So we win after all.' He chuckled. 'It's like playing both sides of a very difficult chess game.'

'You didn't tell me where we are going,' I persisted. I was getting nowhere fast and talking was the only action open to me.

He considered. 'Out of the United States, certainly. My master may be the only one free of nine-day fever in the whole continent, and I don't dare take a chance. I think the Yucatán peninsula would suit us – that's where I've got her pointed. We can hole up there and increase our numbers and work on south. When we do come back – and we will! – we won't make the same mistakes.'

I said, 'Dad, can't you take these ties off me? I'm losing circulation. You know you can trust me.'

'Presently, presently – all in good time. Wait until we go full automatic.' The car was still climbing; souped up or not, thirty thousand was a long pull for a car that had started out as a family model.

I said, 'You seem to forget that I was with the masters a long time. I know the score – and I give you my word of honour.'

He grinned. 'Don't teach grandma how to steal sheep. If I let you loose now, you'll kill me or I'll have to kill you. And I want you alive. We're going places, son – you and me. We're fast and we're smart and we're just what the doctor ordered.'

I didn't have an answer. He went on, 'Just the same – about you knowing the score. Why didn't you tell me, son? Why did you hold out on me?'

'Huh?'

'You didn't tell me how it felt. Son, I had no idea that a man could feel such peace and contentment and well-being. This is the happiest I've been in years, the happiest since —' He looked puzzled, then went on, '– since your mother died.

But never mind that; this is better. You should have told me.'

Disgust suddenly poured over me; I forgot the cautious game I was playing. 'Maybe I didn't see it that way. And neither would you, you old fool, if you didn't have a slug riding you, talking through your mouth, thinking with your brain!'

'Take it easy, son,' he said gently – and, so help me, his voice *did* soothe me. 'You'll know better soon. Believe me, this is what we were intended for; this is our destiny. Mankind has been divided, warring with himself. The masters will make him whole.'

I thought to myself that there were probably custard heads just screwy enough to fall for such a line – surrender their souls willingly for a promise of security and peace. But I didn't say so.

'You needn't wait much longer,' he said suddenly, glancing at the board. 'I'll nail her down in the groove.' He adjusted his dead-reckoner bug, checked his board, and set his controls. 'Next stop: Yucatán. Now to work.' He got out of the chair and knelt beside me in the crowded space. 'Got to be safe,' he said, as he strapped the safety belt across my middle.

I brought my knees up in his face.

He reared up and looked at me without anger. 'Naughty, naughty. I could resent that – but the masters don't go in for resentment. Now be good.' He went ahead, checking my wrists and feet. His nose was bleeding but he did not bother to wipe it. 'You'll do,' he said. 'Be patient; it won't be long.'

He went back to the other control seat, sat down, and leaned forward, elbows on knees. It brought his master directly into my view.

Nothing happened for some minutes, nor could I think of anything to do other than strain at my bonds. By his appearance, the Old Man was asleep, but I placed no trust in that.

A line formed straight down the middle of the horny brown covering of the slug.

As I watched it, it widened. Presently I could see the opalescent horror underneath. The space between the two halves of the shell widened – and I realized that the slug was fissioning, sucking life and matter out of the body of my father to make two of itself.

I realized, too, with rigid terror, that I had no more than five minutes of individual life left to me. My new master was being born and soon would be ready to mount me.

Had it been possible for flesh and bone to break the ties on me I would have broken them. I did not succeed. The Old Man paid no attention to my struggles. I doubt if he was conscious; the slugs must surely give up some measure of control while occupied with splitting. It must be that they simply immobilize the slave. As may be – the Old Man did not move.

By the time I had given up, worn out and sure that I could not break loose, I could see the silvery line down the centre of the slug proper which means that fission is about to be complete. It was that which changed my line of reasoning, if there were reason left in my churning skull.

My hands were tied behind me, my ankles were tied, and I was belted tight across the middle to the chair. But my legs, even though fastened together, were free from my waist down. I slumped down to get even more reach and swung my legs up high. I brought them down smashingly across the board – and set off every launching unit in her racks.

That adds up to a lot of g's. How many, I don't know, for I don't know how full her racks were. But there were plenty. We were both slammed back against the seats, Dad much harder than I was, since I was strapped down. He was thrown against the back of his seat, with his slug, open and helpless, crushed between the two masses.

It splashed.

Dad was caught in that terrible, total reflex, that spasm of every muscle that I had seen three times before. He bounced forward against the wheel, face contorted, fingers writhing.

The car dived.

I sat there and watched it dive, if you can call it sitting when you are held in place only by the belt. If Dad's body had not hopelessly fouled the controls, I might have been able to do something – gotten her headed up again perhaps – with my bound feet. I tried, but with no success at all. The controls were probably jammed as well as fouled.

The altimeter was clicking away busily. We had dropped to eleven thousand feet before I found time to glance at it. Then it was nine ... seven ... six – and we entered our last mile.

At fifteen hundred the radar interlock cut in and the nose units fired one at a time. The belt buffeted me across the stomach each time. I was thinking that I was saved, that now the ship would level off – though I should have known better, Dad being jammed up against the wheel as he was.

I was still thinking so as we crashed.

I came to by becoming slowly aware of a gently rocking motion. I was annoyed by it, I wanted it to stop; even a slight motion seemed to cause more pain than I could bear. I managed to get one eye open – the other would not open at all – and looked dully around for the source of my annoyance.

Above me was the floor of the car, but I stared at it for a long time before I placed it as such. By then I was somewhat aware of where I was and what had happened. I remembered the dive and the crash – and realized that we must have crashed not into the ground but into some body of water – the Gulf of Mexico? I did not really care.

With a sudden burst of grief I mourned my father.

My broken seat belt was flapping above me. My hands were still tied and so were my ankles, and one arm seemed to be broken. One eye was stuck shut and it hurt me to breathe; I quit taking stock of my injuries. Dad was no longer plastered against the wheel, and that puzzled me. With painful effort I rolled my head over to see the rest of the car with my one good eye. He was lying not far from me, three feet or so from my head to his. He was bloody and cold and I was sure that he was dead. I think it took me about a half hour to cross that three feet.

I lay face to face with him, almost cheek to cheek. So far as I could tell there was no trace of life, nor, from the odd and twisted way in which he lay, did it seem possible.

'Dad,' I said hoarsely. Then I screamed it. *'Dad!'*

His eyes flickered but did not open. 'Hello, son,' he whispered. 'Thanks, boy, thanks —' His voice died out.

I wanted to shake him, but all I could do was shout. 'Dad! Wake up! Are you all right?'

He spoke again, as if every word were a painful task. 'Your mother – said to tell you – she was – proud of you.' His voice died out again and his breathing was laboured in that ominous dry-stick sound.

'Dad,' I sobbed, 'don't die. I can't get along without you.'

His eyes opened wide. 'Yes, you can, son.' He paused and laboured, then added, 'I'm hurt, boy.' His eyes closed again.

I could not get any more out of him, though I shouted and screamed. Presently I lay my face against his and let my tears mix with the dirt and blood.

XXXV

And now to clean up Titan!

We who are going are all writing these reports; if we do not come back, this is our legacy to free human beings – all that we know of how the titan parasites operate and what must be guarded against. For Kelly was right; there is no getting Humpty-Dumpty together again. In spite of the success of Schedule Mercy, there is no way to be sure that the slugs are all gone. Only last week a Kodiak bear was shot, up Yukon way, wearing a hump.

The human race will have to be always on guard, most especially about twenty-five years from now if we don't come back but the flying saucers do. We don't know why the titan monsters follow the twenty-nine-year cycle of Saturn's 'year', but they do. The reason may be simple; we ourselves have many cycles which match the Earth year. We hope that they are active only at one period of their 'year'; if they are, Operation Vengeance may have easy pickings. Not that we are counting on it. I am going out, Heaven help us, as an 'applied psychologist (exotic)', but I am also a combat trooper, as is every one of us, from chaplain to cook. This is for keeps and we intend to show those slugs that they made the mistake of tangling with the toughest, meanest, deadliest, most unrelenting – and ablest – form of life in this section of space, a critter that can be killed but can't be tamed.

(I have a private hope that we will find some way to save the little elf creatures, the androgynes. I think we could get along with the elves.)

Whether we make it or not, the human race has got to keep up its well-earned reputation for ferocity. The price of freedom is the willingness to do sudden battle, anywhere, any time, and with utter recklessness. If we did not learn that from the slugs, well – 'Dinosaurs, move over! We are ready to become extinct!'

For who knows what dirty tricks may be lurking around this universe? The slugs may be simple and open and friendly compared with, let us say, the natives of the planets of Sirius. If this is just the opener, we had better learn from it for the main event. We thought space was empty and that we were automatically the lords of creation; even after we 'conquered' space we thought so, for Mars was already dead and Venus had not really gotten started. Well, if Man wants to be top dog – or even a respected neighbour – he'll have to fight for it. Beat the ploughshares back into swords; the other was a maiden aunt's fancy.

Every one of us who is going has been possessed at least once. Only those who have been hagridden can know how tricky the slugs are, how constantly one must be on guard –

or how deeply one must hate. The trip, they tell me, will take about twelve years, which will give Mary and me time to finish our honeymoon. Oh yes, Mary is going; most of us are married couples, and the single men are balanced by single women. Twelve years isn't a trip; it's a way of living.

When I told Mary that we were going to Saturn's moons, her single comment was, 'Yes, dear.'

We'll have time for two or three kids. As Dad says, 'The race must go on, even if it doesn't know where.'

This report is loose-jointed; it must be revised before it is transcribed. But I have put everything in, as I saw and felt it. War with another race is psychological war, not war of gadgets, and what I thought and felt may be more important than what I did.

I am now finishing this report in Space Station Beta, from which we will transship to UNS *Avenger*. I will not have time to revise; this will have to go as is, for the historians to have fun with. We said goodbye to Dad last night at Pikes Peak Port. He corrected me. 'So long, you mean. You'll be back and I intend to hang on, getting crankier and meaner every year, until you do.'

I said I hoped so. He nodded. 'You'll make it. You're too tough and mean to die. I've got a lot of confidence in you and the likes of you, son.'

We are about to transship. I feel exhilarated. Puppet masters – the free men are coming to kill you!

Death and Destruction!

Science Fiction in Pan

Occult & Supernatural

Ghost & Horror in Pan

Ira Levin

ROSEMARY'S BABY   25p

'At last I have got my wish. I am ridden by a book that plagues my mind and continues to squeeze my heart with fingers of bone. I swear that *Rosemary's Baby* is the most unnerving story I've read' – KENNETH ALLSOP

'. . . if you read this book in the dead of night, do not be surprised if you feel the urge to keep glancing behind you' – QUEEN

'a darkly brilliant tale of modern devilry that like James' *Turn of the Screw*, induces the reader to believe the unbelievable. I believed it and was altogether enthralled'

– TRUMAN CAPOTE

A KISS BEFORE DYING   25p
THIS PERFECT DAY   35p

These and other PAN Books are obtainable from all booksellers and newsagents. If you have any difficulty please send purchase price plus 7p postage to P.O. Box 11, Falmouth, Cornwall.

While every effort is made to keep prices low, it is sometimes necessary to increase prices at short notice. PAN Books reserve the right to show new retail prices on covers which may differ from those previously advertised in the text or elsewhere.